"This coul[d] [move] fast," Rye [said with a charming grin.]

Kara kept her response to herself. Not long ago she and Rye Wagner couldn't stand to be in the same room together, and now they'd agreed to stick together for the duration of the trail drive. They'd be working side by side, sleeping side by side. Might something more come of it than keeping each other out of trouble?

To her knowledge no man had ever found her sexually attractive, at least no one she'd worked beside on the range. There was no reason to think Rye would be any different, and yet, she couldn't help wondering, wishing, hoping that maybe...

But no, she was just one more burden that had been heaped on Rye's broad shoulders, and she'd best not start to think otherwise. If she did, she would really be in danger—danger of getting her heart broken.

Dear Reader,

This September, four of our beloved authors pen irresistible sagas about lonesome cowboys, hard-luck heroines and love on the range! We've flashed these "Western-themed" romances with a special arch treatment. And additional treasures are provided to our readers by Christine Rimmer—a new JONES GANG book with an excerpt from her wonderful upcoming single title, *The Taming of Billy Jones,* as well as Marilyn Pappano's first Special Edition novel.

In *Every Cowgirl's Dream* by Arlene James, our THAT SPECIAL WOMAN! Kara Detmeyer is one feisty cowgirl who can handle just about anything—except the hard-edged cowboy who escorts her through a dangerous cattle drive. Don't miss this high-spirited adventure.

THE JONES GANG returns to Special Edition! In *A Hero for Sophie Jones,* veteran author Christine Rimmer weaves a poignant story about a ruthless hero who is transformed by love. And wedding bells are chiming in *The Mail-Order Mix-Up* by Pamela Toth, but can this jilted city sophisticate find true love? Speaking of mismatched lovers, a pregnant widow discovers forbidden passion with her late husband's half brother in *The Cowboy Take a Wife* by Lois Faye Dyer.

Rounding out the month, *Stranded on the Ranch* by Pat Warren features a sheltered debutante who finds herself snowbound with an oh-so-sexy rancher. And Marilyn Pappano brings us a bittersweet reunion romance between a reformed temptress and the wary lover she left behind in *Older, Wiser...Pregnant.* I hope you enjoy each and every story to come!

Sincerely,

Karen Taylor Richman
Senior Editor

Please address questions and book requests to:
Silhouette Reader Service
U.S.: 3010 Walden Ave., P.O. Box 1325, Buffalo, NY 14269
Canadian: P.O. Box 609, Fort Erie, Ont. L2A 5X3

ARLENE JAMES

EVERY COWGIRL'S DREAM

SPECIAL ✦ EDITION®

Published by Silhouette Books

America's Publisher of Contemporary Romance

To Daryl Tumbleson, one of the most accomplished and interesting men I know, with thanks for your help but especially for bringing romance into the life of my best friend in the world. Love you both. D.A.R.

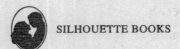 SILHOUETTE BOOKS

ISBN 0-373-24195-X

EVERY COWGIRL'S DREAM

Books by Arlene James

ARLENE JAMES

grew up in Oklahoma and has lived all over the South. In 1976 she married "the most romantic man in the world." The author enjoys traveling with her husband, but writing has always been her chief pastime.

Dear Reader,

What a ride this book has been! From Utah to New Mexico, the hard way. Not for me, mind you, but for Kara Detmeyer. Days spent on horseback, nights spent on the hard ground, working daylight to dark in mercurial weather. Only a *good cowboy* (which is the highest praise, by the way, that one working cowboy can give another) can survive—never mind thrive—in such circumstances. Well, Kara Detmeyer is a good cowboy, gender irrelevant; but that's only part of what makes her THAT SPECIAL WOMAN! for Ryeland Wagner.

It takes a strong, determined individual to excel at the physically and mentally demanding work of ranching, whatever his or her attributes and talents may be. Throw in an old-fashioned cattle drive over a great distance, mix with threats and sabotage, and you have a situation that few could master. Now add a touch of gender bias, a wary young boy and a heart overflowing with love for a single father who's vowed never to love again. Only a tough, talented, stubborn, generous, loving, pure-hearted woman could come out on top of that one! Such a woman is Kara Detmeyer.

She is, essentially, Rye Wagner's exact female equivalent—except in one regard. It takes a certain courage to love as Kara does, unconditionally, without restraint or requirement. It's a kind of courage that Rye no longer possesses and for good reason. So what's a woman to do?

I hope you enjoy Kara's journey as much as I have. Besides, after all, that's the whole point!

God bless,

Arlene James

Chapter One

The old truck rattled across a dry wash in the dirt road and rumbled on toward the low, white house in the distance.

"Place is already going to pot," Kara muttered, and her dog, Oboe, whined agreement from his spot on the seat next to her.

"Don't be silly," her mother, Dayna, said, lifting her silver-streaked, blond ponytail from the back of her neck with a slender hand. "They must've had a rainstorm recently, that's all."

"Plum's only been gone five weeks," Kara remarked. "Looks like that Wagner couldn't keep the place up that long without Plummer around to tell him to do it."

Dayna sighed. "Kara, why don't you like Ryeland Wagner? Your grandfather obviously thought highly of him, or he wouldn't have taken him on as foreman of the ranch."

Kara shook her head. "I don't know. Something about Rye Wagner just—" She shivered. "He makes me uncomfortable."

Dayna slid a speculative glance sideways at her daughter, but Kara didn't notice. Her gaze was trained on the dusty yard of her late grandparent's Utah ranch house. She loved that old house. It didn't have the same kind of personality as the fine log home her parents had built on the New Mexico place, but it was

Plummer and Meryl Detmeyer through and through, from its rough exterior to the glowing red rock hearth standing dead center in the living room and the soft, lush, hand-hooked rug in the master bedroom. Her grandmother had made that rug long before Kara was born, and Plummer had treasured it every day afterward, just as he'd treasured every rocky inch of the Detmeyer Ranch and every hide of every Detmeyer cow that roamed the rocky range. In the same way, Kara treasured the Detmeyer legacy, the ranching concern that reached across three states and five generations.

She brought the old truck to a halt, noting with both satisfaction and trepidation the number of other vehicles parked inside the split-rail fence that marked the ranch house yard. Her cousin Payne's convertible was there, along with Uncle Smith's luxury sedan, and Plummer's new double-cab pickup truck, as well as another vehicle that looked like a rental. Kara's heart did a flip-flop at the sight of her grandfather's shiny new truck. It was his last indulgence. The rental, she presumed, belonged to the attorney who would read the will.

Reaching down, Kara switched off the engine of her battered old truck. She took a deep breath and closed her eyes briefly. Dayna Detmeyer reached across the seat and squeezed the top of her daughter's shoulder. "It'll be okay, honey. Plummer always took care of everything, didn't he?"

Kara sighed. "I know. It's just that with Daddy and Grandpa both gone, it only leaves Uncle Smith to oversee the business, and all he really cares about is his bank in Denver. He'd been trying to get Grandpa to sell forever."

"Have some faith. Your grandmother's bound to have some say."

Kara nodded, but she remembered too well how delicate and aged her grandmother had looked at the funeral, how diminished she'd seemed to be. It was as if Plummer's death had taken the heart right out of the old woman. Kara feared it had done even more than that. She feared, for some reason, that Plummer Detmeyer's death had taken the heart right out of the family itself. Losing her father had been a severe blow, but losing Plummer little more than a year later might well mean the finish, at least of the business. Yet it was unthinkable that somewhere on this earth there should not be a Detmeyer ranch. Plummer would have made some provision. He had to have done. He just had to.

Oboe whined in a bid for freedom. Being cooped up in the cab of the old truck all the way from Farmington, New Mexico, was a trial for him. Four hours without a good run or a pit stop. Poor baby. "All right, all right," Kara said, ruffling his thick black-and-white coat. "Go find something to bark at."

Oboe answered her with something between a snort and sneeze that could have meant anything from "Move it, sister," to "I adore the ground you walk on." Kara got out of the truck, and the dog bounded out after her, racing off toward the corrals.

Kara smiled. "He hates living in town."

"He's not the only one," Dayna said with a laugh, and let herself out of the truck.

Kara made a face. It was true. She'd never gotten used to the traffic and the constant swarm of people, the cement and the brick. She hated her job waiting tables, hated the featureless little apartment where they lived. She mourned the loss of her horses and the rolling, lush green of the Chama valley, the utter silence at dawn, the vastness of a night sky so empty of reflected artificial light that the heavens lifted into an infinity strewn with diamonds. Her cousin had said at her father's funeral that Lawton Detmeyer's death marked the end of an empire, but the truth was that the empire days were long gone for the Detmeyers. Kara knew that. Yet Plummer and Lawton had wrested good livings from the two remaining parcels of what had once been a vast enterprise that rivaled that of the robber barons—until Law had been accidentally killed. That in itself had almost put an end to the New Mexico operation.

Kara still felt the shock of it every time she thought about her father's failure to insure his own life. That, together with the sudden downturn in the beef market, had almost put the place into receivership. As it was, they'd had to sell off all the stock and equipment to meet the demands of creditors and pay the taxes. Kara and her mother had moved a hundred and twenty miles west to Farmington in order to support themselves until the market turned around and they could somehow afford to re-stock the ranch.

Plummer's personal decline had started then. The financial pressure had been too much for him. With his younger son gone, his will to live had faltered as certainly as his seventy-six-year-old heart. He had rallied for a while after Rye Wagner had taken the job as foreman at the Utah ranch. He had, in fact, seemed to adopt Rye, transferring his affection and his esteem for his younger son to the new foreman. That, along with Rye's distant, faintly disapproving attitude toward her, had not sat well with Kara. Despite the fact that he looked like every cowgirl's dream, from his gray eyes and splendidly drooping mustache to his large-knuckled hands and big, booted feet, Kara resented the lanky, good-looking cowboy.

It was true that Plummer's judgment had always been sound. What Plummer hadn't known about cattle and ranching was yet a mystery to God Himself, in Kara's opinion. But still she couldn't quite conquer the uneasiness that she felt every time Ryeland Wagner came within spitting distance of her.

Ah, well. She wouldn't have to worry about that much longer. After today, she'd never have to see Ryeland Wagner again. It irked her that Plummer had specifically requested Rye's presence at the reading of the will, but this was surely the last time she'd ever have to look into his pewter gray eyes and feel that he was taking her measure and finding her wanting.

Shaking out her long legs, Kara put a hand in the small of her back and stretched out the kinks before following her mother toward the low, sun-bleached ranch house where she had spent so many idyllic summers. At five feet nine inches and one hundred forty pounds of pure muscle, Kara was no lightweight, but she felt diminutive the instant Payne swept down on her from the porch, his long, thick arms coming around her.

"Hey, little cousin. Thought you'd never get here."

Kara laughed, her blond ponytail bobbing, and kissed Payne on the cheek, smiling up into blue eyes very like her own. "Hey, yourself, cuz. Been here long?"

Payne drew back and grimaced at her. "Got here last night. Dad insisted. He seemed to have this idea that Grandmother would know every detail of the will and give it to him early." The sparkle in his eyes said that Smith Detmeyer had yet again underestimated his parent. Kara couldn't help a smile. Uncle Smitty's run-ins with the old folks were legendary. Somehow Smitty just didn't operate on the same plane as his parents and his brother. It was a good thing, again in Kara's opinion, that

Smith had opted to go into banking instead of taking an active interest in the ranching operation. She only hoped that he would continue the policy now that Plummer was gone.

She clamped a hand onto Payne's bulging forearm. "So how is she?"

"Okay. Sad. Smaller, somehow."

Kara nodded. "Yeah, that was my impression last time. She seemed so fragile."

"Well, I'd say she's recovered a bit of the old spunk," Payne told her, eyes sparkling. "She sent Dad to his room last night."

"You're kidding!"

He chuckled and leaned close, whispering into her ear, "The really funny part is that he went."

Kara had to press a hand to her mouth to keep from laughing aloud. "Poor Smitty!"

"Well, he should've known he wasn't going to get anything out of her. Law, now he could have had her spilling the beans in no time."

Kara shook her head. "Dad wouldn't have asked."

Payne looked chastened. "You're right, of course. I only meant that he knew how to talk to his parents."

"That he did. Now, then," Kara said, changing the subject briskly, "how are you?"

"Can't complain."

"Make another killing in the stock market recently?"

Payne shrugged noncommittally. Dayna came back to the door, pushing open the screen to poke her head out.

"You two coming in?"

"In a minute," Payne answered. "We can't get started until Wagner shows himself, anyway."

"Well, your father seems a bit anxious," Dayna said, and Payne and Kara traded loaded looks. "Don't keep him waiting any longer than you must."

"Wouldn't dream of it," Payne said.

Kara added, "If Rye doesn't show up soon, we'll go looking for him, Mom."

"I'll tell that to Smitty." Dayna pulled back inside and closed the screen door. Payne stepped up onto the porch and walked over to one corner to lean against the railing, arms and ankles crossed. Kara followed.

"So, all's well in Denver, huh?"

"I know you can't fathom the attraction," Payne said, "but the city has a lot going for it. What have you got against theater and sports and good restaurants, anyway?"

She hitched up a shoulder. "Nothing. They're just in the city, that's all, and since when have you taken an interest in the theater?"

Payne's eyes took on a special glint. "Well, actually, since I met this little actress at one of mother's events."

Kara groaned. "Not another of your women!"

"Sweetie, that phrase may have to be reduced to the singular soon."

"You don't mean it!"

"I do."

Kara let her mouth hang open. "Good grief, you're actually thinking of settling down. Will wonders never cease?"

Payne laughed. "You're not going to say, 'It's about time!'?"

"No, but it is."

"Look who's talking," he retorted. "You're only two years younger than me, you know."

"It's that thirty thing," Kara teased. "You're over the hump, and I'm not."

Payne's grin turned lethal. "So, still no man in the picture for you, hmm?"

"I have other things on my mind."

"That could be changing, you know," Payne said softly.

Knowing perfectly well that he was trying to prepare her for the likely loss of the ranch where she had grown up and the life she had lived, Kara turned away—and caught sight of Rye Wagner as he left the little house on the hill that came with the job of foreman. A chill ruffled along the flesh of her arms, despite the weight of the shirt and jean jacket that she was wearing.

"Wagner's on the way."

Payne straightened. "I don't get it. Why'd Plummer mention him in the will? He's only been here, what, seven, eight months?"

"Something like that."

Payne's mouth set in a harsh, bitter line. "Yeah. Well, apparently he fit the bill in Plummer's estimation. Unlike myself."

"That's not true," Kara protested. "Plummer understood that

this life isn't for everyone. He was proud of you and all you've accomplished. He wouldn't have let you handle the finances otherwise.''

Payne relaxed and put on a smile. ''I know. It's just that the appeal of Ryeland Wagner purely escapes me.''

Kara turned back to watch as Wagner approached. She didn't much like the foreman, either, but Plummer had always known a real cowboy when he came across one, and he'd sung Wagner's praises for months before his death. She had to believe that Wagner was capable, honest and hardworking, even if he was as prickly as cactus. For the first time she wondered what Rye Wagner was going to do now. Unless she missed her guess, Wagner wasn't the sort who could easily go to another kind of life, either. No, he was the genuine article, cowboy down to the soles of his boots, rancher to the bone. Where would he find another job in this tight market?

Oboe loped up to Wagner's side and fell into step with him. Wagner looked down at the black-and-white shepherd, obviously speaking, though Kara could not decipher the words at this distance. Oboe shook his head and made that almost absurdly human sound of his as if actually replying to something Wagner had said. Wagner spoke again, cocked his head and reached up to reposition his hat, all the while eating up ground with that long, athletic stride of his. Kara couldn't help a slight smile. They might have been pals, two very human pals, only one of them had four feet.

As they drew nearer the porch, Oboe kicked up his tail and scampered ahead. He ran lightly up the steps and over to Kara. As if to let her know that she was still number one in his book, the dog went up on his hind legs, forepaws resting on her hip, and gave her that snort-sneeze of his. Laughing, Kara rumpled his fur. Oboe answered with a real bark. Payne reached out to duplicate her actions, which the dog tolerated but ignored. He didn't seem to like Payne, but apparently put up with him for Kara's benefit. She found it rather embarrassing.

''Hello, Wagner,'' Payne said, switching his attention to the cowboy.

Rye ignored him, doffing his hat to Kara. ''Miss Detmeyer.''

''Mr. Wagner.''

''That's a right smart dog you've got there,'' he said drily.

Payne gnashed his teeth, but Wagner continued to ignore him by opening the screen door and walking into the house.

"Arrogant son of a—"

Kara threw an arm around her cousin's shoulders. "Oh, don't let him get to you. He won't be around much longer, anyway."

Payne ducked his head, and when he lifted it again, he was smiling wryly. "You're right. We'd better go in now."

Kara took a deep breath. "Guess so. No sense standing around out here dreading it."

Payne stepped to the door and swung it open, bowing from the waist. Kara swept inside, Oboe following right on her heels, head and tail aloft as though he were a king receiving his due. Payne brought up the rear, the screen door slamming lightly behind him.

The family had gathered in the living room, claiming seats on the sofas and chairs arranged around the fireplace, with Rye Wagner on one side and the lawyer on the other. The attorney had placed his briefcase on a small table, pushing aside a genuine Victorian lamp, and was digging through the contents. Rye leaned against the wall, frowning beneath that magnificent mustache, his hat in his hand, silent and watchful. Kara went straight to where her grandmother sat.

Meryl Detmeyer was a tall, rawboned woman with long, white hair that she wore pinned in elaborate loops and rolls against the back of her head. Her blue eyes had paled over the years, but nothing could dim the intelligence that shone through them. They softened now as Kara bent to hug the old woman's neck. Meryl's skin felt dry as paper, her bones brittle as straw beneath Kara's touch.

"How are you, Grandma?"

"As well as can be expected, dear. Glad to see you."

Kara went down on her knees at her grandmother's feet, her eyes filling with tears. "It's so hard with him gone, isn't it?"

Meryl nodded. "I always believed I would be the first to go. I counted on it. Seems selfish now. My consolation is that Grandpa didn't have to go through being left behind."

"He loved you so much."

A dreamy look darkened Meryl's blue eyes. "Yes," she whispered, smiling. "Yes, he did." Suddenly her eyes grew sharp again. "It's time, young lady, that you had a man of your own."

Kara gasped, "Grandma!"

"Hear, hear," Dayna agreed.

"Mom!"

Payne laughed, and Kara sent him a daggered look. "Watch it, cuz," she said. "I have ammo, now, a certain rising interest in the theater."

He stifled the laughter and pressed his lips together, zipping a finger across them. Faith, Payne's mother, was not so circumspect. The instant she caught the reference, she spilled her guts. "Oh, yes, Meryl, did I mention that Payne is keeping company with a certain Denver debutante who has a professional interest in the theater?"

"A debutante, no less," Kara teased, wide-eyed. Payne narrowed his eyes and made a wringing motion with his hands.

Faith ignored them, as she usually did, crowing, "Everyone says she's really quite a good actress, and she's certainly beautiful! And the family... My dear, the family is impeccable. Old, old money. Deep, deep roots. I have hopes. I have great hopes."

Meryl turned a discerning gaze on Payne. "And do you have hopes?"

Payne's smile was bright. "Actually, I do."

Meryl smiled and stretched out her hand, softening. "I'm glad. I'm very glad."

Payne caught her fingertips with his and moved close. Bending, he kissed her forehead. He sent Kara a wink as he straightened. She telegraphed her gratitude with a grin. He had certainly taken the heat off her.

Smitty harrumphed sharply and said, "Let's not count our chickens before they hatch." A sentiment everyone else chose to ignore.

The small, balding, middle-aged attorney cleared his throat. "I believe we're all present, so I'd like to begin."

Kara rose and quickly moved to stand behind her mother at end of the sofa. The attorney extracted from his briefcase several stapled documents, which he began passing out.

"For those of you who do not know me, I am Ardel Canton, and I've been Plummer and Meryl's attorney for nearly thirty years. In that time the document in your hands has been altered in a number of ways. At one point Plummer had willed everything to his wife. Later he changed his will to leave everything to his two sons. Then after the death of his son, Lawton, he changed it yet again. The final version, with the addition of two codicils, was made some five weeks ago.''

"Five weeks!'' Smith echoed. He turned a scathing glare over his shoulder. "I don't suppose that would have anything to do with Wagner.''

"In a way it does,'' Canton affirmed, "but first things first.'' Ardel Canton cleared his throat yet again and lifted the cover sheet on the document in his hand. "The first order of business, as I'm sure you will note, deals with the widow. 'To my dearest Meryl,''' he began reading, and suddenly Kara could hear her grandfather's gravelly voice saying the words he had no doubt dictated himself.

"I leave my undying love and eternal gratitude. You have been the light of my life, at times my conscience, and always my strength and support. Forgive me for being the first to go and for doing what I now must. I trust you will understand, as you always have, and uphold my wishes in this matter without deviation. Upon my death, I leave my dear wife the home to which I brought her as a bride, the six acres upon which it stands, including all the outbuildings herein detailed....''

"I think we can leave off the listing,'' Canton said and flipped the page while Meryl sniffed and wiped her eyes. He continued reading, "''As sole recipient of the proceeds of my life insurance, policy number...''' Canton moved on down the page, continuing with, "''In the amount of three hundred and eighty thousand dollars, the principal to be invested and dispersed as herein detailed, providing her a yearly living, it is my express wish that she make no monetary gifts of any size to anyone, including family members, until a minimum of three years after the date of my death.'''

Canton paused to let this sink in, and Meryl said with some amusement, "I'm not to give away my own money, am I?''

Ardel Canton had the grace to look uncomfortable. "It was Plummer's express wish.''

"Well, I think it's preposterous,'' Smith announced.

Canton kept his gaze on Meryl. "He said you'd understand.''

One corner of her mouth crooked up in a near smile. "Proceed, Ardel."

He cleared his throat again, obviously a nervous habit, and plunged ahead.

"To my son Smith Detmeyer, I leave my unconditional love and my hunting trophies, knowing that of all my possessions, he appreciated those the most. I beg him to accept them in the same manner with which they are offered. To my grandchildren—"

"What?" Suddenly Smith was on his feet, flipping through the stapled pages furiously. "He left me his *hunting trophies?* His damned *hunting trophies!* My God, had he lost his mind? I'm his only living son! He can't do this to me!"

"Actually," Canton said lightly, "he could and he did. Now if I may proceed..."

"You may not! This is absurd! It's criminal!"

"I assure you it's all perfectly legal."

"But if he didn't leave it all to Uncle Smitty or Grandmother, who did he leave it to?" Kara asked.

"I am coming to that," Mr. Canton said in a harried voice.

"Who's left?" Payne said quietly, and traded looks with his father.

Who, indeed? Kara wondered. Certainly not her mother or Aunt Faith. But then that left only Payne and herself and— Oh, no. He wouldn't.... She tried but couldn't stop herself from turning to look over one shoulder. Rye Wagner leaned insolently against the wall. He smirked and shook his head as if to say she was a fool for even thinking it. She quickly turned her gaze forward again.

Her grandmother was scolding them. "Everyone just shut up and let Mr. Canton read! Proceed, Ardel."

He strained his neck, and Kara winced, beginning to dread those throat clearings. He made a gargling sound and began flipping pages. "There are a number of minor individual bequests detailed on the following pages. However, since the main concern is the Detmeyer ranching properties, we'll move on to page seven." He began to read again.

"All real business properties, including all stock, structures, equipment and supplies, other than those entailed to the historical home, henceforth known as The Business, with the exceptions heretofore mentioned and that to follow—is left *in partnership,* with all the attendant provisions and restrictions, to my beloved grandchildren, Payne Smith Detmeyer and Kara Ann Detmeyer."

Kara felt weak. It was a toss-up, for a moment, whether or not her legs would even continue to hold her. She swayed forward and gripped the back of the sofa, dimly conscious of her mother's hands covering hers. Gradually, Canton's voice penetrated the haze into which the bequest had plummeted her.

"It is my deepest regret that The Business is no longer the robust enterprise that I and my late son, Lawton, have been honored to oversee. That being the case, it is my wish and intent that my heirs will exercise one of two options which I dictate as: *(a)* Selling the assets of The Business, i.e. the Utah and New Mexico properties in total, the equipment and stock, omitting only those items delineated for personal bequest as set forth in this document, for equal division of resulting monies after settlement of outstanding obligations, debts, fees and taxes, and *(b)* selling the Utah property, omitting only those items as mentioned above, for settlement of outstanding obligations, debts, fees and taxes, while transferring all equipment and stock held by The Business to the New Mexico property to be operated by the partnership, allowing the continuance of The Business in hopes that its viability may be maintained."

"Hardly a sound option," Smith stated solemnly.

Meryl said nothing, merely maintained her expectant posture. Dayna gripped Kara's hand, smiling.

"What about the codicils?" Payne asked. "Do they alter our options?"

Ardel Canton swiped a hand over his balding pate. Kara imagined the poor man was sweating despite the chill in the air.

"They do, indeed. As to the first codicil, if you will turn to page eight..."

Papers rustled as everyone flipped to that page, Kara included. Canton skipped the throat clearing this time and instead shot a glance toward the far wall. Kara felt Ryeland Wagner's sudden interest, his growing presence. It was as if he had absented himself mentally until that glance, and now he was fully there, dominating the entire room with nothing more than his attention.

"'To my friend and foreman, Ryeland Wagner,'" Canton read, "'I leave two months' severance and the pickup truck, ID number—' we'll skip those particulars for the moment '—in free and final title, including payment of all pertaining loans, taxes and fees, fully realizing that said bequest will totally consume the cash reserves of The Business as held in account with First National Bank, Salt Lake City, Utah.'"

"For heaven's sake!" Faith gasped. No one had to say that the double-cab, dual-axle, top-of-the-line vehicle had cost in excess of fifty thousand dollars, or that both Smith and Payne had argued vociferously that its purchase was both unnecessary and unwise.

Kara turned another look over her shoulder. Rye Wagner was staring at the crown of the hat he held in both hands, a wistful, sad smile tilting up one corner of his drooping, multicolored mustache. A swatch of medium brown hair fell over his high forehead, contrasting with his deeply tanned skin and the wide bands of silver at his temples. His pewter gray eyes were sheltered with thick rows of lashes mottled in the same fashion as his mustache, a dozen shades of brown flecked with silver. A pale scar crinkled at the corner of his right eye, and Kara found herself wondering how he had come by it. Belatedly she became aware of the angry words swirling around her.

"Preposterous!" Smith was saying. "*I get hunting trophies*, while *he* gets a brand-spanking-new truck and a wad of cash handed to him on a silver platter!"

"I'm afraid those were your father's wishes," the attorney retorted.

"And his wishes will be followed!" Meryl stated flatly.

Smith's glare and red face proclaimed that he held the attorney at fault somehow, along with Ryeland Wagner.

Payne lifted a hand as if requesting permission to speak, and the attorney tacitly granted it by pausing.

"The term *in partnership* seems to imply that the restrictions of a business partnership apply."

"That's correct. In essence, the conditions of the late Mr. Detmeyer's will creates a business partnership in which both parties must come to agreement concerning the operation and or dispensation of the properties."

"In other words, Kara and I must agree before either of us can do anything with the ranches."

"Exactly."

"Can you tell me why my grandfather set it up this way?"

Canton cleared his throat. "I'm afraid that comes under the heading of attorney-client privilege."

"I see." Payne looked down at the paper in his hand. Kara sensed that he saw something there that she did not. All that mattered to her at the moment, however, was that her grandfather had done his best to protect the ranch. Her eyes filled with tears.

Canton said, "Now to the final codicil," and Kara lifted her chin, blinking determinedly.

"I hope it reclaims the cash and the property he gave to that ranch hand!" Smith grumbled loudly.

The "ranch hand" in question quietly lifted himself away from the wall and moved forward. Suddenly Kara's mouth went dry. Why was Ryeland Wagner at her elbow? It was almost as if he meant to lend her his aid, and yet he couldn't possibly know what this last codicil contained. Could he? She glanced to the side and found Rye Wagner's smoky gray eyes trained on her. She tilted her head in confusion. His expression revealed nothing.

"This last provision," attorney Canton said after the ritual clearing of the throat, "is most unusual but, I assure you, completely legal. Plummer made sure of that, and he was most insistent about its details. Please refrain from comment until I've read the entire section." He took a deep breath and plunged in.

"Knowing each of my grandchildren and in consideration, I freely admit, of my own heartfelt desires, I have wrestled with a means by which to fairly and rightly ensure the continuation of the Detmeyer family and the great legacy with which our forebearers have gifted us. To wit, in order to preserve the most viable of the properties and the life-style enjoyed by generations of Detmeyers and some remnant of the ranching concern that once made the name of Detmeyer great, I leave this as my last express wish.

"I charge and challenge my dear granddaughter, Kara, to undertake, with the direct guidance, advice and assistance of Ryeland Wagner, his consent being granted, the commission of a certain exercise with the following results. If, within six weeks from this date, Kara and Ryeland together, with those assistants of their own choosing, can successfully move a minimum of three hundred head of cattle from the Utah property to the environs of the New Mexico property owned by The Business, in the same fashion and the great tradition of those of old, that is, enacting the modern equivalent of the vaunted tradition known as a *trail drive,* the New Mexico property, cattle, and all equipment, supplies and assets held by The Business, shall be hers and hers alone, with the express wish that she manage it in accordance with her heart's desire and mine. To this end, I have outlined—"

"This is absurd! Beyond absurd!" Smith cried, ensuring that Canton did not get his wish, nor could he have truly expected to, considering the shocking contents of that codicil.

Kara herself could hardly believe her ears. Perhaps she had misunderstood the legal jargon. Perhaps she was dreaming. She couldn't think beyond the words that kept running through her head.

New Mexico property. Hers and hers alone. In accordance with her heart's desire and mine. Her heart's desire and mine. Hers and hers alone. And all she had to do was drive the cattle to New Mexico in the same manner as her ancestors might have done—with the guidance, advice and assistance of none other than Ryeland Wagner. Who had given his consent.

He had known. He had known exactly what this final codicil to her grandfather's will had contained—and he had agreed to go along with it. Deaf to the storm raging around her, Kara turned to the man standing at her side. Ryeland Wagner met her gaze unflinchingly. His solemn gray eyes said that he didn't understand it, either, nor did he give a fig why Plummer had set things up this way. He had given his word; everything else was academic. As if that look told her all she needed to know, he gave a slight nod, put on his hat and walked out.

Chapter Two

Rye shook his head. They could shout till the cows came home, but it wouldn't change anything. Plummer had planned too well. He still couldn't quite believe that he'd let himself be talked into doing this thing with Kara Detmeyer, of all people. Cool, blond, blue-eyed, shapely Kara. She didn't like him any better than good old Payne did, and Payne hated his guts, had since the moment they'd laid eyes on each other, and it had been mutual even then. Somehow, Payne was the reason Plummer had come up with this scheme. Rye still couldn't fathom it. What had Plummer expected to accomplish? He could've left the place outright to anyone he'd chosen, but he'd chosen to make it conditional—on the completion of a trail drive, of all things! With Rye right in the middle of it.

He stepped down off the porch and started across the dusty yard. Behind him the screen door opened and slammed closed.

"Just a minute!"

He sighed and turned reluctantly to face her. She marched right up and stood toe-to-toe with him. She was tall enough to look him right in the eye with only a slight tilt to her chin. Oddly, he liked that, which was more than enough to spark his flight response. He stepped back and to the side as casually as he could manage, aware that his pulse was slamming. "Don't get in my face," he told her harshly, despite feeling foolish. It worked. She backed off.

"Sorry. I just want to ask you a question."

He rubbed a hand over his mustache, feeling his own frown. He knew what Champ would say about that. Champ would say, "Daddy, your mouth is hiding again." He wondered what Champ would say about his trembling hands. Rye nodded. "All right. One question, then I've gotta go."

She gulped. "Why'd he do this?"

"Haven't the faintest notion. Now if you'll excuse me..." He turned away and started walking again.

"Wait!"

"One question, Miss Detmeyer," he said over his shoulder. But suddenly she was in front of him, not behind him, her arms stretched out straight and locked, her hands on his chest. He reversed himself, spinning away. "Do you mind? I have to get back to my boy!"

"You knew he was going to do this," she said. "You had to!"

"Yes," he admitted, rerouting around her. "We'll discuss it after dinner. Or don't you think my son gets hungry like other boys?"

She let him go, but he could feel her frustration and curiosity like physical entities that rode his back all the way up the hill. He pushed them away as he stepped through the door into the little house that had been more home for him and his son than any other. Champ was stretched out on his belly on the living room rug, thumbing through a catalog. Borden Harris, the horse wrangler and the only hand left on the ranch, sat in the rocker in front of the window, braiding a leather riata. Rye hung his hat on a hook on the wall and turned toward him.

"How'd it go?" he asked, his curiosity obvious.

Rye shrugged. "It went. They're all shouting at each other down there. I figured I'd get supper on. Care to join us?"

"Don't mind if I do," Bord said.

"Thanks for keeping an eye on this rug rat," Rye told him, kicking his son's boot affectionately on his way to the kitchen.

"No problem," Bord said. "I only had to skin his head a time or two."

"Did not!" Champ giggled, rolling over onto his back.

"Well, how d'you explain that bald spot back there then?" Bord teased.

"Is not!"

"It didn't rub off all by itself."

"Uh-uh!"

Rye chuckled as he walked on into the kitchen. Champ was fun to tease because he tended to take everything so seriously, sometimes too seriously. He'd sure taken the old man's passing hard. But no harder than his father, if the truth be told.

It still hurt Rye to think of the old man being gone. He would never forget everything the old man had done for him. And that truck. If he lived to be a hundred, he'd never get over that damned truck! Plummer must have intended from the beginning to see it go to him. Plummer had known his heart was bad, and the cash flow had been nothing more than a trickle at the time he'd bought the thing—just after Rye's own truck had burned its motor into a lump of coal. It hadn't occurred to Rye that Plummer would leave it to him. Rye's eyes watered; he wouldn't give in to tears.

For more reasons than he could count, Rye would have bossed a trail drive all the way to hell and back if the old man had asked him to. Fortunately, he only had to go as far as New Mexico. After that, he had no idea where he was going or what he was going to do, but he would think of that later.

He got out a cast-iron skillet and a bag of potatoes. Working quickly, he spooned shortening into the skillet and set it over a burner on the propane stove. Then he began peeling the potatoes, rinsing them and slicing them. When the grease was just about hot enough to start smoking, he tossed in the raw potato slices and jumped back to keep from getting splashed. When the hot grease settled down, he went back to work, opening cans and dumping their contents into various pans until all four of the burners were covered. The end result was a meal of potatoes fried into a kind of brown mush, corned beef hash, green beans and creamed corn, that, too, a little on the brownish side. It wasn't the fancy fare they'd be having down at the big house, but the atmosphere was decidedly more convivial.

* * *

Dinner was a tense affair. Payne was smiling and easy, but Kara sensed an underlying tension in him, too. Smith was just plain belligerent. He'd made no secret about his feelings. He didn't like being left out of the principal portions of the will, and he didn't like this trail drive nonsense that would effectively cut out his son, too. Kara couldn't blame him, but she'd make that drive anyway and make it on time with all the stock required, and she'd do it with Rye Wagner's help, no matter how much it galled her.

Aunt Faith, for her part, behaved as if it were all Kara's fault, conveniently forgetting that Kara had had no more idea what Plummer's will had contained than anyone else—with one obvious exception. But he wasn't around to receive their slings and arrows; Kara was. And she figured it was a small price to pay for the right to keep her home. Poor Meryl just seemed sad, her grief still too real for anything else to matter. Kara allowed her grandmother her grief, and did her best to ignore her aunt's and uncle's animosity. Smith wouldn't let it lie, however.

"It's not fair," he said for perhaps the hundredth time. "Father knew I'd be hurt. He did it on purpose."

"Don't be silly," Meryl countered wearily. "Your father did what he thought was best, period."

"Staging a cattle drive? How could that be best? Especially with one person winding up with everything at the end of it!"

"You wouldn't be complaining if that person was Payne," Dayna pointed out defensively.

"As it should have been, if not myself!" Smith retorted.

"I'm not a rancher," Payne put in smoothly. "Grandfather obviously wanted someone who would try to make a go of the ranch. That would, naturally, be Kara."

"Thanks, cuz," Kara said softly.

"No thanks necessary," he replied. "And there's no point kicking and screaming. Why he did it doesn't really matter, only that he did." He kept his eye on his plate as he cut into his steak. "I'll admit I'm a little hurt, but that doesn't mean I don't wish you the best."

"I appreciate that," Kara said. "Frankly, I'm not sure I'd be so good about it if the tables were turned. But I promise you that it won't be for nothing. Detmeyers have ranched this country almost since there were cattle to herd, and it won't end with me, I swear.''

"Let's hope you're right," Payne said lightly, and adroitly changed the subject. "My compliments to Angelina, Grandmother. These steaks are perfection, as always.''

"I'll tell her you said so,''· Meryl said in acknowledgment, forking up a bite of asparagus.

Smith said nothing more, but it was obvious that he had no intention of being mollified. Kara sighed inwardly and forked steak into her mouth. The beef was wonderful. She took pride in the fact that it had been raised right here and willed the minutes to pass until she could meet Rye Wagner. They had much to do, much to decide—and not a minute to lose. She'd already jotted down dozens of things that needed to be done.

Finally everyone began to leave the table. Kara headed down the hall toward the small room that her grandfather had long ago appropriated as his study. The door was closed, but she didn't bother to knock before opening it and walking inside. Ryeland Wagner was already there and on the telephone. He sat in her grandfather's chair just as Plummer himself had done, his booted feet propped on the corner of the desk, the telephone trapped between his shoulder and his ear. His hat was parked on top of the desk lamp just as Plummer's had often been, and he welcomed her into his domain with a nod and a flip of his hand, for all the world as if he were Plummer Detmeyer himself. But he wasn't.

Anger and resentment swept through Kara. She marched straight to the desk and knocked Rye Wagner's feet off her grandfather's desk with a whack of one hand. The chair bumped upright, and Rye's frosty eyebrows bumped up several notches with it.

"I'll call you back, George," he said smoothly into the telephone receiver, then reached across the desk and dropped it into its old-fashioned cradle with the rotary dial. "What's wrong with you?" he said to Kara. "Dinner not up to your lofty standards?"

"Dinner was excellent!'' she snapped, walking around the end of the desk to his side. "What's wrong with me is *you!* You're *not* my grandfather. This is *not* your office, your desk, your chair, your anything! I'll thank you not to treat it as though it were!''

"Lady, you've got some nerve," he told her, glaring up at

her. "I've parked my butt in this chair more times than you can count and, yes, propped my feet on the desk—with Plummer's full blessing. He gave me the run of the place the first day I came here, the office, the house, the whole damned ranch. But then, he was a generous man and a damned fine one, an aberration among the Detmeyers, seems to me."

Kara gasped, outraged. "You arrogant ass!" She leaned forward, getting in his face very much on purpose, her hands braced on the arms of the chair. "I'll have you know my father was as fine a man as ever—"

Suddenly his gaze ratcheted up to her face, and she realized belatedly that he hadn't exactly been paying attention to her words. She started to look down at whatever had distracted him, when he threw up his hands, knocking hers from the arms of the chair and barked, "Button up your blouse!"

Shocked, Kara snapped upright and dropped her gaze straight down. A couple of buttons had indeed slipped their holes. She clapped a hand over them. Before she could do more, he was on his feet and in *her* face.

"Don't try that stunt again! Flaunting your body won't work with me!

Red flared behind Kara's eyes. Rage strangled her. She couldn't even close her mouth, let along force words through it. She took the only other option that seemed open to her, her right hand swinging out to connect sharply with his cheek. His head snapped to the side and then back again. Suddenly she was facing the angriest man she'd ever seen. It was like one of those cartoons, the enraged bull snorting visible fire from his nostrils and eyes. Her hand was still hanging in the air between them, and he grabbed it. Instinctively Kara shoved against him, succeeding only in toppling him backward and down into the chair again. As he had a hold on her, she went down on top of him, knocking the chair back, so that their boots hit the hard edge of the desk, feet and legs tangling as they struggled independently to keep the chair from tipping all the way over. Rye clamped an arm around her waist. She flung her own across the back of the chair. Then the chair rocked forward again and they were safe. Nose to nose.

Kara gasped, and felt her breasts swell against his chest. Anger had fled in the face of fear and embarrassment, and now suddenly something else had taken its place, something that raised her body temperature alarmingly and sent her heart rate into triple time, something that drew her gaze to Rye Wagner's mustachioed mouth like a magnet to a lodestone. His hand flexed against her back, fingers spreading, pressing. Awareness flashed through her. She felt every square inch of his body against hers with abnormal clarity. And then he let go of her hand and cupped the back of her head beneath her ponytail. Her heart stopped. Her breath seized in her lungs. Something tightened in the pit of her belly. She could almost feel the prickle of his mustache. And then the door opened and her mother walked into the room.

"Kara, I've been think—ing..."

Kara shoved upward. Rye practically threw her onto her feet and followed her up so quickly that the chair sprang forward like a sling and rolled against the desk. His hand caught in her hair, sending the rubber band that held it shooting across the room. Kara stumbled and sat down hard.

"Kara!" Dayna gasped.

Rye reached for her, yanked back, and reached for her again. She slapped his hands away, grabbed for the corner of the desk and crawled her way back onto her feet, pushing hair out of her face. Rye was again staring pointedly at her chest. She looked down at the open buttons and slapped a hand over them hard enough to bruise herself.

"Kara! Are you all right?"

"Yes!" Her voice squeaked like a rusty hinge. She cleared her throat and thought inanely of attorney Canton. "Oh! I—um... s-so—clumsy!"

"Clumsy!" Rye echoed. He stared at Dayna for a long moment, his face flaring red, and then he blinked and said, "She fell."

"I saw that!"

"Before, I mean. She fell before...she fell."

Kara forced a laugh. "Yes, I...I don't know what's gotten into me. I'm so clumsy all of a sudden. I think I've had— It was all a shock. Today. Everything. It was—" She made herself swallow whatever other words were about to fall out of her mouth and lifted her chin, her free hand going to her tumbled hair. She *forced* herself to face Rye. "About those details..."

"I'll have...them together...soon."

She looked away, saying briskly, "Yes, have them ready for my approval in the morning."

"For your—" He strangled the last word and said tightly instead, "In the morning. Fine."

She had her nose so high in the air that she could hardly see where she was going, but she went, anyway. "Thank you. Well good night I'm more tired than I thought," Kara said as quickly as possible. She swept past her mother and down the hall.

Dayna Detmeyer followed, stopping to lean her shoulder thoughtfully against the wall just outside the door to the study. Significantly, that door slowly creaked closed a moment later. Dayna's mouth wiggled. A chuckle sputtered out. She lifted a hand and pressed it against her lips. After a bit she let it fall and lifted her eyes upward. "Plummer, you old cupid," she whispered. "God love you." And then she took herself off, smiling.

She knocked this time, not because she thought he deserved any special consideration, but because it was one more way to put off the dreaded meeting. Her face still pulsed red when she thought of the ridiculous tussle that had taken place the night before—and its aftermath. She could not even bear to think of that moment when she'd realized she was in his lap, her blouse unbuttoned, her body behaving absurdly, her gaze pinned hopefully on his mouth. How could she have wanted him to kiss her? How could she have felt such...*longing?* And how was she going to face him now?

He negated that worry by yanking open the door himself. And there he stood, a harried look on his face, his smoky brown hair tousled, a clipboard braced against one hip, a pencil sticking out of his mustache. He plucked the pencil out of his mouth as if it were a cigarette. "Oh. Hi. Want some coffee? Angelina just dropped off a pot." He glanced over his shoulder and added wryly, "And enough sweet rolls to feed a whole crew, which, incidentally, ought to be our first order of business. A crew, that is." He seemed to realize just then that he was still blocking the doorway and hopped back. "Oh. Come on in."

She slipped inside, still too nervous to look him in the eye and murmured, "Coffee sounds good."

He got busy in front of one of the filing cabinets. Waving a hand negligently, he said, "Help yourself." A second or two later he added, "Rolls are good—if you haven't had your breakfast."

"I haven't," she confirmed, helping herself to a mug of brew and a fat, golden brown roll dripping with white icing. Angelina had thoughtfully supplied napkins to go along with the treats but no plates or flatware. Kara held the roll gingerly in one hand and the coffee mug in the other, then carefully positioned herself on one of a pair of scarred wood kitchen chairs that Plummer had appropriated years earlier and parked in front of his desk.

Rye slammed closed the drawer of the file cabinet as if warning her that he was about to join her, which he did, pulling out the other chair and straddling it. He dropped the clipboard onto the desk and slid it toward her with the tip of one finger. "Okay. Top page there, that's the crew I've put together so far. First name, that's Borden Harris. You probably know him. He's...*was* your grandfather's wrangler—and our first volunteer. Most of the other hands on the place left soon after Plummer...soon after his passing. Can't blame 'em. They're working men, gotta have that regular paycheck, and word came that there was steady work up in Montana."

"Why didn't you go?" The question just sort of slipped out between the sweet roll and the coffee.

He shot her a disgruntled look, a muscle working in the hollow of his jaw, and after some delay said, "I promised Plummer." He pointed at the second name. "Now George Marshal, he's—"

"Because of the trail drive," she said, wanting it perfectly clear.

He didn't look at her or move his finger. "Yeah. Now. George is a friend of mine from my rodeo days."

She had to bite her tongue to keep from saying, "I didn't know you rodeoed." Instead she said, "I assume he knows his way around a cow."

"Absolutely." He half rose from his chair, reached across the desk and poured himself a cup of coffee, talking all the while. "George is a fine hand with a rope. He'll be a lot of help. But beggars can't exactly be choosers, and since we're not paying, we definitely fall into that category." He sipped from his cup and pointed to another name. "Pogo Smith is a rancher, about fifty-five, a good working cowboy." He paused, and his gaze fell on the plate of rolls. Kara pushed it closer and peered once more at the clipboard.

"Who's this Dean Schuster?"

He reached for the roll and bit off a chunk of it, gulping it down with hardly a chew. "Another friend of mine. He's no great shakes as a cowboy, frankly, but he can sit a saddle all day without falling out of it, and he has an asset nobody else I know has."

"Really? What's that?"

"A motor home. I figure it's as close to a modern day chuck wagon as we're gonna get. And for the record—I checked this out with Plummer and the attorney, too—we're allowed to use whatever modern equivalents we want, so long as we don't load up those beeves and ship, fly or float 'em to New Mexico."

"Then so long as the cows walk, we're in compliance with the terms of the will."

"Exactly."

"Hmm." She licked icing from her fingers and took a drink of the strong black coffee. "Okay, that's four, six counting you and me."

"Seven, counting Kanaka."

"Who?"

"Everybody calls him Shoes. That's not his real name. His real name means something like 'life-giving waters,' but since he's a farrier—"

"He shoes the horses, hence Shoes."

"Right. He'll keep our horses shod and our tack in good shape, plus a hundred other little things I don't even want to think about, and he's an able cowboy."

"A good man to have along."

He set his cup on the desk, and for the first time actually looked her straight in the eye. "You're not taking issue with a single one of them. That makes things a lot easier than I expected. Thanks."

She lifted an eyebrow. "You expected a fight?"

"Frankly, yes."

She shook her head. "I have a practical mind, Wagner, and like you said, beggars can't be choosers. I'd sign off on a crew of circus clowns right now, provided they could ride facing forward. Now, what else have you got?"

He munched his sweet roll thoughtfully. "I've made a list of supplies."

"So have I." She plunked her coffee cup down and dug a folded sheet of paper from her shirt pocket, saying as she unfolded it, "I'll show you mine if you show me yours."

He gagged on a piece of roll, got it down, coughed to clear his throat and reached for his coffee cup. Kara cocked her head worriedly.

"You okay?"

"Fine," he croaked. "Uh, what's o-on the list isn't as i-important, really, as where we're going to get it."

"I've been thinking about that," she admitted. "Grandpa made it plain that Grandma wasn't to give me money."

"I don't think he was worried about that, actually, but never mind. I think I know where you're going. Meryl can't give you money, but nothing was said about supplies."

"My point exactly."

"This place has a fully stocked pantry," he said, "and with the hands all gone..."

"I'll bet she'll thank us to get it off her hands."

"One problem. Those supplies could be construed as assets of the business, and old Pain-in-the—er, Payne would be perfectly within his rights to refuse them to us."

"Payne wouldn't do that," she said definitely.

"You don't think so?"

"Of course not. And he's not a pain in the anything. He's been more than decent about this whole crazy thing."

Rye didn't try to mask his doubtful look. "If you say so."

"Honestly, I don't understand your dislike of him. He hasn't done anything to you."

"Nope. Can we get back to work now—or are you picking another fight?"

"I'm not picking a fight!"

"Well, that's what it looks like to me."

"That's stupid! Why would I want to pick a fight with you?"

"Beats me, but here you go, getting all hot around the collar."

"I am not!"

"Oh, no? Then what're you shouting about?"

"I'm not the only one shouting!"

A chuckle from the doorway shut them both up. Dayna again.

She leaned against the doorjamb and folded her arms. "Is this a private fight or can anyone wade in?"

"We're not fighting!" they exclaimed in unison.

Dayna fairly chortled, a hand pressed to her mouth. "No?"

Kara bit her lip and looked away. *Of course* they were fighting...about fighting. To her surprise, a grin wiggled across her mouth. Rye coughed. Sort of. It wasn't convincing enough to hide his chuckles. Kara looked at him in amazement—only to find him looking at her with the same expression, and suddenly they both burst out laughing. When the moment of hilarity passed, Kara was embarrassed again. Heavens, what was it about this man that made it so hard for her to be in the same room with him? She gulped down the bottom of her coffee and trained her attention on her mother.

"Did you want something, Mom?"

"Sure did, sweetie. I want to give you something."

Dayna sauntered around to the end of the desk and propped a slender hip against it. At fifty she was still a very attractive woman, still slim and fit. Her face had a few lines, but they were soft and feminine, as was the gray sifted liberally through her long blond hair. She wore her jeans and boots like they were lace and silk, a trick Kara had never learned to manage. Kara wore jeans and boots because she had to wear something, and skirts didn't cut it on the range—and because she'd never worn much of anything else. Only rarely did she put on a dress, and then it was usually a simple, tailored costume, like the uniform she'd had to wear to wait tables. The few times she'd been forced by circumstance to wear ruffles and frills, such as the time she'd been drafted as a bridesmaid in her mother's cousin's wedding, she'd absolutely hated the sight of herself. But her mother could turn out in bows and rhinestones and look like she'd been born to it. Kara wished, suddenly, for some of her mother's innate femininity, which was probably the very last thing she needed to make a trail drive.

"You say you want to give me something?" Kara asked, forcing her mind back to the matter at hand. It was then that she noticed her mother was holding something behind her back. She slowly drew it out and placed it on the desk.

"I want you have this—to help with expenses."

Kara's jaw slowly dropped. Rye whistled and leaned closer to take a good look at the elaborate squash-blossom necklace laid out lovingly next to the desk blotter.

"Mom, you can't want to part with that!"

"Not particularly," Dayna admitted lightly. "But it's the only thing I have of any real value, and I know your father would want it to go for this particular cause. He loved the place as much as you do, Kara, and he only gave me the necklace because he couldn't think of anything else to give me at the time. I hardly ever wore it, not that I haven't treasured it, but I'd have been as proud and happy with a collection of box tops—as you well know."

Kara bounced a glance around the room, heading off the tears that burned at the back of her eyes, while Dayna explained to Rye.

"Once," she said, "when Kara was a little girl, she started saving box tops for a prize. I think it was a set of walkie-talkies. Anyway, that was the year she realized that Christmas was more about gift giving than gift getting. Her father got a rock with a groove filed in it. I got the box tops." Her voice thickened. "I still have them. We buried Law with that rock."

Rye said quietly. "I know what you mean. My boy, Champ, likes to cut photos out of catalogs and glue them to paper. You'd think they were the real thing the way he gives them out. He says they're promises. I have every one he ever gave me."

"I knew you'd understand," Dayna said. "You'll get as much for the necklace as you possibly can, won't you, Mr. Wagner."

"Yes, ma'am, I surely will. And my name's Rye or just Wagner, if you prefer."

"Thank you, Rye. Well, I promised Angelina I'd help her turn out the beds in the bunkhouse, if you'll excuse me."

Rye got to his feet as she left the room. Kara couldn't trust herself to look at him. How had he known that the best thing to do, the only way to keep from hurting her mother's feelings, was to just accept the necklace and make it work for them as best it could? She'd known he had a son, of course, but she hadn't thought much about what kind of father he might be, whether he could have anything in common with her own. Maybe that kind of sentimentality was something all fathers felt. But no. She knew better than that. All she had to do was to look at her uncle Smith to know that wasn't so.

Kara got up and edged toward the door, saying, "I'd better talk to Meryl about those supplies."

Rye nodded, walking around the desk. "We'll meet again later."

"After lunch?"

"Fine."

"You, uh, you're welcome to eat with us."

"Thanks, but my boy will be expecting me."

"I see. Okay. Well, later, then."

"You bet."

But she couldn't quite go yet. She swallowed hard and said, "Thanks, Rye. I wasn't quite up to handling my mother's gift, but you were. Thanks."

He didn't look up from the papers he was shuffling. "Sometimes it's easier from the outside looking in."

"Thanks, anyway."

He nodded. "You're welcome."

She left with the confusing realization that she was looking forward to coming back.

Chapter Three

Rye dropped his hat on top of the file cabinet, curly brim up. A scratch at the door sent him walking back to it. When he opened it, Kara's dog, Oboe, sneeze-snorted, his ruffed head bobbing up and down, lifted his tail and pranced in as if he owned the place. He went straight to the corner of the desk and lay down, so that Rye would have to step over him to get to the chair.

"Well, hello, boy," Rye said, going down on his haunches to scratch the dog's ears. "I know a young man who would dearly love to make your acquaintance." Oboe flopped over onto his back so Rye could scratch his belly. "Yeah, my Champ would dearly love you."

"Why don't you introduce them?"

He looked over his shoulder. Kara stood in the doorway. From this perspective, her long, jeaned legs seemed to go on for yards until they blossomed into nicely rounded hips. Her belt cinched in a much smaller waist, gathering in the fullness of her shirt necessary to cover the generous bosom above. Heavens. Long legs and an hourglass figure to boot, not to mention all that blond hair. He remembered the feel of it, the way it swung heavy and thick and glossy when freed. Damn. He was in trouble. He gave the dog one final, absent pat and rose to his full height.

"How was your lunch?"

"Fine. But you didn't answer me. Why don't you take Oboe to meet your son later?"

"All right, I will. Champ will like that. Thanks."

"Champ, that's his name?"

"Yeah. Speaking of names, why'd you call the dog Oboe? Seems funny, naming him after a musical instrument."

For answer, she snapped her fingers and patted her thigh. The dog flipped up onto its feet and snapped to attention. "Speak, Oboe, speak."

The critter tossed back its head and let loose a series of deep, mellifluous *ooooow-ooow-ooows* as distinctive as anything Rye had ever heard.

Kara clapped her hands and said, "Good boy!" The dog snapped his jaws shut, cutting off the sound, and darted across the room for his reward, placing his front paws against Kara's side. Laughing, she rumpled his fur roughly. "Oh, you're such a good boy. Yes, you are."

He made that snort of his, as if saying, "Of course!"

Rye said, "I've never heard anything like that, not the howl, not that sneezing thing he does."

"Oh, he's one of a kind, all right," Kara replied proudly. "You should see him work cattle."

"He's good?"

"The best. Dad trained him, and he had a way with animals. He'll be a help to us on the drive."

"Glad to hear it. Listen, I've been meaning to mention something to you."

Kara looked up from rubbing the dog. "What's that?"

"I'll be wanting my son to go along with us. He's just a little kid, but not used to being separated for long, and when we leave here with the drive, we won't be coming back."

Kara snapped her fingers and pointed at the floor. The dog plopped down on his belly. She brought her hands to her waist. "If you don't mind my asking, have you given any thought to what you're going to do after the drive?"

He shrugged. "Guess we'll bunk in awhile with my folks

down in Durango. Something will come up. And speaking of Durango, that's our next order of business.''

"How so?"

He moved around behind the desk and flipped open the oversize file folder there, crooking a finger at Kara. "I want you to come here and have a look at this." He unfolded a large, detailed map as she walked over to the front of the desk and leaned forward, craning her head around. "No, come on this side. This is important. We don't need any misunderstandings." Kara lightly walked around the end of the desk and stood next to him. He slid over, putting some space between them and tapped the map. "We're here."

"Okay."

"Now, your grandfather mapped out a route for us. He called in a lot of favors to ensure us crossing rights and, whenever possible, holding pens, all the way south to the Utah-New Mexico border and on into Farmington, then east to the Chama Valley. I've broken it down into segments. Say we average fifteen miles a day—I think that's reasonable, considering the terrain. It'll take us twenty-two days. That's cutting it real close in my book, considering we haven't even started rounding up the beeves yet. *And* we have to cross the Navajo reservation. It's not mountainous, as everything north of it is, but it's dry as a bone. Water could be a real problem, not to mention the fee they're asking for crossing rights." To show her what he meant, he picked up a sheet of paper and pointed out a figure in Plummer's own handwriting.

"Yow!"

"My feeling exactly," Rye said drily.

"But do we have a choice?" Kara asked.

"Yes. And your grandfather thought of this himself." He returned to the map. "We angle across Colorado to Durango, then head southeast through the Chako Indian reservation to New Mexico and the Chama Valley. That cuts the trip to eighteen days. And I can guarantee you a welcome rest stop just south of Durango."

"How's that?"

He smiled. "I just told you. My folks are there. My father and older brother ranch as fine a piece of property as you'll ever see right there." He stabbed the map with a forefinger.

"Sounds fine to me. So why didn't Plummer pick the Colorado route?"

He knew she'd come to that question quickly. "One real important reason." He pulled a letter with the envelope stapled to it from the pile of papers on the desk and handed it to her, explaining as she skimmed. "The Chakos refused him permission to cross."

Kara finished scanning the letter and let it drop with a frown of disgust. "So it's back to the Farmington route. Darn."

He shook his head. "I say we take our chances in Durango."

"But if the Chakos—"

"They refused *him*," Rye pointed out. "Not me. I think I can get their permission."

She studied him long and hard. "How? If Plummer couldn't do it, what makes you think you can?"

Rye raked his fingertips through his mustache, considering how much to tell her. He'd been considering that very thing from the beginning, and he still wasn't certain how much to divulge. He hadn't said anything to Plummer. It was just too hard to talk about, and whatever he told Kara to win her cooperation, he knew he wouldn't tell it all. Finally he said, "I need you to trust me on this. Suffice it to say I have a little influence Plummer didn't have and let it go at that."

She folded her arms beneath her breasts, and he wished devoutly that she hadn't. It showed him, in a way that even last night's glimpse of her impressive cleavage had not, just how much she had going for her. He got busy folding up the map. She said, "I'm not sure I can do that. We're talking about my whole future here, about keeping my home and my way of life. Maybe you don't know how important this is to me."

"I think I do," he said more gruffly than he'd intended. "I have to worry about making a living, too, you know."

"It's not about money!" she exclaimed, shoving at his shoulder to make him face her again. "It's about a way of life that my family has embraced for generations. I won't let that go easy."

"I never thought you would," he told her softly.

"So tell me," she came back.

He sighed, knowing he wouldn't have been satisfied if the boot had been on the other foot. He'd give her part of it. Only part.

Because his personal business was his own—and it was too tough to explain. "Shoes Kanaka. You remember we talked about him this morning."

She frowned. "The farrier."

He nodded and said, "His uncle is one of the more influential chiefs."

Kara's mouth fell open. Being from the general neighborhood, she understood more than the average individual would. "Shoes Kanaka is Chako and he lives off the reservation?"

"Not exactly."

"Not exactly! The Chakos are notorious for clinging to the old ways. They don't allow their children off the reservations."

"They don't forbid their children to leave," he told her. "It's just that they discourage it, and most choose to stay. Shoes chose to come and work for my family up in Durango several years ago. That's how he picked up the trade."

"And you think he can get us permission to cross the reservation?"

"Something like that." The rest he absolutely would not tell her. It didn't matter anyway. "The important thing is that we have an 'in' with the tribal council. I'm sure, for certain considerations, they'll allow us to cross."

"What considerations?"

He hung on to his patience by sheer dint of will. "I don't know yet, but you can bet it'll be a whole lot lighter on your pocketbook than dealing with the Navajos. What I need from you right now is a decision one way or the other. You say Durango, I fire off a letter to Shoes's uncle *today*. Shoes will take it to him personally. You say Farmington, we've got to raise some major funds *pronto*. So what's it going to be?"

She had the bluest eyes in creation, and she used them just then to plumb him tip to top, her pale lashes sparkling clean. It was all he could do to stand there for it. He didn't like being probed. It made him feel naked, vulnerable, as if all his secrets were exposed. His hands curled into fists. His gut clenched. His jaws locked. Finally he felt her pull back.

"Durango," she said. "And you must know that I've just put my whole future in your hands."

He gulped, nodded, and forced his gaze back to the folder. Actually, Plummer had done that weeks ago, and it had felt like a burden then. It felt like the weight of the whole world now. But Plummer had trusted Rye to see this through, and come what may, Rye would do just that. Miss Kara Detmeyer was just part of the package, another detail to be handled, endured and put behind him.

He uncurled his fists, made his jaws relax and said, "Now, about that list of supplies..."

"So he's shortened the trip, has he? My, my. Next he'll be walking on water."

"Payne!" Kara glared at her cousin, who grimaced over the rim of his glass.

"Sorry, cuz. It's nothing to do with you. I just don't like the man, that's all."

"No, really?"

"Well, last I heard you weren't exactly enamored of the guy, either."

Heat threatened to climb her throat and blossom in her cheeks. She willed it away and her gaze with it. "He's not my favorite person, true, but I do have to work with him. And you asked how it was going."

"I do have a minor interest in the enterprise," he pointed out glumly.

She set her cup on the edge of the coffee table and reached across the couch to take her cousin's big, powerful hand in hers. "Payne, I'm sorry. I know this is awful for you, and I've been thinking. We could always operate the New Mexico ranch through the partnership. All we have to do is agree to it. Mom and I would live there and oversee the day-to-day operations, and you could continue to take care of the—"

He was shaking his head. "No, I can't ask you to do that. Why should you when you can have it all with the trail drive. Besides, that's the way Plummer wanted it. I guess that's what gets to me most. He didn't just want to give you a chance, he wanted to cut me out."

"That's not true! I know it isn't. If it were, he'd have chosen some other way to do it, because, believe me, this trail drive is a long way from a sure thing."

"Yeah?" He tossed back the last of his bourbon. "How so?"

She hadn't expected to have to answer that question, hoping her assurance would be enough to set his mind at ease, but she had little choice now. She put a hand to her head, sighing wearily. "For one thing, this Colorado route's no sure thing. Rye thinks he can get permission to cross the Chako Reservation even though Plummer couldn't."

Payne sat up a little higher, concern on his chiseled face. "What happens if he doesn't get it?"

"We head to Farmington," she said dismissively, not even wanting to think about it. "Other than that, there's the crew. Big question marks, every one of them—except Borden Harris."

"You mean the horse wrangler?"

"That's right. I figure if he worked for Plummer, he has to be good."

For a moment Payne seemed lost in thought, the ghost of a smile on his lips, as if he, too, was remembering how gifted Plummer was at this ranching business. "Right," he muttered after a moment. "What else?"

"Money," she said flatly. "Mom's been generous, and Grandpa paid as many fees ahead as he could, but I'm still having to sell my car, and even that won't give us much of a cushion."

"That's too bad," Payne said thoughtfully. "How much is the crew costing you?"

"We're feeding them," she said, "and that's it. They're all volunteers. Some folks like a challenge, I guess."

"Guess so." He shook his head and looked into his glass. "Not my idea of a good time, riding all day, sleeping on the ground at night, eating God knows what."

"Working like dogs," she added, "wearing dirty clothes, getting sunburn during the day and frostbite at night."

He chuckled. "You must want that ranch awful bad."

"It's my home," she said simply. "Just think what you'd do to save that big house in Denver."

He cut her a sudden look and said solemnly, "You have no idea."

"Oh, yes, I do," she assured him, "because that's exactly what I'd do to save the ranch."

His glass hit the coffee table with a clunk, and he laid a long arm across her shoulders. Leaning in, he brushed aside her bangs to kiss her in the center of her forehead. "That's why you're so special to me, kid," he said. "You've always understood me like no one else ever has."

Kara laughed, happy to have this display of affection. He was the closest thing she had to a brother, after all.

"Well, I'm ready to turn in," he said, getting up.

"Oh, Payne, I've been meaning to ask you something."

"What's that, hon?"

"It's about the inoculant serum in the cooling shed."

"Cattle inoculations?"

She nodded. "Grandpa bought it in big batches. Cheaper that way. It's stored in the big refrigerators."

"Yeah, I know. What about it?"

"I want to use it. We can't move these cattle until they're properly inoculated, and it was purchased for that purpose. But technically it belongs to the partnership. The foodstuffs we're using probably do, too."

"No, they don't," he said matter-of-factly. "Dad asked Canton for a detailed inventory, and I've taken a look at it. The foodstuffs aren't on the list. I'm not sure why, but they aren't."

"Well, what about the inoculant? Do you mind if we use it?"

Payne shrugged, then smiled. "Why not? It's not good for anything else. It can't even be resold."

She went up on her knees in the corner of the couch, smiling at him. "Thanks, cuz. I knew you'd be a sport about this."

He thumped her on the top of the head. "I'm a soft touch where you're concerned, and you know it."

She grinned cheekily. "I was counting on it."

"Brat."

"But you love me, anyway."

"Darned if I don't."

"It's mutual, you know."

"Yeah, I know." He winked. "Good night, kid."

"Night."

He left her there in front of the fire and went down the hall toward the bedrooms at the back of the big, rambling house. She sat with her chin on her drawn-up knees and contemplated the days to come. What she'd told Payne was true. This cattle drive was no sure thing. Any one of a million details could go awry—

and undoubtedly would—but she wouldn't let that stop them. She wouldn't let anyone or anything stop them.

"What do you mean you can't cook?"

Kara rolled her eyes at the frazzled cowboy. "I didn't say I couldn't cook *at all*. I can rattle around in the kitchen enough to keep myself from starving."

"Terrific." He frowned, and Kara couldn't keep from giggling. His frosty brows drew together. "What?"

She wiped the grin off her face. "Oh, nothing. It's just that when you do that—" she indicated that she was talking about his mustache by raking her fingertips over her top lip "—your whole mouth disappears under that scrub brush of yours."

His scowl deepened, but then a grin broke out from beneath the shield of his mustache. "My boy says the same thing, says my lips are hiding."

Kara laughed. "You're really crazy about that kid, aren't you?"

His expression immediately turned wary and a little sheepish. "He is my son, after all."

"And you really seem to take joy in that fact."

Clearly uncomfortable talking about his emotions, Rye leaned an elbow against the top of one of the file cabinets and said lightly, "We're getting off the subject."

Kara would much rather have talked about him than this newest problem, but she dutifully applied herself to the latter. "Right. We need a cook."

Rye scratched his neck. "I can talk to Pogo. Champ and I spent a week fishing with him once, and his camp cooking wasn't half-bad. Maybe he'll do it."

"We need him on that flank," she reminded him.

"We need a lot of stuff," Rye said wearily, rubbing his eyes with forefinger and thumb.

"You need some sleep," Kara said, unfolding from her grandfather's chair behind the desk.

He shook his head. "I'm all right. I'll rest when we get these cows to New Mexico. I want to go over the map and agenda with you. More than one of us needs to know where we're supposed to be and how we're supposed to get there."

"I'll take them to my room and study them tonight."

"That won't get it. We're really dealing with two trails here. The chuck wagon and rigs have to stick to the roads, but the herd rarely can. So we have to rendezvous on a daily basis, twice if we want to eat lunch. That means pinpointing rendezvous and campsites *exactly* and knowing just how the other group's going to get there. This thing has to be closely coordinated."

"Okay, but that means that whoever ramrods the vehicles has to know this stuff by heart, too. Why don't we wait and go over it with—"

"But that's you," he said.

Kara stared at him an instant, sure she'd misunderstood. But no, there hadn't been much to misunderstand. She folded her arms and leaned a hip against the edge of the desk. "What do you mean, that's me?"

He gaped at her like he couldn't believe she was asking such a question. "I thought it was understood. I'll be ramroding the herd. You'll be taking charge of the vehicles."

"What gave you that absurd idea?"

"It's not absurd!" he said. "I drive the cows. You drive the chuck wagon—or the tack truck or whatever you want—so long as you have those vehicles where they're supposed to be, lunch ready and camp set up."

"I'm not going to sit around some campsite all afternoon waiting for you to get my cows down the road!"

His shock and frustration were almost comical to watch. Disbelief came and went, his mouth gaping open then snapping shut again to disappear beneath the overhang of his mustache. It was truly a magnificent mustache, Kara couldn't help thinking. She wondered what he'd look like without it, then decided that he couldn't look any better than he already did. The man was fine, no doubt about it. She'd always known he was physically attractive, of course, but now that she was getting to know the whole package, the physical attributes were somehow enhanced. In point of fact, she was enjoying Rye Wagner, even while she resisted the very real temptation to reshape his head. He was doing a creditable job of getting a handle on his temper at the moment, clenching and unclenching his fists and jaw while his face pulsed red.

"Now listen, Kara," he said, striving mightily to sound reasonable, "this will be nasty, physically draining work. None of us is going to be up to it in the beginning. I'll be walking funny myself for a few days. You can't possibly—"

"Don't even go there, Wagner," she warned. "You don't know me well enough to risk it. I'll telling you now, though, I can match you hour for hour, minute for minute all day long. Anything you can do, *I* can do. Those are my cows, dammit, and—"

"They'll *be* your cows if we get them to New Mexico, you mean."

"That's right, and I mean to see that they get there step by ornery step, if need be. It's what I do best, Rye. Honestly it is. You don't want me getting up your dinner, not when I can do so much better working those cows."

He looked more than a little doubtful, but he decided—wisely—not to argue the fine points, sticking instead to the obvious. "But we need someone to take care of the camp."

"You're right," she said. "We need a cook, a domestic engineer *extraordinaire*." She snapped her fingers, amazed it hadn't occurred to her before. "I think I may have the answer to our problems. Hold on." Quickly, she stepped over Oboe, slid past Rye and went to the door. Yanking the door open, she called for her mother. "Mom! Mo-o-m! Mo-ther!"

An answering cry came from some far corner of the house. In moments Dayna Detmeyer appeared, an oil rag in one hand, the corners of a towel knotted in the belt loops of her jeans as a makeshift apron. "Good grief, Kara, what's wrong?"

"We need a cook," Kara explained, "and someone to drive the chuck wagon, er, motor home."

"It's a small one," Rye put in.

Dayna opened her mouth to reply, but Kara wanted to be very sure that she knew what she'd be getting into. "It means breaking camp after breakfast every day, delivering lunch to the crew on the move, then locating the new campsite and setting up camp every afternoon. Plus there's laundry to think about and—"

"First aid," Dayna supplied. "Someone's thought about first aid, haven't they?"

"Yes, ma'am," Rye assured her.

"And we need a cell phone," Dayna mused. "For emergencies."

"Got it," Rye said. "Several, actually."

"Someone needs to call ahead and let the owners know the herd will be crossing their land that day," she pointed out. "Wouldn't hurt to check in with someone every night and let them know where we are, either."

"My folks just south of Durango will be expecting those calls," Rye said, pleased that their minds seemed to be traveling on the same track.

"Then you'll do it?" Kara asked excitedly. "You'll come with us?"

"If you don't," Rye said, "then would you please tell this stubborn daughter of yours that she has to take on the job? There's no one else to do it, and—"

"I will not!" Kara exclaimed, glaring at him. "And that's final!"

"Well, somebody has to!" Rye pointed out hotly.

"You're shouting again!"

"I'm just trying to make you understand that we're out of options here! You have to—"

"I don't have to do a damned thing, Wagner!"

A shrill whistle split the air and nearly deafened both of them. They clapped their hands over their ears and, as one, turned amazed stares on Dayna Detmeyer, who calmly removed her fingers from her mouth and said gently, "I've been trying to tell both you hardheads that I've had every intention from the beginning of being in on this thing."

"But you never said—" Kara began.

"When have I had a chance?" Dayna interrupted firmly. "You two have been closeted in here for days, barely taking time to eat or sleep, let alone carry on conversation."

Kara blinked at that. They had been spending an awful lot of time together, but then they had an awful lot of work to do. "We've been busy," she muttered.

"Yes, I know. I've heard the shouting." She cut a look between her daughter and the bemused cowboy with the magnificent mustache. "You two just seem to strike sparks off each other."

Kara felt her face color slightly. Sparks. Yes, she'd definitely felt a few of those.

Rye cleared his throat. "Do you think you can handle this

job? What I mean is you'll have to cook for eight, three times a day, besides making rendezvous at noon and setting up camp at night.''

Dayna's mouth twitched. "I think I can handle it.''

"Of course she can handle it,'' Kara said, insulted on her mother's behalf. "Who do you think did all the cooking for our outfit?''

"Well, not you, that's for sure,'' Rye retorted.

Dayna laughed. "Trust me, Rye, Kara's a damn sight better hand with a rope than a skillet.''

"I tried to tell him that,'' Kara grumbled.

"It's settled then. The chuck wagon's my venue,'' Dayna said.

"Uh, there's one other thing,'' Rye said.

"Oh?''

"My son, Champ, will be along. He's eight, so he won't be able to ride with the herd. That means he'll have to stay with the camp rigs. I'll need you to keep an eye on him, if you don't mind.''

Dayna smiled. "Not at all. I love kids. We'll get along fine.''

Rye breathed a sigh of relief. "That's great. Thanks.''

"Don't mention it. Now then, how many other vehicles will be going along and who else will be behind the wheel?''

Rye rocked back on his heels. "I figured we'd rotate, try to give everybody a break from the saddle now and again, but starting out we'll have Shoes Kanaka—he'll be bringing his farrier's truck and a horse trailer. Bord Harris, our wrangler, will drive my truck, which we'll use to haul our tack, feed, personal gear and another horse trailer. Dean Shuster will drive your truck, which will be outfitted with a water tank. I figure you and Bord to be permanent drivers with our other three hands taking turns.''

"That leaves just you and me on horseback every day,'' Kara said.

"And four riders to manage the herd,'' Rye said. "We can squeeze out five, if we have to, by hopscotching the rigs. That means—''

"Driving two ahead,'' Dayna said, demonstrating her understanding of the concept, "then taking one back with two drivers to pick up the third.''

Rye nodded. "We won't be moving those cows much more than fifteen miles a day, so it's really not that much driving.''

"But with all the cooking involved and setting up and breaking camp and the thousand and one other things that are going to come up," Dayna said, "it'll do."

Rye nodded. "I'd say you've got a pretty good handle on the job already. What we have to do now is familiarize you with the route." He waved her over to the desk, and the two of them bent their heads over the map. Kara watched from the other side.

More than an hour passed before Dayna straightened, stretched and sighed. "I'll study these carefully. Meanwhile, Kara, we'd better decide how we're going to handle our own move. If we're not going to pay another month's rent on that dingy apartment, we've got to get to Farmington and box up everything, then move it to the ranch. Then we've got to hightail it back here and—"

"Oh, and I have to sell my car!" Kara exclaimed. "And pick up my paycheck."

"And have the utilities shut off."

"And turn in my uniforms so I can get the deposit back."

"And leave a forwarding address. We'd better get hopping."

Kara's mind was humming with details again. She'd have to give her plants away. They'd never survive weeks untended out at the ranch. And her bank account in Farmington would have to be closed. And there was the cleaning deposit at the apartment to wrangle out of the manager. And...she looked at Rye Wagner, fully aware for the first time that he essentially held her entire future in his hands. She smiled. Plummer had taken good care of her, after all, very good care.

Chapter Four

The move from Farmington back to the ranch took days longer than Kara expected, but at last she and her mother were on their way back to Utah. They stuck as closely as possible to the itinerary set for the cattle drive, familiarizing themselves with the roads and terrain. It wasn't possible, of course, to drive the exact route. For one thing, they were doing it backward. For another, the cattle would be moving across country that modern vehicles couldn't easily negotiate, but it was helpful to know what facilities would be available to them via the roads that the vehicles would be using from rendezvous to rendezvous and campsite to campsite. That, too, added to their time away, however, so that when Kara and Dayna finally got back to the ranch in Utah, they were the last of the crew to arrive.

They dragged in about 8:00 p.m., tired, bedraggled and hungry. Kara was surprised to find her cousin in residence, along with the agent for some concern interested in purchasing the Utah property not left to Meryl in Plummer's will. Kara couldn't help feeling that it hadn't taken the carrion long to start circling the corpse, but Payne quietly pointed out that they did have obligations to meet apart from her own personal "venture." She was too concerned with her own business, however, to pay much attention to the rest of it. As unfair as it was, she gladly left that end of things in her cousin's large, capable hands. Payne, bless him, didn't seem to mind. No one, in fact, seemed to mind leaving her out of anything.

Kara sat on the porch in the dark and listened with growing chagrin—and no little envy—to the sounds of celebration wafting down from the little house on the hilltop. Rye and his buddies were having a happy reunion, it seemed. No doubt they were making plans for the drive, happily dividing up the responsibilities and storing up memories of what was sure to be an experience none of them would ever forget. She ought to be up there, she told herself. She was a major part of this enterprise. She admitted, only to herself, that she felt a little hurt at being left out. Logically, she knew that Rye probably didn't even know she was back, but that didn't make her feel any better. She decided that she would go up and let him know that she was here and ready to go to work.

As soon as she stepped off the porch, she wondered where Oboe had gotten to. She'd left him behind when she and her mother had returned to Farmington to take care of their business there. He'd whined a protest when she'd climbed into the truck without him, but she'd known that as badly as he hated to be cooped up, it was far kinder to leave him where he had the run of the place than to take him with her. Now she worried that he'd taken advantage of his freedom to wander away, perhaps in retaliation for the months spent unhappily caged in that tiny apartment in Farmington. But then she was apt to credit the animal with far too many human traits.

The night air was crisply cool. Kara felt the unmistakable bite of autumn in the air. That bite would grow fierce teeth before they reached New Mexico. She tilted back her head and surveyed the brilliance of the stars strewn across the black heavens. This would be her ceiling for weeks to come. Her spirits and her steps quickened as she climbed up the hill. Soon she recognized the sounds of harmonica and guitar. No, guitars, plural. They drew her on even more quickly than before. When she knocked on the door, she was surprised to find it opened by a small boy with a round face topped by an ink black pelt cut closely to his head.

His father's gray eyes looked back at her from that sun-browned face. From his side, Oboe leaped at her.

Kara caught him and went down on one knee to give him a good rubbing. "Well, hello, old chum. I was wondering where you'd gotten to."

The boy frowned, straight black brows drawn together sharply. "Who're you?"

"I'm Kara. You must be Champ." She stuck out her hand, but the boy scuttled back before bolting away, Oboe at his heels. "Da-a-d!"

A second later the music stopped. Then Rye appeared, guitar in hand.

"Hey, Kara. About time you got back. Come on in and let me introduce you."

She stepped up into the crowded room. All of its occupants were on their feet. They were a motley crew, ranging in size from tall and lean to short and squat and in coloring from freckled skin with red hair to brown with black. The boy was absent. Rye made the introductions. The men respectfully nodded, and some offered handshakes. When the formalities were complete, it was Rye's friend Pogo Smith, tall and leanly muscled with silver hair and bright green eyes, who offered Kara refreshment from the sideboard laden with chips and dips, white bread sandwiches, beef jerky, peanuts and cold beers. A plate of hard-boiled eggs and pickles had been wiped clean except for flecks of yolk and streaks of brine. Kara helped herself to sandwiches and beer.

"I'm starved, actually. Thanks."

Borden Harris vacated a rocker for her, one like those that had graced the porch of the big house for as long as she could remember. Kara sank down into it gratefully. As soon as her bottom hit the seat, the men all scrambled for places, perching on the old sofa and its rickety arms, the end of the battered coffee table and a windowsill. Rye leaned his guitar in a corner and took the one other chair in the room, leaning forward with his hands pressed together, his elbows on his knees.

"Me and the boys were just enjoying a little music," Rye said needlessly.

Kara swallowed the bite of sandwich she'd grabbed and nodded. "I heard. Sounded pretty good. Guess we won't be lacking for entertainment around the campfire."

"Chances are that most nights we won't be much in the mood for music or anything else by the time we get to camp," Rye said. "We'll be dog-tired and aching all over, ready for food and sleep, and not necessarily in that order."

"Speaking of dogs," Kara said between bites and swigs, "he seems to have adopted your boy."

"They're back in Champ's room," Borden said.

"The boy's shy," Pogo added.

"Oboe seems to think he's a calf to be herded," Rye said with a chuckle.

Kara nodded. "He's protective, all right. Once down in Farmington, I was getting ready to take him for a walk—he hated that apartment—and I heard the most awful caterwauling. I looked out the front door and found Oboe holding the neighbor's little girl by the seat of her pants. Seemed she'd gotten out of the apartment without her mother knowing it and was trying to get down the open stairwell. She was two, maybe three years old. Kid would have fallen to her death if not for that dog."

"I had a dog once tackle a snake to keep it from getting me, a rattler," Pogo said. "Damn, I miss that dog! Er, pardon me, ma'am."

Kara waved away the apology. "My dad always believed animals were a lot smarter than we give them credit for. He and Grandpa told me about an old dog they used to have when Dad lived here in this house before he and Mom married."

"I know what dog you're talking about," Rye said. "Plummer swore that if he made that old hound mad, it would take its bowl and blanket and move up here until he apologized."

Kara nodded. "Dad said the same thing. He said the dog would only go home again if *he* made it mad or Grandpa apologized."

Everyone laughed, and soon dog stories were the order of the day. Kara strongly suspected that some of them were sheer fabrications, but she was enjoying herself too much to worry about a little thing like that. Before long the sandwich plate was empty, the chips were reduced to mere crumbs, the dips congealed and all the bottles on the table were empty. Only when Oboe appeared, whining to be let out for the night, did she realize that considerable time had passed. She glanced at her wristwatch and swallowed a gasp.

"I better be going, too," she said, getting to her feet. "Everyone will be wondering where I've gotten to."

"We'd all best turn in," Rye said, standing. "We have an early morning and a long day of round-up ahead of us tomorrow."

"What time were you thinking to start?"

"First light."

"I'll be ready."

Rye seemed mildly surprised. "You really intend to ride out with us to round up the herd."

"Damn straight. It's my herd, you know—provided we get it to New Mexico on time."

"We'll get it there," Rye said flatly, and she grinned to let him know she'd baited him. Waving to the others, she added, "See you bright and early, boys."

Farewells and polite rejoinders were made as she and Oboe wound their way to the door. Rye was right behind them. "Be careful walking down. It's dark out there."

"Oh, I'm not worried," she said dismissively. "In a way, this is my own backyard."

"Not for much longer," Rye muttered. "Old Payne didn't waste any time getting the place on the market."

Kara sobered. "I know. But there are creditors to be satisfied, and Payne takes his responsibilities seriously."

"Humph."

She shook her head, stepping down through the door, and turned back to look up at him. "You just can't credit Payne with any good attributes, can you?"

Rye groomed his mustache thoughtfully with his fingertips, then said, "Nope."

Kara rolled her eyes. "You're a hard man, Wagner."

"And make no apologies for it," Rye confirmed.

Exasperated, Kara turned away. "Thanks for the food and the introductions. See you in the morning."

"If you insist."

"See you in the morning," she repeated.

Rye made an exasperated sound and closed the door. She set off down the hill. Oboe had taken himself off the instant the door had been opened, but he rejoined her now, his business concluded.

"So," she muttered to the dog, "you've adopted Champ Wagner, have you?"

The dog sneezed and wagged his tail.

"Not very friendly, is he?"

That elicited no reply at all.

"Guess he's too shy for his own good, poor thing," she mused. "Well, he'll warm up once we hit the trail." She thought suddenly of the quiet stillness of Shoes Kanaka. He had been a calm island of serenity in the happy, garrulous chaos of five other more outgoing personalities. Of average height and stocky build, he wore his black hair long. His teeth, when he briefly smiled, were a startling white against the smooth red-brown skin of his face and a stark counterpoint to the whites of eyes crowned with black pupils and near black irises. Something about his face felt familiar. Roundish and a bit flat, its high, broad cheekbones triggered some vague correspondence. She shook her head, quite certain that she'd never seen the man before. She couldn't even remember meeting anyone similar to him. Yet, something about him nagged at her. And then she knew.

It was the boy. Of course! The resemblance was undeniable. If Shoes Kanaka was not closely related to Champ Wagner, she'd eat her hat. So Kanaka was not Rye's only connection to the Chako tribe. But why then had Rye not simply said so? What was it Rye Wagner didn't want her to know? She sighed, troubled by this new mystery, but then a lot of things troubled her about Ryeland Wagner. Too many. She promised herself that she'd know every one of his secrets by the time the drive reached New Mexico, and suddenly the weeks ahead held even greater import for her. Whatever Rye said, there would be evenings around the fire when frank talk and deep discussion would lay them all bare. She could hardly wait.

Rye walked back inside to a barrage of comments and questions.

"You didn't say she was good-looking."

"She fit right in, like one of the boys."

"That mother of hers anything like her?"

"Wanda wouldn't like it, so don't none of ya'll clue her in."

"That fiancée of his has a ring in his nose all right," Kanaka commented quietly of George, to general laughter.

"You reckon she's gonna last the day tomorrow?"

Rye deigned to answer only the last question. "I wouldn't count on it. Damned fool woman wants to be a man, but we all know she hasn't got what it takes."

"Including the equipment," Dean cracked, and they all laughed again, all but Rye. He didn't think it was funny. He didn't know why, he just didn't. Seemed to him that she deserved more respect than that, but again, he couldn't say why he thought so. Except...

"She's still the boss, and don't forget it. I may be ramrod, but Plummer made it pretty plain who he expected to have the final say."

"Still," Dean said worriedly, "you wouldn't cave in to her if you knew you was right. Would you?"

Rye kept his expression and voice neutral. "You know me better than that. You all do." It was a reference to a knowledge shared uncomfortably by all, and Rye was sorry he'd brought it up. "You boys better get on down to the bunkhouse," he said. "Shoes will help me clean up here."

They all knew Rye Wagner well enough to recognize an order when they heard one, however friendly. They filed out, one by one, Dean taking along his own guitar and George his harmonica.

"See you in the morning."

"Sleep well."

"Damn, I can't wait to get at them cows!"

Rye shook his head at that. "Dean's enthusiasm is a product of his ignorance," he said after the door closed behind them.

Taking the direct route, as always, Kanaka said, "What will you do about the boy?"

Rye shrugged and began gathering empty beer bottles. "Nothing to do."

Kanaka cut him a sharp glance. "He'll see her as a threat."

Rye snorted. "That's ridiculous. Kara and I barely tolerate each other."

"That could change."

Rye shook his head. "It won't."

Kanaka sighed. "If not that one, then another woman will mean something to you someday."

"Don't count on it."

"You can't believe that you will always live alone."

"Drop it, Shoes."

"You tell the boy nothing to help him accept that one day another woman will enter both your lives."

"I said, drop it."

"You will not make him understand his mother's faults, will not allow that she might love him as she could not love you."

"That's enough!"

Kanaka sat thoughtfully for a moment, then rose in that languorous, graceful way of his that made him seem so much larger than he actually was. "You must accept, Ryeland, that this drive will change everything. You made sure of that when you wrote to my uncle."

"I'll deal with that when the time comes," Rye said through his teeth.

"All right. But how and when will you deal with the rest?"

Rye turned on him. "There is no more, damn it! Except in that convoluted Indian mind of yours!"

Shoes Kanaka gave his friend a pitying look and said quietly, "She came to see you tonight. You, no one else. Oh, she was polite to the rest of us, but she was looking at you. There is more. Much more. And I don't think you are unaware of it, whatever you say."

He walked quietly from the room, his footsteps so light that they were silent. Rye put a hand into his hair and reflected bitterly that he'd get to clean up by himself. He wouldn't think of anything else. He refused to help his son accept a possibility that he himself rejected utterly. No matter how attractive he found Kara Detmeyer.

Kara bent forward from the waist, pressed her hands against the top rail of the stall and arched her back until the muscles warmed. Next she placed one booted foot on the bottom rail and lunged forward, bending her knee. She lifted her foot even higher so she could stretch her groin muscles as well. Then she switched legs and went through the process again. Limber and strong, she belted on her heavy leather chaps, shrugged into a down vest, and settled her brown felt hat so that it rode in back just above the base of her ponytail and sat low over her eyes in front. Pulling on rough-out gloves made supple by long hours of use, she slung a coil of grass rope over one shoulder, canteen and bridle over the other, and hoisted her saddle from the middle rung of the gate where she'd perched it minutes before. She shuffled out into the corral, her saddle weighing heavy against one knee.

Her horse was waiting right where she'd told Bord to tether him. She tossed smiles at the cowboys in various stages of saddling their own mounts, heaved her saddle onto the top rail, and approached the head of the big bay that had been her grandfather's favorite.

She scratched the horse's chin, speaking directly into his nostrils. "Hey, Bets. How's it been, hmm? Missing the old man, are you? Yeah, I know. I know." The horse shifted restlessly, and a figure appeared at her elbow.

He offered a saddle blanket of bright scarlet. "You sure about this, ma'am?"

Kara smiled at the wrangler. "I'm sure, Bord. I helped my grandfather break this horse. We're old friends, aren't we, Bets."

"That's sure a strange name, All Bets Off."

"Not so strange when you understand that my grandfather was the only one—of the many who tried—to tame this monster, and even he was by no means certain of success."

"Ah, wasn't covering any bets on this one, was he?"

"None." She petted the gelding's long, narrow nose. "But you fooled them all, didn't you, boy? You weren't as ornery as you were smart enough to pick the best master of the lot."

"Need any help?" the wrangler asked solicitously, sparking Kara's irritation.

"No."

"Okay. Fine. Just thought I'd ask."

She ignored him as he backed away, hands aloft. She told herself that she shouldn't be so touchy. Men had been offering the "little woman" help as long as she could remember—until they discovered that in many ways she was a better hand than any of them—and she wasn't exactly little, either. She should be used to it by now.

She dismissed the thought and quickly blanketed and saddled the horse. When she'd tightened the cinch sufficiently, leaning into the big bay with her shoulder while pulling with both hands, she secured the girth strap and lowered the stirrup. That done, she forced the bit between teeth the size of her thumbs, pushed the strap up over flicking ears and buckled the chin chain, despite snorts and an energetically wagging head. With her gear tied down, she took the reins firmly in hand and removed the halter, hanging it on the fence post. Then it was just a matter of mounting up. She noted that she was in the saddle sooner than most of the men, Rye the only exception.

Catching the eye of the wrangler, who waited expectantly at the gate, she nodded to indicate that he should open. He paused long enough to look questioningly at Rye before swinging the iron gate out, putting his back to it and hitching his elbows over the top to hold it there. Rye moved his big blue-gray Morgan through it at a canter. Kara lightly flicked the end of her reins against the bay's shoulder and walked it out of the corral. Drawing alongside the wrangler, she sidestepped the horse until her leg brushed the wrangler's chest. Then very casually she brought her face down to his, hat brims brushing.

"Mr. Harris," she said softly, enunciating each word crisply, "you second-guess me again, and I'll ride your face into the dirt. Rye's the top on this operation, just as he's been here on the ranch, but I'm the Detmeyer, and don't you forget it."

The wrangler shut his gaping mouth and finally managed, "Yes, ma'am," though a host of unhappy emotions flitted across his long, lean face

She straightened in the saddle and wheeled the horse away, reasonably certain that she'd made herself understood. Cantering after Rye, she turned her mind to the task ahead.

Kara quickly tired of the sun's glare and dug out her shades. Rye seemed to bristle at her every word, but she ignored him and went on about the business of rounding up the cattle and culling them. They had decided to take along three hundred and twenty-five head. Just in case anything happened, they didn't want to risk arriving at the end of the trail with fewer than the three hundred cattle specified in Plummer's will. That in mind, she was determined to take along only the strongest, healthiest stock, which meant personally inspecting every heifer and calf.

No steers or bulls would be making this trip. They didn't need the headaches that moving bulls in company with heifers would involve, and the steers were good only for the meat packers. It made no sense to drive such animals across three states, walking all the meat off of them, just to sell them at depressed prices after they got them there. Better to take along principal breeding stock and future sellers. The bulls could come later. Besides, if they didn't reach the New Mexico holding in the time allotted and with the herd stipulated, they wouldn't be needing those bulls, anyway. It would be relatively simple to have the more aggressive critters shipped out to the ranch after the drive, but culling them from the gathering herd would make the present work more difficult. The drovers could count on spending a good deal of time driving off unwanted cattle rather than merely rounding up the desirable ones.

And there was more work ahead. Once the herd was assembled, it would be necessary to inoculate every head and treat them for parasites, as well as any obvious health problems. Branding would be foregone in favor of tagging because it would be faster.

Meanwhile, those cows had to be driven, dragged and enticed out of rocky ravines, shrubby rills and hidden vales and moved to the eastern flat where sizable holding pens and a strong chute would aid the work of culling, inspecting and treating the herd. When the crew was assembled at the eastern flat, Rye assigned partners before dispatching them to select areas. Shoes went with George Marshal, Borden with Pogo Smith. Rye took Kara and Dean Schuster with him. Oboe appeared like magic and padded along to one side of the three-rider group, well away from the hooves of the horses.

Dean, obviously, was the least experienced. Kara knew that Rye either put her in that category with Dean or considered her a downright menace. *Well, live and learn,* she thought wryly. It didn't take long for the first lesson to present itself.

In a deep gully not a half mile from the holding pens, they found two heifers being nosed proprietorially by a big bull. He did not take kindly to their interference, especially when they spooked the nervous young heifer in which he seemed most interested, causing her to pull herself out of the ravine by her front legs and scamper for a covering of brush about two hundred yards away. Kara dropped a loop around her neck on first throw, then dragged her a safe distance away in the opposite direction of the brush, while ordering Oboe to cut out that bawling bull.

Rye recovered from his surprise quickly enough to get on the bull and drive him away, dog nipping at its heels. Dean managed to keep the older cow in the ravine by simply riding his horse into the breach.

Rye returned, leaving Oboe to harry the frustrated bull a little longer. He rode right up to Kara, who had retrieved her loop and driven the heifer back down into the ravine with the one Dean was holding. Rye pushed his hat to the back of his head and took off his sunshades. He didn't compliment her work, didn't even acknowledge it. He did something better. He asked, "What do you think? Should we leave Dean to keep 'em bunched or pull some scrub down into the ravine to block it?"

She considered. "Why don't we block the ravine and leave Oboe? That way, the cows won't wander and if the bull returns, Oboe can drive him away again."

He turned his horse toward the bushes. "I'll get to work on the scrub."

She called her dog with a sharp whistle, then ordered him to keep the cows before sending Dean off to help Rye cut scrub. While the two cowboys did the hacking and dragging of dry brush, Kara consulted a contour map of the area. By the time the men had blocked the ravine, she had decided where to head next. She couched her decision as a suggestion; Rye agreed without comment.

They drove twenty-two head into the holding pen before lunch. Kara got down and took care of her horse without complaint, though her backside was screaming from the long hours in the saddle. Dayna and Meryl came out in Dayna's old truck to dispense lunch. Thick sandwiches, potato chips and pieces of fruit were wolfed down with cans of cola and bottles of tea. No one went away hungry, but no one exactly ran for a horse afterward, either.

They had intended to work the same horses all day, but it was evident that the horses were suffering at least as much as their riders. Rye sent Bord and his tack back to the house with Dayna and Meryl to gather another string, while everyone else lay down in the dirt for some rest, saddles as pillows, hats as shades. Kara knew she needed the respite and settled down to it gratefully. In about a second Rye was shaking her awake.

"Up and at 'em, cowgirl."

She got up and stretched, uncaring what the others did. When she was sufficiently limbered, she went to saddle her horse—and was the first one mounted. Since Borden, as wrangler, had to take responsibility for the extra horses, he was excused from round-up for the afternoon. Rye sent Dean in his place as partner to Pogo, leaving Kara teamed with him.

An hour later they were driving a balky bunch of cows out of a narrow box canyon. The wall on the left was a tall stair step of shallow shelves that crumbled away whenever one of the cows tried to escape that way, while the wall to their right was a sheer cliff of rock about thirty feet high. Not liking the way the sand and shale crumbled and slid around on that left canyon wall, they rode close to the cliff wall on their right, venturing out from it only to ride around large boulders and other debris that blocked the narrow natural path.

Kara could never say just what alerted her. They'd been hearing the trickle and thump of small falling stones since they'd ridden into the place known as Spear Canyon. She'd almost blocked out the nerve-racking sound, but something fairly screamed "Watch out!" at her, and she looked up. Two stones were falling toward them, one about the size of a five-gallon bucket. The other looked like it could crush a sports car, not to mention a man on horseback. Kara saw it and understood the danger, all in a split second. She reacted instinctively, grabbing the cheek piece of Rye's roan's bridle and spurring her own in the same instant. Wheeling about, they were well up the opposite wall, slipping and sliding, when the boulders crashed down onto the path, raising a cloud of dust and scattering the cattle so that they bolted in different directions.

Rye spat curses, first at those boulders and then the cattle, one of which actually retreated back down the canyon the way they'd come, while the others galloped ahead. When they could both breathe normally again, they looked at each other with mutual relief.

"How the hell did you know?" Rye asked.

Kara shrugged and shook her head. "Couldn't tell you. I just suddenly knew something was wrong and where to look for it."

Rye removed his hat and lightly whacked it against his thigh, causing his horse to shift and sidestep. "I'd be dead now if you hadn't known and reacted."

Kara looked at the big boulder in the sand. "Maybe both of us."

Rye followed her line of sight and said flatly, "Me definitely." He put his hat on his head and tugged it into place before looking her square in the eye. "You can ride my elbow any time," he told her with a grin.

She laughed. "Okay."

He put a hand to the back of his neck and shuddered as if shaking off the willies. Then he glanced over his shoulder and wheeled his horse. "Well, I'm after that stupid hide bag that ran back up the canyon. You get on out of here and see if you can gather up any of the others."

She nodded. "See you up on top."

He glanced once more at the boulder then back at her before giving her a nod. She knew as he cantered away that she'd seen the glint of admiration in those gray eyes. What surprised her was how glad she was to have finally seen it—and how upset she'd have been if he hadn't gotten out of that rock's way.

Chapter Five

Dayna Detmeyer laid a mighty fine table. Tired as he was, Rye felt a spurt of enthusiasm at the sight of chickens roasted to a rich brown, fluffy whipped potatoes and a whole sideboard covered with an amazing variety of green and yellow vegetables. She set freshly baked yeast rolls on the table and announced two kinds of pie for dessert. The men waded into the bounty like hungry bears. Kara ate well, too, but Rye was aware of an undercurrent of worry there. He shared it...even, he hoped, surpassed it.

The day had not been as productive as he'd hoped. He and Kara had brought in the most cattle, and he judged at first glance that a fourth, maybe a third, of them would have to be culled. They'd have left most of them on the range if not for the fear that the others would just spend more time dragging them in. Seasoned cowhands could be expected to do the culling before driving the select head to round-up, but a volunteer crew of mostly nonworking cowboys could not be expected to recognize at a glance which cattle to drag in and which to drive off, with the exception of the few bulls. So the most efficient way to go about it was to drag in everything, cull them at one time, and drive off the undesirables. That, unfortunately, slowed down things, but not as much as having every crew drag in the same rejected cows over and over again. Still, he'd hoped to have at least half the herd by the end of the day, and they hadn't met that goal. At this rate, it would take an extra day just to assemble the herd, never mind culling and treating them. Time was not the only problem on Rye's mind, however.

That had been no natural rock slide that had nearly squashed him like a bug today. He'd been riding this country long enough to know that rock and earth slides were a constant threat in some places, and he'd witnessed his share. He'd never seen a really big rock fall all on its lonesome. Boulders that big just didn't roll off some ledge. Instead, the ground gradually gave way beneath them, raining down a shower of small rocks and a slide of dirt alongside the monster. And yet, today one big rock and one monster boulder fell straight out of the sky and nearly pulverized him—and Kara, too, except... It had felt like someone had targeted him specifically. He tried to tell himself that he was being paranoid, but he couldn't quite make himself believe it. So how had those rocks tumbled? He decided to take a little drive before he turned in for the night.

Naturally, circumstances conspired against him. He'd barely cleaned his dessert plate before Kara appeared at his shoulder.

"I think we'd better take another look at our projections," she said, rolling her shoulders and working at her neck muscles with both hands. He knew just how she felt. He was beginning to tighten up, too, and she was right about those projections, but tonight was not the time. He shook his head.

"Not tonight, Kara. I've got something to do."

She didn't take being rebuffed easily. "It couldn't be more important than being sure we meet our deadline."

"Tell you what," he said, rising gingerly. "You take a look at the projections tonight, and I'll go over them with you first thing in the morning. How about we meet in the kitchen for coffee?"

She wasn't pleased. Her frown left little doubt. Nevertheless, she reluctantly nodded. "If that's the best you can do."

"I'm afraid so. See you in the morning." He shoved his chair up under the table and caught the eye of the one friend he knew could be of service to him in this circumstance. "Shoes, could I have a word with you?"

The other man nodded once and went back to his pie with his customary concentration. Anyone but Rye might have taken it as the surliest of reluctant compliance, but Rye knew his friend well. He took a moment to thank Dayna Detmeyer for the meal, praising her abilities. The handsome woman smiled.

"Thank you, Rye. I thought I'd treat you boys tonight. Even with the convenience of a modern kitchen in the mobile home, I won't be able to do yeast rolls and pies on the trail. We'll have to settle for biscuits and cobblers then."

"I'm betting you'll get no complaints from anyone, least of all me," Rye told her.

"We won't go hungry," she assured him with a wink.

Rye chuckled. "Ma'am, you're too modest. Your cooking is enough to make this mongrel crew forget they're not being paid."

Dayna laughed, clearly pleased. "We Detmeyer women like to hold up our ends of things," she said.

Rye couldn't prevent a glance in Kara's direction. "You sure do," he admitted softly, and Dayna's smile grew.

"She knows her stuff," Dayna said, following the line of his glance. "Her father saw to it, and he was his father's son, after all."

Rye nodded. "Yes, ma'am. I can see that for myself." He rubbed an earlobe, momentarily withdrawing into himself. "Never seen a woman like her," he murmured.

"She's one of a kind," Dayna said proudly.

Recovering himself, Rye shot her an embarrassed look. "Yes, ma'am," he replied noncommittally. "Thanks again for the meal. Lookin' forward to breakfast."

"Good night, Rye."

"Night, ma'am."

He went out through the kitchen, not bothering to so much as glance over his shoulder to check if Shoes was aware of his leaving. He was standing deep in the shadows beside the back door when Shoes let himself out the same way and turned unerringly to face him.

Advancing soundlessly, Shoe asked, "What's up?"

"Think you can read some sign with the aid of a flashlight?"

Sturdy white teeth flashed. "Or without."

"Let's get the truck."

A small shape slipped out of the shadows. "Dad, can I go?"

Rye looked at Shoes. How had Champ gotten so close without them knowing it? The big Indian shrugged. "He's Chako."

Rye lifted his eyebrows. He'd have to watch the scamp a lot closer from now on. He waved a hand inclusively. "Come on."

Champ was so excited he could hardly sit still on the slow drive out to the canyon. Shoes regaled him with a history of cattle drives past—from both sides of the trail, Indian and white. By the time Rye guided the big truck up the rough, steep path that flanked Spear Canyon, he was pretty caught up in the tale himself.

"And so the steel rails were laid," Kanaka said, "and instead of driving their herds to the railroad, the railroad came to them, and there was no need for the big drives any longer."

Champ cocked his head at this and said, "I bet it was more fun the other way."

Rye chuckled. "I don't know about fun, but it sure was more work." He brought the truck to a stop, the headlamps picking out a deep crevice that rainwater had cut into the ground. Had rain undercut that hunk of mountain that had almost squashed him?

"We'll have to walk from here." He took one of the flashlights from the compartment in the dashboard and handed the other to Shoes. "Son, you stay behind us, understand?" Champ nodded. "Let's go." He shut off the engine but left the headlamps on. He let himself out, turned on the flashlight and opened the door for Champ. They met Shoes in front of the truck. "Latch on to my belt, Champ." He felt the small, strong fingers curl around the waistband of his jeans. "Lead on, Shoes."

Kanaka began swinging his light in a slow, purposeful arc as he trudged up the slope, while Rye kept his trained on the trail ahead. Shoes stopped and shined his light to one side. "Footprints."

"So someone was up here earlier."

Shoes nodded and went on as before. Eventually, they came to a place where a huge boulder might have rested. If so, the boulder had not sat on top of the canyon wall but had actually occupied a notch in its side at the top. Kanaka signaled for Rye and Champ to back up, then went down on his belly and crawled to the edge of the canyon. Peering over, he shined his light downward. Small rocks scattered. Dirt slid from beneath his shoulders. Shoes scrambled backward out of danger.

"That's it," Shoes said, whipping dust from his shirt. "He must have scouted out this spot when you were up inside the canyon, then waited for you to come back."

"But how did he move it?" Rye wanted to know.

Shoes kept dusting himself off even as he followed his light in an ever widening circle. Finally, he stopped. "Here."

Rye led Champ to the spot where Shoes trained his light. It was a small ravine filled with scrub, and someone had poked a fence post down into it. "He did the same thing I did," Shoes explained, "laid on his belly. Then he used the post to loosen the boulder and, at the right moment, shove it free."

Rye laid a hand between Champ's shoulder blades and pressed the boy to him, a feeling of danger suddenly overwhelming him. He eyed Shoes in the dark above the twin beams of their lights. "Any way to tell who it was?"

Shoes Kanaka shook his head. "Naw. It's too rocky around here to get good prints. About all I can tell you is that he was wearing boots, not shoes, certainly not athletic shoes, and he has a big foot."

"How big?"

"Bigger than your elevens."

Rye looked down at his own feet thoughtfully. "Okay. Let's get back. I'm ready to sleep where I stand."

Champ was tired, too. He was sound asleep in the back seat of the double-cab truck long before they got back to the compound, allowing Rye a chance to speak frankly with his friend.

"Someone tried to kill me, Shoes."

"I'd say so."

"But why?"

Shoes pulled a deep breath. "Who stands to benefit from your death?"

Rye didn't have to think long. "Di'wana?"

Shoes chuckled and shook his head. "My cousin has no reason to wish you dead. You may not believe it, but she does not wish death for the father of her son."

"But who else stands to gain a thing from my death?"

"My point exactly," Shoes said. "If you die, my cousin gains custody of her son, and I may inherit a fine new truck, but what else happens?"

Rye tightened his hands on the steering wheel. "The trail drive is at least delayed, I should think."

"At least," Shoes agreed drily. "And if both of you and Kara should be killed?"

Rye knocked his hat back with his hand, muttering words he didn't usually allow to be spoken in front of his son. "Someone's out to stop the drive."

"That's my take."

Rye gritted his teeth. "Any bets as to who it is?"

Shoes just looked at him.

"All right. I don't want word of this to get out. Those falling rocks were an accident, as far as everyone else knows. I'll have a private conversation with the local law just in case something else happens."

Shoes nodded. "You aren't going to tell her?"

"Think she'd believe it?"

Shoes didn't answer that.

"I have to do something. She's in danger." Rye sighed. "I'll just have to keep her in sight."

Shoes turned a smile to the night-painted window. Rye ignored it. He had more than enough to worry about already. He wondered if the old man had had any inkling what he was stirring up when he'd made his plans for this drive. Rye didn't suppose it mattered now, but he wished with all his heart that Plummer had left him out of this mess. Or that Kara Detmeyer looked more like the man she seemed determined to be.

Kara licked the tip of her mechanical pencil and scribbled a number into her tally book. "Well, we did better than yesterday, but we're still going to be short. I've been thinking how we can speed up the process, and I thought maybe you could take a couple hands and go out in the morning to round up. You know what I'm looking for, so you can cull as you go and not worry about anyone else bringing in your rejects. Meanwhile, I'll be here, sifting through the herd we've already collected."

Rye frowned and leaned a forearm across his saddle horn. "I

don't much like that idea. I'd prefer for you to do all the culling. It's your herd, after all. You ought to go out with us. I reckon a half a day ought to do it.''

Kara shook her head. "Your way we'll lose half a day. My way, we gain it. I've already told you I trust your judgment."

"Yeah, but I'd rather have you with me."

She blinked at that. Had he just suggested that he didn't want to be parted from her? Or was she hearing what she wanted to hear these days? No doubt it was the latter. She sighed. "Time's more important than any other consideration."

"Not *any* other."

"Name one."

He straightened and took off his sunglasses to rub a hand over his face, his horse shifting beneath him. "Kara, can't you just humor me in this?"

"Why should I?"

"Because I asked you to!"

She couldn't quite believe what she'd heard, then suddenly she knew that he wasn't telling her something. "Okay, Wagner, what's going on?"

Rye slumped in his saddle. "Dammit, Kara, why do we have to make a big deal of this?"

"Either explain yourself or forget it, cowboy. You're not making much sense."

He covered his face with both hands, the reins dangling between his fingers, and muttered what sounded suspiciously like a very foul word. Finally, he dropped his hands, straightened, and kneed his horse closer. "I want your promise that you won't repeat what I'm going to tell you. I don't want him to know that we're on to him."

"Him?"

"Them. Whoever. Promise?"

"All right."

He took a deep breath. "You're in danger. Someone's trying to hurt, maybe even kill you."

She waited for the punch line. When it didn't come, she laughed anyway. "That's absurd."

He reached out and took hold of her reins, leaning closer still. "Shoes and I went up on Spear Canyon last night, and we found proof that someone pushed those rocks down on us. We even found what he used to do it. Now I think that smacks of something more than a prank, don't you?''

She was too shocked to reply right away. Eventually the information clicked into place in her brain. ''You were the one nearly killed.''

He shook his head. ''Even if whoever dislodged those boulders knew I was the one riding on the inside, he couldn't be sure you wouldn't be hurt. This is serious, Kara, and I'm not letting you out of my sight until I know you'll be safe.''

She braced one hand on her thigh and tried to take it in. It was almost more than she could comprehend. ''This just can't be.''

''Kara, I wouldn't lie to you about something like this.''

She stared at him a moment. ''No, of course, you wouldn't, but... There has to be some logical explanation.''

''I'm listening.''

She cocked her head, trying to come up with one. She took a deep breath. It was a mistake. It had to be. ''Look, Wagner, it was dark last night. You can't be sure about this.''

''Shoes was there. Ask him.''

She didn't want to ask Shoes Kanaka any such thing. ''Whatever's going on, we're not joined at the hip. You can't be with me twenty-four hours a day. You'll just have to trust me to take care of myself.''

He clamped his teeth. ''Kara, if he's trying to stop this drive, he'll try again.''

''You don't have any proof that anyone is trying to stop the drive. In fact, you don't have any proof at all, or else you'd have the law out here.''

''I talked to the law last night.''

That rocked her. He really believed someone had pushed that boulder off on top of them. ''And?''

He clamped his jaw shut, a muscle flexing in its hollow. ''They were supposed to take some pictures this morning, but when they got out there the area had been swept clean.''

''By whom?''

''By whoever doesn't want to get caught!''

Kara shook her head. ''I just don't get this. Why would someone want to hurt the two of us?''

''To stop the drive.''

"That's crazy. The only one who stands to gain at all from that— Now wait just a minute. I know you don't like Payne, but this is ridiculous!"

"Did I say anything about Payne?"

"Who else would benefit?"

"I don't know! I just know that I'm not letting you out of my sight!"

He did sound genuinely concerned, and while that pleased her, she couldn't credit his conclusions. "I'll be extra careful."

He shook his head. "Not good enough."

"I'll be certain that I'm with someone all the time. Will that set your mind at ease?"

He looked her square in the eye. "I want you with me."

"Well, we can't sleep together! How are you going to protect me then?"

His face pulsed a dull red. "I've already thought of that. Starting tonight, we're going to be sleeping around the campfire, all of us. We'll tell the crew that it's kind of a trial run, to help them figure exactly what to take on the trail in their bedrolls so they'll be as comfortable as they can be."

Kara blinked at him. It was a pretty ingenious plan. "Okay. I'll go along with that."

"Good. Then we're riding out together, right?"

Kara rolled her eyes. "Maybe I ought to remind you who saved whose life yesterday when that rock fell! I'm not a child, and I'm nobody's idiot. You've done your part by warning me. Now back off, Wagner, and do your job. That means helping me get this herd on the trail and to New Mexico by the deadline."

"Dammit, Kara! You aren't taking this seriously!"

"Trust me to take care of myself!" she argued.

"How can I, when you show no signs of taking the danger seriously?"

"I'm sorry, Rye. I can't help thinking that there's been some mistake, but I will be careful, I swear."

He was as mad as that bull they'd driven off from his heifers that first day. "You're bound and determined to get yourself killed, aren't you? Fine, then. I'll be damned if I'll come riding to the rescue when you willfully put yourself at risk!"

He yanked his horse around and cantered away. "Fine!" she shouted after him. "You take care of you, and I'll take care of me!'' He didn't so much as acknowledge he'd heard her. Kara slumped back into the saddle, thinking over all he'd said. Attempted murder. It was like something out of a movie. Things like that just didn't happen to people like her. And yet...if that boulder had been pushed, then Rye, at least, was in danger. But who could hate Rye enough to want him dead? She shook her head. She knew so little about the man that it was impossible to even guess, but that didn't matter as much as making sure nothing happened to him.

Suddenly, riding out with him wasn't such a bad idea. Darn. She hated eating crow.

It was late when she finally found a moment to speak with him again. He'd decreed that they would sleep around the campfire that night, just as he had told her he would. No one quibbled. Sleeping on the ground was something they all had to get used to, anyway. She put together her bedroll just as her father had taught her, and picked a space. She wasn't particularly surprised when Rye threw his bedding down on one side of her and Shoes on the other. She'd showered and changed into fresh clothes, which she would sleep in tonight and wear all day tomorrow, but Rye had yet to clean up and change.

He was crouched down, spreading out his blanket roll when she stepped up behind him and laid a hand on his shoulder. He froze for an instant, then went on about his business, finishing the job before rising to his feet and carefully turning to face her.

"Got some complaint about the sleeping arrangements?"

"No. I just need a minute of your time. In private."

Nodding, he turned and walked away, obviously expecting her to follow. He picked a spot in clear sight of the others, but far enough away that they wouldn't be overheard. "Get it out. It'll be my turn in the shower in a minute."

"I've been thinking. You're right. We better stick together."

He lifted an eyebrow. "And what brought you to that conclusion?"

She shrugged. "Let's just say, I figure we ought to keep an eye on each other. That way, whoever the target is, someone will be looking out for him, er, or her."

He chuckled. "Cowgirl, are you looking out for me?"

She met his gaze defiantly. "Why not? You're looking out for me. And after all, I have already saved your hide once."

He rolled his eyes and pulled at his earlobe. "You aren't ever going to let me forget that, are you?"

She shook her head smugly. "Not a chance."

He laughed. "Okay. Here's the deal. You'll watch my back, and I'll watch yours. Agreed?"

She stuck out her hand. "Deal." His bigger one swallowed it and pumped her arm.

"All right, now we're building up a head of steam. I might as well tell you just what I'm thinking so I know we'll be on track together." He waved an arm, indicating the camp. "I know every one of these men. They're my friends. But just for the sake of argument, let's say that they're all vulnerable to enough money... Take George, now. He's had a few good years on the rodeo circuit, but he's engaged to be married, and take it from me, rodeo and marriage don't mix too well. The temptation to stock away a windfall might be too much for him. I don't believe it for a minute, but just for the sake of argument, let's say it's so. We can't be too careful. See?"

She folded her arms. "What about the others?"

He tugged at his ear. "Pogo, now, I'd stake my life he's an honest man, but he's also getting a little long in the tooth, and this cowboy life isn't an easy one. I'd be surprised if he had more than a week's pay to his name. Could be, he's thinking about retirement."

"And Dean?"

Rye shook his head. "Dean's got money, more than he knows what to do with. Dean's got a head for business, and he's made good use of it. On the other hand, it's the greedy man who most often gets rich. Now, Dean's always been generous with me, but I've heard some others complain that he could be tighter than Dick's hatband. So I have to consider him vulnerable, too."

"And Shoes?"

Rye hung his thumbs in his waistband. "Shoes Kanaka is the one man in this world that I'd trust with my life and, more important, my son's life. But then, to tell you the truth, I trust them all."

"That just leaves Bord Harris."

"Bord's not easy to know," Rye said. "I've worked with him nearly half a year now, and he's never been anything but friendly and helpful, but to me he's the least known. Still, Plummer hired him, and Plummer was as fine a judge of men as I've ever known. If he ever had any misgivings about Bord Harris, he never said anything to me. That's about all I can tell you."

Kara frowned. "I don't suppose you've checked everyone's whereabouts yesterday afternoon?"

He slanted her a smug look. "Suppose again. I paired them up, remember? Everyone was with someone else. Except Bord. But his work was all done with his usual thoroughness, and Angelina saw him around the barn twice that afternoon. He could've taken the truck out and done the deed, but he'd have to have been darn lucky not to have been seen at it. Besides, he seemed as surprised as everybody else when we talked about it at dinner last night. No, I'd bet my last dollar that none of the crew was involved, but I don't know it. That's why I don't want to take anyone else into my confidence just now."

She nodded. "Okay. Better safe than sorry, as they say."

"Exactly."

"I don't want Mom getting wind of it, either. She's upset enough just thinking it was an accident."

"Then it stays between the three of us for now—me, you and Shoes."

"The three of us," she agreed.

"By the way, Shoes will be keeping an eye on you when I'm not around, understand? I don't want you going anywhere without one of us. Okay?"

"Okay. Now you promise me."

He looked at her like she'd grown two heads. "Promise you what?"

"That you won't go off without me or Shoes."

He rolled his eyes. "Oh, please!"

"Listen, Wagner, what's good for the goose is good for the gander. From now on the two of us are sticking together."

"Isn't that what I said this afternoon when you nearly bit my head off?"

She didn't let him rile her this time, admitting flatly, "Yes. And you were right."

He pretended to stumble backward and clamped a hand over his heart. "I may faint."

She laughed. "That'll be the day. Okay, so we ride out in two big groups tomorrow and finish the round-up, then we—you and I—cull the herd. Agreed?''

''Agreed.''

''And you won't go anywhere without me or Shoes along. Right?''

He folded his arms.

''Right?''

Finally, he nodded. ''Oh, all right.''

''Fine. Go get your shower. If I wanted to smell horses all night, I'd bed down with the remuda.''

He rolled his eyes. ''What? You aren't going to insist on taking a shower with me?''

''I'll just stand outside,'' she said, hooking her thumbs in her empty belt loops and grinning.

He shook his head. ''This thing could get real complicated real fast,'' he said, stroking his mustache with his fingertips. ''We're going to have to set up some kind of protocol. I'll think on it before I go to sleep. Meanwhile, we'll just have to keep on our toes.''

They strolled up to the little house on the hill. She wondered if he was sad to leave it, but didn't want to ask. They went inside, and he led her down the hall that divided the building to his bedroom. She waited outside the door while he gathered his things together, then went into the living room after he started his shower water in the little bathroom. Not long ago she and Rye Wagner couldn't stand to be in the same room together, and now they'd just agreed to buddy-up for the duration. They'd be working side by side, eating side by side, sleeping side by side. Might something more come of it than keeping each other out of trouble?

To her knowledge no man had ever found her sexually attractive, at least not one she'd worked beside on the range. There was no reason to think Rye would be any different, and yet, she couldn't help wondering, wishing, hoping that maybe... But no, she was just one more burden that Plummer had heaped on Rye's broad shoulders, and she'd best not start to think otherwise. If she did, she would really be in danger—danger of getting her heart broken.

Chapter Six

Kara opened her eyes to a gray sky streaked with vivid pink, bright yellow and purest blue. Her back ached, and her throat felt thick and clogged. She cleared it, stretched and lifted a hand to rub away a tickle on her nose, but she froze in the process, suddenly aware of a warmth and a heaviness that wasn't her own. Looking down, she found a hand, a big one, in the hollow of her shoulder. The long, blunt fingers were closed tightly in the fabric of her red-and-white-checked shirt. She followed the hand to a thick, corded wrist, the cuff of a chambray shirt and a sleeve that led to a thick, knotted shoulder, Rye Wagner's shoulder, neck and face. Beneath his arm, his son snuggled under his blanket, only the blue-black hair at the crown of his head visible. With that one arm, he'd managed to hold them both safe through the night. Kara smiled.

A presence at her other side drew her attention in that direction. Shoes Kanaka crouched next to her. Baring his big white teeth in a smile, he lifted a finger to his lips in a signal for silence. Then, very carefully, he reached across her and gently pried loose Rye's fingers. Rye sighed and drew back his hand, letting it fall atop his blanket. Kanaka's hand closed around the top of her arm as he helped her to her feet. He stood with his fingertips poked into his back pockets as she first shook out, then stomped into her boots. With a jerk of his head, he led her away from the sleepers.

"I'll walk you to the house."

"Thanks."

He said nothing more for a few steps, then, "He's afraid for you."

She stopped and looked him straight in the eye. "It wasn't an accident. You're absolutely certain?"

He tucked his hair behind his ear and nodded. Kara sighed, and shook her head.

"I'm not the target. I can't be. The only two people in the whole world who have anything to gain by my death are the very two who love me the most."

Kanaka hung his thumbs in the curves of his front pockets. "You are wondering who could want Ryeland dead."

"Yes. Can you tell me?"

"No."

She narrowed her eyes. "Can't or won't?"

He didn't answer, just returned her stare with his fathomless black eyes. She kicked at the sand and resumed their stroll toward the house. "Could Champ be in danger, do you think?"

He seemed genuinely shocked that she asked. "No, I don't think so."

"Because you think it's tied up with the trail drive, don't you?"

"Yes."

She shook her head. "I can't believe that."

He nodded. They had reached the front steps, and Kara was feeling some urgency for a few moments in private, but she had to know one more thing. "You'll help me protect Rye, won't you, and Champ, too?"

He stared at her for a long moment, and then he laughed. His face utterly transformed in that moment. Suddenly he was handsome in a noble, almost untouchable way. "Yes," he said, "I will help you protect Rye. And Champ. And I will help Rye protect you—and Champ." He folded his arms, hands tucked into his armpits. "We will all protect one another," he said jovially. "We will be our own tribe. The Trail Drive Tribe." He held the door open for her, chuckling and shaking his head.

It seemed an absurd reaction to Kara, but she didn't know the man well enough to make judgments yet. Shrugging, she hurried up the steps and inside.

Rye swung up into the saddle and turned his mount toward Kara, who waited patiently, one arm draped across her saddle horn. What looked like a small posse rode at her back, everyone but Shoes and Harris. "Okay, boys," he said, "keep your eyes and ears open. We're heading due west. We'll only be bringing in keepers, so run 'em every one by me or Kara. Got it?"

He received a chorus of affirmative replies and turned his horse. "Let's ride." He hardly noticed when Kara fell in beside him, her sorrel effortlessly keeping pace with his big gray. They covered ground quickly, the dog roaming off to one side, always within sight. They were eighteen, nineteen minutes out when suddenly the dog drew up short, spun in a circle and bayed in those clear, bell-like tones.

"He's found something. Don't know if it's cows, though." Kara turned her horse, and Rye followed, the other three right behind him. They approached a small rise over which Oboe had disappeared a moment earlier. Kara went over first. She was sitting still atop her prancing horse when Rye drew rein beside her. He pushed back his hat, failing at first to comprehend what he was seeing.

"Somebody count," he said finally, choking out the words as the others made sounds of shock. After a moment, Pogo and George rode over for a closer look.

"My God," Kara whispered, "who would do such a thing?"

Rye watched Oboe pick his way through the dozen and more corpses. The sandy ground was dark with blood. Behind him he could hear Dean puking. Pogo got off his horse and carefully nosed around, while George took a count.

"I don't know," Rye said, "but he obviously meant to scare us."

"It's working," Kara whispered.

Rye looked over at her. "You okay?" She nodded, her mouth pressed together in a whitish line. He wanted to get her away from the carnage but didn't dare let her ride off alone and couldn't yet leave the scene himself. "Why don't you see about Dean?"

She shook her head. "He'll be embarrassed. Besides, I want to know what they find over there."

Rye nodded. She was tough, that woman, tough and smart. He let his leg brush hers and settled down to wait. Pogo mounted up, and he and George rode to meet them. Kara whistled for Oboe, and the dog, too, abandoned the investigation. "Well?" Rye said as the two men reined in.

George pushed his hat back on his head. "Twenty-two," he said morosely.

Pogo took a deep breath. "All select heifers from what I can tell."

"Son of a bitch!" Rye swallowed bile. "What else?"

"Ain't been dead long," Pogo went on, looking off into the distance. "No carrion around yet. You'll want to get somebody out here, but it looked to me like there was three or four of 'em. They were shooting bolts, like they do at slaughterhouses."

"A quiet way for killing," Rye said darkly.

Pogo nodded. "That's what I figured, too. Can't tell you why they were cutting their throats after. Don't make good sense unless they were going to butcher 'em."

"Maybe we scared 'em off," George said.

Rye shook his head. "No. We didn't scare anybody off, but that's what they're trying to do to us. That's why they cut their throats. They wanted as much blood and gore on the ground as they could manage." He looked at Kara. "This has to do with the drive."

She bit her lip and lowered her eyes. "I just don't understand how anyone could do such a thing."

"Well, someone sure as hell did," Rye said bitterly. "You got that cell phone on you?"

She nodded and twisted around to fish it out of her saddlebag. Flicking it open, she handed it to him. "Who're you calling?"

"Same person I called last night," he said, meaning the law.

She nodded sadly, staring down at her hands as he put through the call and relayed the details.

"We'll send one of the men back to lead you out," he said

into the telephone. "I'll see you if you're still around when we get in at lunchtime. If not, I'll give you a call later on."

He folded up the phone and handed it back to Kara. "George," he said, "think you can handle this?"

"You bet."

"Okay. Good man. The rest of us are going after cattle." He looked at Kara. "You up to it?"

She lifted her chin and nodded.

"All right. You tell 'em back at the flat, George, that we've gone out after cattle. Those sons-a-bitches might as well know they didn't succeed in putting us off the round-up." He paused to look at Kara again. He didn't much like her stillness or silence or the whiteness around her mouth. "You with me on this?"

She took a deep breath. "Yes. I'm with you."

He reached across the space between them and gripped her hand, then abruptly released it again. Embarrassed for what might be construed as a show of sentiment, he twisted in his saddle. "You with us, Dean?"

Dean shamefacedly wiped his mouth on his shirtsleeve and nodded. "Yeah."

Rye adjusted his reins. "You tell 'em, George," he said. "You tell 'em we'll be in with a herd of select come noon. We're driving this herd to New Mexico, and no damned fiend is going to keep us from it."

George nodded and whipped his horse into a canter, heading back in the direction from which they'd come. Rye turned his horse and led the group at a trot away from the scene of the carnage. They rode for half an hour before Oboe picked up a whiff, and it was another ten minutes before they finally came across a milling group of cattle. The reason for the unrest soon became obvious as two bulls squared off against each other. One of them trotted off without much effort on Pogo's part, but the other dug in and bellowed a warning. Oboe went for him, fang and claws, snapping and scratching at the bull's muzzle. The bull tossed its head. Its horns had been blunted, but one of them had a jagged end that could have done serious damage. Rye threw a rope at it, and so did Kara. A slap or two in the face in addition to Oboe's harrying, and the bull turned and trotted. They drove it a good distance away, then Kara sent Oboe back to contain the nervous cattle, while she went along with Rye to investigate sounds coming from a draw at the base of the hill.

They found four more heifers and big calves there and drove them up to join the first group. Then Oboe was off over the hill, and before they knew what was happening, they'd scared up almost forty head. Rye checked his wristwatch. Ten forty-five. "Should we go on in or keep at it?"

Kara looked around as if expecting to find someone else that he could be speaking to, then shrugged. "Let's go in."

Rye rose in the saddle and swung an arm at Pogo. "Let's take 'em home!"

Pogo heeled his horse at the cows, scaring them into a trot, but they instantly veered off after an old mama cow that headed over the hill. Kara spurred her horse after it, dropped a loop and dragged the cow behind her in the direction they wanted the herd to go. The cow bawled and tried to dig in, but Rye whacked her across the rump with the end of his rope and she went docilely after that, a near-grown calf at her side. They slowed to a walk pretty soon, cows not being much for exercise. Habitually they followed their noses from one blade of grass to another and then went off in a lazy search for water. Only rarely did they bolt in a panic. This lot settled into a slow, easy gait, nose to tail behind Kara's horse and followed her all the way to the flat. The local deputy was waiting when they got there.

"Pretty nasty scene back there," he said to Rye. "One of my men backtracked them to a road east of here. Looks like they parked a truck and a trailer, unloaded mounts, cut the wire and came in that way. They probably picked the cattle up along the way. Puzzle is why they picked that spot for their butchering."

"Oh, I think I can answer that," Rye said. He brought his hands to his hips, one knee cocked, and pitched his voice so that it carried around the entire flat. "They knew we'd be coming that way this morning. It was common knowledge around the camp and compound. They wanted us to find their killing field. It's an attempt at intimidation. They...*he*...someone is trying to stop this trail drive before it even gets started."

The deputy nodded. "You might be right. So what are you gonna do?"

Rye looked at Kara, who stood quietly to one side. Slowly she lifted her gaze to his. He was troubled by the puzzlement and pain that he saw there, but then she lifted her chin and said, "We're going to drive this herd to New Mexico." Something like pride filled him.

Rye turned his gaze back to the deputy. "You heard the lady."

The deputy nodded and resettled his hat. "I'd appreciate it if you'd keep in touch."

"Count on it."

He spoke with the lawman for a few more minutes, uncomfortably aware that Kara had wandered off. When the deputy climbed into his four-wheel drive to leave, Rye instinctively turned her way. She was climbing into the saddle of a neat little Appaloosa that he knew was one of the best cutting horses on the place. Bord was leading his favorite toward him. A big, fast dun that could turn on a dime. Rye had never seen a cow that could get by him on that dun. Nevertheless, he wondered if he ought not to call a halt, give Kara a few minutes to come to terms with what they'd found out there on the range. Then he shook his head. What was he thinking? Giving that woman orders was like spitting into the wind and about as effective. Besides, if she was a man, he'd let her take the lead, believing she knew best how to deal with her own emotions. Funny he should think of that.

He mounted up and joined her in the holding pen. She'd already put Dean on one gate and had George backing him up on horseback, his rope looped out and ready. Bord climbed onto the second gate, with Pogo behind him pulling on his gloves. Working wordlessly, Rye helped Kara split the herd. Then she picked her gate and nodded to her man. He took the other one, and they went to work, separating the culls from the select and driving them out the gates, where George or Pogo picked them up and hazed them out. Occasionally some stubborn critter didn't want to leave the herd, and the outside riders would have to rope it and drag it until it decided freedom was a better deal, after all.

They'd made a good dent in the herd by the time Dayna drove up with lunch, but Kara seemed not to notice until Rye waved off the men and rode into her line of vision, putting a halt to the work. "Trying to show me up?" he asked with a grin.

She shook her head. "No. I was just... No."

He understood perfectly. Gazing off into the distance, he gave the others a few seconds to fix their attention on the lunch truck before turning his smile on her again. "Well, I'm ready for a break. You set a mean pace, woman." But she had already turned her mount and was riding slowly toward the gate. Rye bowed his head, uncertain what to say or do next. He decided to just keep giving her space.

It turned into the proverbial situation of giving her an inch and having her take a mile. By the time he'd secured his horse and loosened the saddle girth, Kara had disappeared. Momentarily alarmed, Rye elbowed his way to the head of the line and demanded of the only person he knew who might have an inkling, "Where is she?"

Dayna shoved a barbecue sandwich and a bowl of coleslaw into his hands. "Shoes trailed her over the rise."

Absurdly relieved, Rye frowned. "Anybody tell you what happened this morning?"

Dayna nodded, turning a stricken gaze at him. "Afraid so." Her gaze flickered away again, as if she didn't want to discuss it. He could understand that. Kara was another matter.

"She's not acting like herself today."

"Yes, she is," Dayna told him. "She's acting exactly like herself. You just don't know her yet."

"Well, how could I? I've never seen her all quiet like this. She's usually wrangling with me over every little detail."

"She'll be wrangling again in no time, not like it was when Law died." Dayna shook her head. "It was months before I could get a rise out of her back then."

Suddenly Pogo appeared at Dayna's elbow. "Let me lend a hand, ma'am," he said, scooping sandwiches out of the hot box in the back of the truck. "You and Rye look like you need a few minutes."

Dayna sent him the sparest of looks and moved away from the truck without so much as a word of thanks. Rye followed her, poking his plastic spoon into his shirt pocket and tucking the plastic bowl of coleslaw into the bend of his elbow. He unwrapped his sandwich with one hand and bit out a huge chunk. The thinly sliced pork with sweet sauce was dark, so tender it fell apart in his mouth.

"What's your read on what went down out there this morning?" Dayna asked, her fingertips slipping into the front pockets of her jeans.

Rye gulped and wiped the corners of his mouth with the pad of his thumb. The barbecue went down sour as he thought about what he'd seen. "Somebody wants this drive stopped, and he'll be as cruel as he needs to be to see it done."

Dayna nodded. "I was afraid you'd say that."

"Any idea who it might be?"

Dayna shrugged. "Someone hoping to get both properties cheap, maybe."

"Or maybe just someone hoping to get both properties, period."

Her gaze rose to meet his. "Smitty could do something like that."

Rye shook his head. "Smitty's not one of the heirs."

"If it's Payne's, it's Smitty's," Dayna said flatly.

Rye considered that. "Okay, so there's Smitty, some nebulous hopeful buyer, and there's Payne."

"Meryl suggested it might be one of the creditors hoping to force an early settlement."

Rye held up four fingers. "Okay, that's four possibilities."

"Could be a disgruntled former hand, too, according to Meryl."

He shook his head. "No, I don't think so, not anyone I ever met. Every one of those boys was pretty broken up when Plummer went. I didn't sense resentment or anything there."

"So Payne's number one on your list," Dayna deduced correctly.

He cocked his head, trying to find more than a gut instinct behind his reasoning. "He stands to gain the most."

"But he loves Kara," Dayna told him, "almost as much as I do. We often thought that if they weren't cousins... Well, let's just say that Law preferred him as a nephew."

Rye's stomach turned over. The succulent sandwich in his hand suddenly looked about as appetizing as a cow patty. He folded the paper over it with one finger. "I better check on her. She's been gone for a while."

Dayna just smiled and folded her arms. "I figure she'll be ready to bite anytime now. Don't say I didn't warn you."

Rye gave her an arch look and strode away. Truth be told, he'd relish getting bitten right about now. His appetite had returned by the time he'd climbed the hill. He found Shoes standing just on the other side, his hands tucked into his armpits.

"What're you doing?"

"Keeping my distance." Shoes nodded in Kara's direction. She was sitting alone at the base of the hill, her forearms on her knees, staring off to the east.

"She said anything to you?"

Shoes nodded. "Oh, yeah." He repeated, word for word, what she'd told him. Rye felt his jaw drop. He'd used those words himself, of course, but somehow coming from her they were shocking. Suddenly he was chuckling.

"Damn, she's something, isn't she?"

Shoes folded his arms a little tighter. "She works and acts like a man, but I think she's really a lot of woman."

This was straying into territory Rye was eager to avoid. He changed the subject. "She had any lunch?"

Shoes shook his head. "Me, neither, and I think I better get me a piece of that pig before it's all gone. Why don't you go down there and see if she's morphed back into a human?"

Rye grinned at him. "Yeah, you go ahead." He started down the hill. Well, she was biting, but something about the set of her shoulders bothered him.

She heard him coming and swiped at her face. He grimaced. Damn if she wasn't bawling. She snapped over her shoulder, "I thought I told you to—"

"Nope, not me," Rye said cheerfully. "If you'd told me that, my ears probably would've caught fire."

She stiffened, then slumped forward in a kind of huddle. He sat down next to her and made himself comfortable. "What do you want?" she asked huskily.

He looked regretfully at his sandwich and shoved it at her. "You won't believe what your mother is peddling down there. I mean, it's a travesty."

Her head whipped around. He saw the glitter of tears in her eyes, the smeared tracks of them on her dirty cheeks. It bothered him more than he'd even expected it to. Damn.

"What're you talking about?" she demanded, yanking the sandwich from his hand.

"Taste it," he said, watching her unfold the paper and look

at the spot where he'd taken out his bite. She turned it slightly and took a small bite out of the side.

"There's nothing wrong with this," she said after chewing awhile.

He plucked the spoon out of his pocket and plunged it into the milky coleslaw. "I know. She's spoiling the hands rotten. They're going to be expecting four-star-restaurant treatment before we're halfway to New Mexico. She just might have ruined them for life."

Kara rolled her eyes and took another bite of his sandwich. He let her munch on that awhile, then traded her the coleslaw for what was left. She looked at the spoon he'd just pulled from his own mouth, then she turned it over and put it in her own, sucking on the bowl. He went hard as stone, just like that, and it nearly choked him, his jeans suddenly cutting him in two, lungs seizing up. He swallowed, trying to breathe normally, and concentrated on the sandwich she'd nibbled. He gulped the rest down in three bites, thankful he didn't wind up hacking and with her beating him on the back. He wadded up the paper and stuffed it into his shirt pocket. She handed him the coleslaw back. He was hurting, and his hands were shaking so badly that he bobbled the bowl, nearly spilling the last few bites.

"Careful," she said, wiping her hands on her thighs. She sighed and stared off into nothing while he gingerly finished off the coleslaw and tried to concentrate on not squirming or tugging at his jeans.

When he'd scraped the last bit from the bowl, she abruptly stood. He looked up, unsure he could do more without doing himself bodily harm, but suddenly she was bending toward him, one hand on his shoulder, the other pushing back his hat brim.

"Thanks," she said, and tilting her head, she placed a slow, lingering kiss right next to his mouth, almost in his mustache.

It burned right through him, nearly doubling him over when it reached his groin. He sat dazed while she straightened, dusted her hands together and said, "Well, this isn't getting any work done." She started up the hill. "You coming?"

He swallowed and murmured, "In a minute."

It was several, actually, before he could stand, and then he had to talk himself out of running fast in the other direction. But then he told himself that it was just a friendly little kiss, just a friendly thank-you for sharing his lunch with her. What the hell had he been thinking? He was still hungry! And she was probably working already, making him look like a darn fool.

He beat the dust off the seat of his pants. He'd dropped the empty bowl and spoon. Bending, he swept them up in one hand, fishing the sandwich paper out of his shirt pocket with the other. Crushing them together, he carried them up the slope and over the top of the rise. He made a determined effort not to look for Kara, and that was why he was halfway down before he realized Kara wasn't working at all.

She was throwing herself into Payne Detmeyer's arms, laughing, and taking his big fat head in her hands to kiss him on the cheek. Rye's jaw dropped. The son of a bitch had very likely slaughtered nearly two dozen head of prime cattle just to unnerve her and here she was throwing herself at him! He watched Payne catch her up and whirl her in a circle, the pair of them laughing like maniacs, and Rye reassessed. No, Payne didn't kill those cattle. He'd had it done. Payne didn't have the guts or grit to do the dirty work. Rye wanted to put a bolt in his brain. He'd gladly pay for the opportunity. He went down that hill with murder in his eye, but the instant he drew near, Kara flew from Payne's arms right into his own. He nearly fell over. Luckily, she was jumping up and down exuberantly, which made it all seem perfectly reasonable behavior on his part.

He got an arm around her waist and pulled her off him. She was grinning like an idiot.

"Isn't it wonderful?"

"Isn't *what* wonderful?"

"Payne's good news!"

Now he knew she'd definitely slipped a cog. "What in blue blazes are you talking about?"

"Payne's getting married!"

Rye blinked at her. Payne was getting married, was he? Excellent. He found a smile breaking out, and he turned it on Payne Detmeyer. "So, the big man's getting hitched, is he?"

Detmeyer laughed, all affability. "I asked her last night. She said yes. We were on the phone for hours."

"Well, well," Rye said. Did he smell alibi?

Kara cleared her throat and bounced back toward Payne.

Damn if she wasn't acting just like a woman now. Rye thought wickedly of nailing her boots to the ground.

"I'm so happy for you," she said, sliding an arm around Payne's thick waist. He tweaked the end of her nose.

"I knew you would be. That's why I made sure you were the first to know."

"Ah, thanks, cuz," Kara purred, going up on tiptoe to kiss Payne's cheek. She sure did kiss a lot all of a sudden, Rye noted sourly.

"Aren't we going to cull those cattle?" he asked through a fake smile.

Kara wilted, but she tried not to show it. "Yeah, you're right. We better get to it." She hugged Payne. "You take care, and I expect to hear all about the wedding plans as soon as I get to New Mexico."

"Sure thing. But you're the one who needs to take care of herself. Promise me, now."

"I promise."

"Good." He hugged her once more, then dropped his arms. She bounced away and started off toward the corral, flipping him a wave. Rye started after her. "Wagner."

He stopped and turned around. "Yeah?"

Payne leaned back against the fender of his splashy convertible and folded his arms. "I want you to take care of her for me," he said quietly. "She's important to me."

"More important than a few thousand acres?"

Payne smirked. "I knew you'd try to blame me for that ghastly prank, but I was at the house all night, on the phone for most of it."

Rye stepped close, his fists on his hips. "Prank? I don't think so."

Any hint of affability left Payne's face. "I meant what I said. If anything happens to her, it'll be your fault, and I'll personally hold you responsible."

"Anything happens to Kara," Rye said, getting right in old Payne's face, "you won't have to come looking for me. I'll be bringing it to you. She may think you're sweet enough to spread on toast, but I know rot when I smell it."

Payne chuckled, looking not in the least intimidated. "You

don't know what you're talking about. You've been talking to cows too long.''

"That's right," Rye said. "Dead cows, and they're every one saying your name."

Payne Detmeyer's heavily handsome face was menacing . "If I was going to cut throats," he said darkly, "I'd start with yours.''

Rye grinned. "Okay. Anytime you want to try, just come on. But remember this. I'm not nearly so easy to kill as a herd of dumb cows.''

Payne's eyes glittered dangerously for a moment, but then he dropped his gaze, eyelids lowering, and the easy smile was back. "You better get back to work, Wagner," the big man said, as if he had the right to order Rye's actions and expected unquestioning obedience. "You've got a big job cut out for you." He opened the car door and slid inside. Rye caught it and shoved it closed.

"It's a job I intend to do well," he said. "Plummer wanted Kara to have that ranch, and I mean to see she gets it."

Detmeyer wrenched the key, grinding the ignition, and threw the transmission into Reverse. Rye backed up, aware that Payne would have run him down if he'd thought he could get away with it. Well, let him try. The more Payne focused on him, the safer Kara would be.

He grinned wolfishly as he yanked his gloves from his hip pocket and strode toward his mount, pulling them on. So the kissing cousin was marrying, was he? Good. He only hoped old Payne-in-the-Butt's intended was a virago who would sink her claws deep into the puke's hide and keep him close to home from the wedding day on. He wouldn't have to worry about Kara then, no matter what happened.

Not that he would once this damned fool drive was over. Not by a long shot. Not even if Plummer Detmeyer whispered in his ear from the grave.

Chapter Seven

Kara felt one hundred and ten percent better. Yes, someone was definitely trying to nix the drive, but it wasn't Payne. She just knew that it wasn't. She had never really thought it was, and yet, somehow it had helped to see him, to feel his love and concern for her. She was so excited for him, so happy that he was getting married.

Whoever was trying to scare them off—and she felt certain that's all they were trying to do—wouldn't succeed, because she and Rye were taking the herd to New Mexico, period. She wouldn't think of those slaughtered beeves anymore. Instead she would concentrate on getting the job done.

With freshened resolve, she pushed everyone ruthlessly. They worked hard, and as a result had the herd culled to three hundred thirty-one head and a quarter of those treated and ear-tagged before nightfall. She slept like a rock and hit the ground running before daylight.

Owing to the previous day's experience, they had their treatment technique down to a fine science. George and Dean would load the animal into the chute from the rear, George on horseback with a loop ready. Then Dean would press it by shoving on the plunge gate until the cow stuck its head out the opening in the front gate. Once the cow was locked down, Pogo pried open its mouth and ran in a pill pusher, ejecting the thumb-sized tablet far into its throat. At the same time, Kara reached through the spaces in the pipe that made up the walls of the chute and shot an injection, prepared for her by Shoes, into the animal's flank. Finally Rye stapled a colored and numbered tag into the cow's ear, and they turned it out into the corral by dropping the front gate, jumping out of the way and letting the animal run over it. Then the front gate went back up, the rear one was opened, and the process started all over again. They were turning out about one per minute and had the whole herd done an hour or so after lunch. It was time to pack for the drive.

Rye had decided the previous day to start posting a guard on the herd. He'd teamed the men in pairs, George and Bord, Pogo and Shoes, himself and Dean, leaving Kara as the odd one out, and assigned them four-hour rotating shifts. Kara spoke to Dayna, and together they presented Rye with an ultimatum. Either they played equal roles or the men could start feeding themselves. Rye looked at the lunch truck, its hot box securely bolted and the key tucked into Dayna's pocket, and reluctantly relented. He drew up new assignments while munching on pasta salad and tuna sandwiches. The new pairings consisted of George and Bord, Pogo and Dean, Shoes and Dayna, and himself and Kara, working in three-hour shifts. Pogo and Dean had first watch that afternoon.

Rye and Kara were each pulled in a dozen different directions as they organized, reorganized and then attempted to streamline the whole outfit. Ultimately, they had it together. Foodstuffs and cooking utensils went into the motor home generously provided by Dean. Shoes took the extra tack into the farrier's wagon with him. Rye's double-cab truck was for personal gear and bedrolls—stored out of the weather in the second cab—and horse feed, which was covered with not one but three tarps in the truck bed. Dayna's old rattletrap became the water wagon, the bed given over to an enormous collapsible plastic container, which, with the addition of two short lengths of rubber hose, became a cold shower. The motor home would provide the occasional hot shower, if and when they could keep the water heater tank filled. In addition to the two trucks, motor home, and farrier's wagon, they had two four-horse trailers to pull, allowing them to keep at least half of their remuda rested at all times. That meant they had four drivers and four riders, unless circumstances required them to leapfrog the vehicles in order to put more riders in the field.

Thank God Rye had packed up his and Champ's household items and shipped them off to his folks in Durango days earlier. That left only a couple hundred minor items, such as extra tires, tools, cleaning supplies, a set of collapsible tables, flashlights, lanterns, medical gear, ropes, pickets, paperwork, maps and even a laptop computer complete with Internet link and fax—again, courtesy of Dean—to be organized and dispersed, along with a strongbox, a goodly sum of cash, a few toys, a radio, a dozen extra pairs of work gloves, an arsenal consisting of a shotgun, a rifle and a handgun licensed in five states and registered to Pogo, two guitars and a harmonica. In addition, they had three cellular phones among them, one belonging to George, one to Dean and the other to Kara.

Packing up a trail drive was only slightly less involved than moving a small city. They were all tired, confused and frustrated, and Kara didn't appreciate it much when Rye stated disgustedly that he'd survived years on the rodeo circuit with nothing more than a clean change of clothes, a shaving kit, a road map, his saddle, a rope and a picking string. Now he was hitting the road with a whole ranch in tow, he pointed out acerbically, including a woman and a kid.

"Two women," she reminded him, hurt that he'd just done what so many others had before him.

He seemed hardly to hear her as he was called over to help Shoes decide whether or not it was worth the space and effort to take along a small acetylene torch.

It came their turn to guard the herd just before dinner. Dayna packed them a small feast which they carried out to the holding pens with them. Fried chicken, mountains of mashed potatoes rising above gravy seas, stewed vegetables, chocolate cake, yeast rolls. They gobbled it up with unabashed gusto, as if it had been days instead of hours since they'd last eaten, their plates balanced atop their knees, paper napkins tucked into their collars. Dayna had been extremely generous, and Kara couldn't finish her portion. Rye polished off her leftovers with barely a pause to catch his breath.

"I hope we packed enough food," Kara said drily, still slightly miffed at the insult she felt he'd dealt her earlier. "If the rest of the men eat like you, we won't get to Colorado on what we have."

"We can always buy extra along the way," Rye said dismissively, wadding up his napkin and dropping it in the bag Dayna had provided for their refuse. Henceforth, they would be very sensitive to proper disposal. They all understood the necessity of capturing their own trash, of doing as little damage as possible to properties across which they would cross.

"Somebody better get a second job then," Kara grumbled.

Rye resettled his hat forward and lay back in the dust. They had wedged themselves into the side of the hill, so he was only half reclining at best. "In case you haven't noticed, neither one of us has a *first* job, not a paying one, anyway."

Kara sighed. "True."

He lifted his hat off his face. "Don't sound so glum. It'll work out. Besides, if...*when* we get this herd to New Mexico, you'll be all set up for the future."

"Which leaves only the present to worry about," she pointed out morosely.

He sat up again, shaking his head. "Women! They're never happy, no matter what—"

Kara instantly saw red. She slugged him, hard, rocking him sideways. He grabbed his shoulder. "Ow!"

She clapped her hands over her mouth in mock dismay and babbled in a singsong soprano. "Oh-I'm-so-sorry-did-that-hurt?" She dropped her hands—and the voice—abruptly shooting to her feet. "You arrogant pig, you deserved that! You have some nerve!"

"Me?" he bellowed, getting up to gape at her, eye level.

"For your information, cretin, all women are not alike! No more than all men are! But you want them to be, oh yes, you do! Well, tough! I'm not the soft, simpering, idiotic, dainty little fragile flower you're comfortable with!"

"I never said—"

She stuck her face in his, practically spitting her words at him. "I may not be the delicate type, but I do have talents! I ride as

well as any man! I rope as well as any man! I *think* as well as
any man! And because I do, I give up everything good about
being a woman! I'll be damned if I'll let you hang me with
everything *bad* you think a woman is!"

"What are you talking about?"

The very reasonableness of his tone shocked her into temporary silence. She stared at him, feeling her anger slip away. Pet-
ulantly she folded her arms beneath her breasts, confused when
his gaze dropped to her chest. "I don't like being lumped into
stupid categories."

He ignored that. "What do you mean you give up everything
good about being a woman?"

She rolled her eyes. "Are you so dense that you don't think
I know how you see me?"

"Apparently so."

She sneered at him. "I've been through this a hundred times!
I know exactly how you see me."

He brought his hands to his hips. "Do tell."

Anger dissolved into mortification. Tears suddenly burned the
backs of her eyes, but she'd be hanged before she'd let them
fall. She mimicked his pose, putting her own hands to her hips.
"It's always the same. The instant I stand up to some guy or,
God forbid, prove I'm as capable a cowboy as him, I become
this sexless, senseless *thing,* not quite one of the guys, but definitely not female enough to be noticed or acknowledged for
anything more than the accuracy of my drop. I catch the cows,
I can't be intelligent, too—and forget *attraction.* I might as well
be one of the heifers—except the bulls only see me for the loops
I drop, too."

Rye folded his arms, unfolded them, yanked on an earlobe,
raked his mustache, put his hands on his hips again. Finally he
said, "Now let me get this straight. You think you're unattractive
to men."

She fought the urge to roll her eyes again, giving him a smirk
instead. "I'm not an idiot."

He popped a knee out, shifting his weight. "Uh-huh. So how
do you explain the way everyone stares at your butt every time
you lift yourself out of the saddle to throw a rope?"

She blinked at him. "They do not!"

"They sure as hell do. Why wouldn't they? I do."

"You do not!"

He threw up his hands. "You know what your problem is? You're stupid! You're as stupid about men as you say I am about women!"

"I didn't say you were stupid!"

"Don't you remember what happened the night you fell in my lap?"

She did remember. In torturous detail. Her face, her body, burned with it suddenly.

"Don't you know what would have happened if your mother hadn't walked in?"

She gulped. "Th-that was an accident."

"So? I was still on the verge of kissing you." His voice lowered, softened. "The scary thing is, I'm not sure it would've stopped there."

Shaken, she literally quivered. He would have kissed her. He wouldn't have stopped with just a kiss. But that was then. That was *before*. She shook her head defensively. "I...I don't believe you. Now you wouldn't. Not now."

A muscle spasmed in the hollow of his jaw. He shifted his weight again, rolling back on his heels, legs spread. "Look at me."

"What?"

"Look at me, dammit!"

She wasn't really certain why, but her gaze dropped to the fly of his jeans. She couldn't miss the long, hard ridge pushing against it. Her gaze zipped right back up to his face. "Wh-why?" she asked incredulously.

"You folded your arms."

She stared at him. "I folded my arms?"

"Yes. You folded your arms," he told her, looking pointedly at her chest.

She looked too, gulping. She'd had these breasts forever, it seemed. No one had ever looked at them quite like that. Why did they seem higher, fuller suddenly? This made no sense whatsoever. She shook her head.

"Hell," he said, and then he knocked her hat off with a sweep of one arm and yanked her to him, his hands at her waist. She looked up just in time. His mouth fell on hers and his tongue rammed into her before her eyelids could even drop closed behind her sunglasses, which collided with his and dug into her face. The surprising, slightly prickly softness of his mustache played an exquisite contrast to the hard demand of his mouth. She'd wondered how that mustache would feel, and now she knew that the reality far surpassed any speculation.

The world sped up, spinning off its axis, throwing her off balance, hurling her against him in a full-body slam. She threw her arms around his neck, feeling her breasts move against his chest. He made a sound that echoed inside her, and his hands slid around her waist, then downward, cupping her bottom and pulling her tighter against him. She slid her tongue on top of his, reaching for the back of his mouth.

Something exploded. Suddenly his hands were all over her, rubbing, skimming, clutching. He slid his hand between her legs, pressing the heavy seam of her jeans against her. He splayed it over her belly, kneading, even as he cupped her from behind with the other. When he squeezed her breast, it was almost painful. And hot. Deliciously hot. She was burning up from the inside out. And she needed him to put out the fire, needed him desperately. Perhaps more desperately than she realized, because she pressed so hard against him that he stumbled backward, and suddenly they weren't embracing so much as trying not to topple over.

They rocked back and forth until they found their feet again. He had one hand clamped against the back of her head, the other splayed between her shoulder blades. Her own were gripping handfuls of his shirt at his waist. His mouth worked hers still, his tongue stroking, sweeping, challenging. She wanted more. Her hands twisted in his shirt, and she made a pleading sound, deep in the back of her throat. All at once he broke the kiss and shoved her away from him.

She was too stunned at first even to think. He ripped his sunshades off and pointed them at her, his chest heaving, his hat perched on the back of his head, one side of his shirttail hanging free. "Get away! Get—" He waggled the glasses at her. She stood rooted to her spot. He didn't mean her, surely. He straightened and grabbed at his hat as it slid from the back of his head, cramming it on again. He then folded his shades and made a stab at sliding them into his shirt pocket, missed and dropped them on the ground. They both went for them. He veered off just in time to prevent collision. Kara swept them up and held them out at arm's length. He snatched them away as if rescuing them from a fire.

"I will not," he began, voice cracking.

"What?"

He swallowed. "Never mind. Just..." He tried to wave her away, realized she wasn't going anywhere and retreated himself, striding swiftly toward his horse.

She simply didn't understand what was happening. "Where are you going?"

"Nowhere!" He plopped his hat on the saddle horn and reached for his canteen, unstoppered it and poured the contents over his head. It was as close as he could get out here to a cold shower.

"Oh." Kara clasped her hands behind her back. "I...I thought you were mounting up."

He shot her a murderous glare. "Not in these jeans!"

She blinked, then remembered what she had pressed against so recently and blushed. He raked his hair back, rammed his hat down over it and took a deep breath. "Well, I hope you're satisfied," he drawled sarcastically.

Her mouth jerked into a smile. "Hardly."

"That makes two of us!"

She slid her sunshades off her nose, feeling the indentations they left behind, and squinted at him. "So what are we going to do about it?"

"Nothing! Not a damned thing!"

Disappointment settled in. She tried not to let it show too badly. "Why not?"

He strode back up the slight incline, hands on his hips, and came to a stop slightly above her, forcing her to look up at him. "You will not cut your teeth on me," he vowed.

She didn't deny that she was inexperienced, just stared at him, wishing. Wanting.

"I can't let you," he added softly. "I bleed too easy. The last one nearly bled me to death."

She wasn't surprised. She'd known it. But there had to be a way they could be together. Feelings that hot and explosive just didn't go away. In some part of her, she was certain that they were merely looking for the accommodation. "Was she anything like me?"

He flinched, then shook his head. "No. But it doesn't matter. I'm still me."

"Maybe this time would be—"

"No."

Just like that. "You can't mean that you won't touch me again, that we can't—"

"That's exactly what I mean."

And he did. She could see it on his face, in his eyes. What had felt beautiful and breathtaking to her had seemed like a threat and a mistake to him. She bit her lip and dropped her gaze so he wouldn't see the tears threatening there. She had cried enough lately, more than enough. She tried to find something flippant and clever to say. In the end she just nodded. He stood there a moment longer, then he simply walked away. She slid her glasses back on, even though twilight had softened the glare, and sat down right where she was.

Well, wasn't that just her luck? He was the first man who actually wanted to, but he wouldn't. Still, he wanted to. That was something. Not much, but something. She sighed and looked out over the cattle, standing placidly in the holding pens, munching the hay scattered by the men. She was going to spend her life with a horse between her legs and some cow on the end of a rope. It was what she wanted, and yet it seemed oddly barren now. Nevertheless, it was the life to which she'd been born, and she'd embrace it with all the skill and enthusiasm she'd inherited. She was a Detmeyer. She had a proud legacy and work to do to maintain it. How many could say that? Few. Damned few. She wasn't about to trade it for anything so fleeting as desire, no matter how compelling. She had everything she needed for now, and when she needed more, she'd get it. Somehow.

Nodding decisively, she fixed her gaze on the horizon and her mind on tomorrow. The tears receded. The fires burned low inside her. Eventually the men came, along with her mother and the boy, in a caravan of trucks and trailers and horses. They would make camp on the flat tonight, and tomorrow they'd hit the trail, bright and early. She got up and dusted off the seat of her britches, then reached for her hat and the bag of trash resulting from their dinner. She had work to do, people to see, a camp to set up. Then she'd have a cold, skimpy shower, change and hit the hay. Tomorrow would bring a whole new set of problems, and she'd have them to solve. It was enough, more than enough in some ways. She just wouldn't think about any others. She just wouldn't.

He pitched his bedroll right next to hers, then settled down with his back to her, Champ at his side. The excitement was palpable. He'd spent a good hour with Champ, answering his questions, calming him for sleep. He didn't expect to sleep himself. Wasn't sure he even wanted to. He knew he'd dream about making love to Kara, and he didn't want that. He wanted to kick himself for letting this happen. Why hadn't he just let her think she was unattractive? Why had he had to prove her wrong? Lord, he was an idiot when it came to women. Well, it wouldn't happen again. She hadn't spoken to him or so much as glanced in his direction all evening, and that was fine with him. So why did he feel compelled to speak? He clamped his jaws together, and still it came out.

"Good night."

She paused as if uncertain he'd been speaking to her. Then she softly said, "Good night."

He closed his eyes. An instant later he opened them again and rolled onto his back, turning his head to look at her. "I think we're ready for tomorrow."

To his surprise, she shot him a fleeting, tremulous smile. "I think so. Guess we'll see."

He wanted to wrap his arms around her and hold her close, to whisper in her ear that he was sorry, that she was beautiful, that he wanted to be inside her but he just couldn't take a chance like that, not with a nice woman like her. When had he started thinking of her as nice? He muttered, "Guess so."

She finished smoothing out her sleeping bag and pads, then shifted into a sitting position and tugged off her boots, placing them side by side between her place and his. The nights before she had put them at the foot of **her** makeshift bed. Obviously she wanted space between them now, too. That was good. Sort of. He rolled back to his side, listening as she settled down and wondering why those boots sitting there bothered him so. She flipped the side of the sleeping bag up over her body. She never zipped it, but she'd be zipping it before they reached New Mexico. The nights were cool now. They'd turn downright cold before long. He tried desperately not to think that he could keep her warm. He hitched his own cover higher and reached over to do the same for Champ. The boy was sleeping deeply. Rye closed his eyes and thought about tomorrow, mentally checking off a long list of all that must be done before they moved those cows so much as an inch.

He opened his eyes to the half-light of dawn, and his first thought was how generously her breast had overflowed his hand. For a moment he was afraid that he had touched her again in his sleep, but a careful inventory told him he was safe. Except that he was throbbing hard, and he didn't want to remember the dream that had gotten him that way. He jackknifed up, stomped into his boots without checking them first, glanced at his sleeping son, rammed his hat onto his head and hiked up the hill. He went down the other side and around a boulder to relieve himself. It was a painful process, and he was flirting with frustration by the time he crested the hill again.

The camp was stirring. Dayna came out of the motor home, carrying a large thermos of coffee and a stack of tin cups. Shoes was pulling on his boots. Pogo was hosing water over his face, preparing to shave with the help of the sideview mirror on the water truck. Everyone seemed to be waking except Kara and Champ. Rye went down the hill and straight to Kara's recumbent form. Ignoring Shoes's mumbled greeting, he nudged her between the shoulder blades with the toe of his boot. She jerked and made a little snuffling sound, then rolled onto her back and lifted her arms above her head, stretching like a lazy cat. Her eyes opened, and she smiled up at him, her golden hair fanning out behind her and all rumpled around her face. He hadn't thought that she was particularly pretty the first time he'd seen her, but now something about that round face, the tip-tilted end of her nose, the hugeness of those blue eyes fringed with gold and the softness of her mouth compelled him.

She yawned behind a fist and reached up to ruffle her bangs, asking sleepily, "What time is it?"

"Time to be up," he said tartly.

He watched the memory of what had happened the evening

before come back to her, her smile fading, her blue gaze clouding
and skittering away. He realized unhappily that some part of him
was glad. He wanted her to suffer as much as he did, infantile
as that was, and it shamed him. She sat up and tossed back the
side of the sleeping bag, reaching for her boots. He strode off
toward the water truck to wash as Dayna set up a folding camp
table, announcing, ''Breakfast in ten minutes.''

He hung his hat on the sideview mirror as he scrubbed his
hands and face, brushed his teeth and scraped back his hair. He
didn't feel like shaving. This wasn't Sunday-go-to-meeting time,
and he didn't think the cows would be offended by the day's
growth on his face. He stood in line for his coffee and a plate
of sweet rolls put up by Angelina the day before. They were tall
and light, filled with plump raisins and cinnamon, dripping with
milky icing, and they tasted like ash in Rye's mouth. He choked
them down while going over the list clamped to the top of his
clipboard.

Half an hour later he was kicking sand, angry with the world.
Nothing was going as it should. All his careful plans seemed like
so much nonsense as problem after problem cropped up. He felt
like one of the Keystone Cops, running from one crisis to the
next. Dean turned his ankle first thing. While putting together an
ice pack, Pogo and an oddly flustered Dayna got into an argument. George, meanwhile, couldn't tear himself away from a
long conversation on the phone with his sweetheart, and Champ
disappeared, only to turn up with Oboe as a frantic Rye was
mounting up to go look for him. Rye shouted the boy into tears,
then regretted it and spent some time repairing the damage with
explanations about parental worries and mutual responsibilities,
reminding Champ of the conversation they had days earlier.
Somehow Shoes, Bord and Kara remained calm enough to do
what had to be done, and almost before Rye knew what was
happening, he was swinging into the saddle and giving the order
to open the holding pens and drive out the cattle.

The motley beasts immediately bolted in five different directions with cowboys who ought to know better by now riding
hell-bent for leather after them. Rye sank back into his saddle in
disbelief. Kara stood her horse beside his, staring openmouthed
at the chaos playing out around them. Rye groaned and bowed
his head, wishing devoutly that he could go back and do it all

again, beginning with that kiss the day before. The only problem was that he honestly didn't know what he'd do differently: walk away before he could get his hands on her or strip her and finish what they'd started. He very much feared that it would be the latter.

Kara sighed dramatically and plopped down into her saddle, shaking her head. Then she began to laugh, a chuckle first, then a sputter, followed by a building titter that had him smiling before it erupted into full-fledged belly laughs that sent the horses sidestepping. He looked at her for a long moment, amazed by this woman unlike any other. Then he looked around him with a fresh perspective.

Dean had mounted up with one bare foot sticking straight out, his empty stirrup flopping against the belly of his horse as he chased a running cow. Dayna was throwing tin cups at two confused head that had run into camp and were frantically careening around looking for a way out, turning over everything in sight and trampling it for good measure. Pogo charged to her rescue and got beaned for his efforts. George, riding high, circled a loop around his head with no apparent idea in which direction to throw it, while Bord chased on foot after a horse that had broken free in the confusion and Champ jumped up and down, clapping his hands in glee, Oboe at his side barking at everything and everyone. Only Shoes, assuming his guise of mysterious Indian, rode calmly through the chaos toward them.

He drew up, pushed back the brim of his black hat, leaned a forearm on his saddle horn, his eyes shaded by mirrored glasses and waited for them to calm, thumbing tears of hysterical laughter from their eyes. "What you want to do now?"

Rye took off his own shades, wiped his face dry on his sleeve and looked at Kara. "Well?"

Kara rubbed her fingertips over her eyes beneath her glasses, sucked air and said with a shrug, "Round 'em up."

Rye picked up his reins, saying to Shoes, "You heard her." He touched his mount's flanks with his spurs and cantered off after the main body of the escaping herd, Shoes and Kara falling in behind him.

It was noon before they had the tagged cattle rounded up again and the culls they'd gathered in along the way cut out once more, but at least by then they were working like a real unit instead of half a dozen lunatics on horseback for the first time. They had lunch on horseback, Dayna mounting up to deliver sandwiches, fruit and soft drinks, then collect the refuse. Impatiently Rye positioned his people and had them hold the herd. The cattle milled restlessly, looking for a leader. Rye pointed out the rangy old cow he and Kara had used for leading on that day they had come to think of as the day of the slaughter, and Kara dropped a loop on her, dragging her in the general direction they needed to go. One by one, others fell in behind. For the second time that day, Rye stood in his stirrups, shouting, "Let's move 'em!"

Shaking out his loop, he used the end of the rope to flick the rump of a big, bawling calf. It bolted after its mother. Soon the herd as a whole surged after Kara's leader, the hands riding flank to keep them bunched. Rye rode fast to catch up with her. "Keep 'em at a walk. I'll see the camp moved out and catch up with you."

"No problem."

He trotted back to camp. "I need everybody mounted this morning," he said to Dayna and Bord. "Let's leapfrog the vehicles for now. Wait for us at the first crossing."

"That would be the Detmeyer-Canders fence line," Dayna commented for clarity's sake.

"That's right," Rye acknowledged, climbing down from the saddle and beginning to loosen his girth.

"But that's only about eight or nine miles," Bord pointed out.

"Seven," Rye said unhappily, "but I'm betting it'll take us the rest of the day to get 'em that far. They're as new to this stuff as we are, you know. If we have daylight left when we get there, I'll cut loose Shoes and Dean to help you drive."

"Don't worry about us," Dayna said. "We'll manage."

"I'm counting on that," he admitted. "Bord, bring me a fresh mount. This soldier's done a day's work already, and I have rough riding to do today." Bord went off to do as told. Dayna picked up a lead rope and slid it into place, quickly stripping the horse of bit and bridle. "You don't have to do that," Rye said, lifting off the saddle.

"I don't mind," she said. "I've done this more times than I can count."

Bord led a big bay gelding up to Rye and tossed a fresh blanket onto its back, then went to work with a grooming brush on the other horse while Rye set the saddle. A few moments later, Rye swung up into the saddle once more. "See you at the crossing."

"Take care!" Dayna called after him.

He doffed his hat and spurred the horse into a run. The herd had already left the flat, swarming down the hillside and spilling out into the valley. The crew was trying to bunch them again, sometimes working at odds to one another. Rye rode into the middle of it, shouting orders from the drag position and bringing in stragglers. Eventually, they got them all headed in the right direction again, but the herd was strung out over a mile or more. Rye rode back and forth at a gallop, giving orders and flailing with his rope in a futile effort to bunch them.

Finally he raced to the front and had Kara turn and hold the herd in place, which involved circling them so they wouldn't get restless and take off on their own again. Meanwhile, he raced back to the drag to bring up the others. By the time they had them sufficiently bunched, Kara had circled back and caught up with him. Essentially, they had backtracked. Rye tamped down his impatience and had her lead them out again. It would do no good to rant and rave.

At least Dayna had camp set up, so the weary, frustrated drovers were greeted with the welcome sight of creature comforts. It was amazing how welcome little things like folding lawn chairs, a campfire and a huge jug of iced tea could be. But before they could dismount and relax, they had to put the herd to bed. That meant guiding the cows through a watering hole before driving them into a grassy corner where the barbwire fencing intersected so they could graze, while pickets were driven and a single strand, marked with strips of fabric, was stretched across them, effectively creating a triangular pen. The heady aroma of beef stew was wafting on the twilight air by the time they were finished, and Pogo volunteered to ride guard while the others ate dinner.

Rye climbed down from the saddle with as many groans and hisses as the rest of them. He couldn't ever remember being so tired. Or hungry. Or frustrated. Or satisfied. They'd done it. They'd moved a herd of three hundred and thirty-one wild-eyed cows from holding pens on the eastern flat of the Detmeyer ranch to a makeshift camp on the edge of the property near the Green River State Park.

Tomorrow they would cross onto the Canders Ranch, and if they'd learned anything useful, the next day would find them crossing the Hoffman property. And after that, the Nacker place, followed by the Ender, and the Monticello and on and on until they reached his family's place outside Durango, Colorado.

Beyond that, he wasn't ready to think.

Hell, he was too tired to think, but somehow after dinner he had to pick a new campsite for tomorrow and call Canders to let him know they'd be crossing and take a second look at the watch list and handle three dozen other details before he could shower, say hello to his son and unroll his sleeping bag. He wondered if he'd last that long.

It turned out that he didn't have to.

When he emerged from a less-than-satisfactory cold shower, performed beneath the shelter of a tarp thrown over the top of the truck, he found Kara waiting for him, a map clipped to the top of her clipboard. Other than tossing him his shirt, she seemed oblivious to the fact that he wore little more than a pair of jeans. While he shrugged into the shirt and they walked back to the center of camp, she talked.

"Mom and Pogo are taking first watch, then Bord and George. I don't think Dean can manage it. His ankle's big as a barrel right now. He's got an ice pack on it and says it doesn't hurt, but I don't want to take any chances, so I'm going out with Shoes later. We all agree that you did the work of three men today, and you'll probably have to do it again tomorrow, so you sleep this night. No argument. Now, about tomorrow's campsite. Take a look at this."

She pushed the clipboard under his nose. "The original site has better water and real holding pens, but even if we make the kind of mileage we hope to, it's a day and half away. Fact is, we aren't going to get there tomorrow evening. This one has a meadow that butts a cliff on one side and is undercut on another with a cavern, creating a natural barrier not even cows are stupid enough to go over. I've seen it, so I can tell you that we'll have to string pickets in two places, but together they probably won't involve much more than we did tonight. What do you think?"

"What's the mileage?"

She wrinkled her nose. "About eight miles, not much more than we did today."

He tugged his earlobe thoughtfully. "Okay, so we take it easy tomorrow, give everyone a chance to settle in, and day after we push it hard."

"We can make it within spitting distance of Moab day after tomorrow, I know we can."

"My thought, too. Okay, we've got that nailed. Now I've got to call Walt Canders and let him know—"

"I've talked to him already," she cut in, drawing to a halt. "He says anything we want to do is fine with him. I promised we'd call when we hit camp tomorrow evening. He wants to come out and take a look around at the operation, so I invited him to dinner."

Rye put his hands to his hips and looked at her. The woman was a marvel. "Okay. Anything else I ought to know?"

She rattled off nearly everything on his list and a couple items he hadn't thought of, winding up with, "And I think Dean should drive tomorrow. That ankle may not hurt, but it looks like hell, and I don't think he ought to be riding. God willing, it'll be a short day, so we can make it without him, I'm sure of it."

"All right. I'll talk to him."

"Thanks. I thought it might sound better coming from you."

"I'm the one who ought to be thanking you," he said. "You seem to have thought of everything."

"Well, you were looking a little used up," she told him, "and I figured I might have had something to do with it. That may sound egotistical—"

"It's not."

"But I figure if I was shaken up by what happened yesterday you probably were, too."

He felt a thrill of satisfaction that was immediately purged by sheer terror. "Damn, Kara, don't you hold anything back?"

She ducked her head. "Guess not. Just isn't my way. Sorry if that makes you uncomfortable, but—"

"I didn't say that," he interrupted, softening his voice. He was keenly aware of everything that was going on around them, the many eyes and ears that could tune in at any moment to the small drama unfolding right in their midst, and he still had to jam his hands into his pockets to keep from reaching out for her.

"I admire your honesty," he went on in a near whisper. "So I'm going to return the compliment and be honest with you. What happened has had me on edge ever since. For both our sakes, I wish it *hadn't* happened." She winced, and he hurried on. "But it did, and now we've got to put it behind us. Deal?"

She nodded without looking at him.

He swallowed and went on, wondering why this was so hard when it was so obviously the best thing for everyone. "I appreciate your understanding and everything you've done today. We couldn't have done it without you. *I* couldn't have done it without you. I don't even want to try. So let's call it friends and be done with the other." He stuck out his hand. For a long moment it looked as though she wasn't going to take it, but she stuck the pencil behind her ear and laid her palm against his, still without meeting his gaze. He hoped she didn't. The warmth of her hand in his was about all he could take. He couldn't even make himself shake it. After a moment she yanked it back, flashed him a weak smile and muttered something about having to speak to her mother.

He watched her walk away, feeling empty and alone. So alone. Then his son's bright laughter reminded him that he didn't have to be, and he let it pull him toward the only human being in the world who loved him without reservation, the only one whom he trusted himself to love in like manner. That ought to be enough. When had it stopped being enough?

Chapter Eight

The camp came awake with groans and even a few outright yowls of pain. Pogo and Rye fared better than the others, but only slightly. No one in this day and age spent full days in the saddle, not doing the kind of work they were doing yesterday. Muscles complained vociferously, and their owners gave them voice. Amid the grumbles, Kara got up, hissing and groaning like the others, but then she lifted her arms high over her head, filled her lungs with air and slowly bent forward until she could touch her toes. Carefully, she "walked" her hands forward, alternately flexing her knees to stretch the long muscles in her legs. The relief was immediate.

It was Champ who giggled and asked, "What's she doing?"

"What I want to know is *how* she's doing it?" Pogo groaned.

Kara turned her head first one way and then the other. "I'm stretching. And I'm doing it very *slowly*."

"You're a better man than me," George quipped.

The crack didn't sting as badly as it might have. After all, if a man like Rye was aware of her as a woman, she couldn't be too manly. Nevertheless, the joke irritated. She went to one knee, then up to her feet. She put her hand to her waist and gave

George a cool look. "Oh, I don't think so. You can manage. So let's see you do it."

He chuckled. "No way."

She caught him with a level look. "It wasn't a request."

He stared at her, anger and desperation growing on his face. The anger took precedent. "I'm not—"

"Yes, you are," Rye said offhandedly. "We all are." Kara turned to find him standing in the middle of his bedroll. For an instant she considered telling him to mind his own business. She didn't need his help to enforce her authority. But then she took a look at the incredulous, clearly resentful expression on Champ's face as he stared at his father, and she decided that she'd made enough of a scene for one morning. "Show us again," Rye said blandly, swinging his arms to work out the kinks there.

Nodding, Kara took up her position. "Dean, you stay put. I don't want you putting any weight on that ankle. We'll work out your stiffness another way. The rest of you, listen up." She demonstrated as she spoke. "Arms high. Lift that rib cage. Deep breath. Take it very, very slow. Forward at the waist, back straight. Bend your knees slightly. And walk out your hands—not too far. Now, right knee first. And the left. Keep going."

To her satisfaction, the groans and grumbles dwindled as the stiffness worked away. She talked them back up and gave a few instructions for stretching the muscles without getting down on the ground and rolling around. Cowboys hated that, she knew. By the time Dayna warned that breakfast was about to be served, everyone was moving much more easily. Spirits even seemed to have lifted somewhat, for all except one of them. Kara listened unapologetically when she overheard Champ complaining to his father as they washed up on the opposite side of the truck from her.

"What'd you do that for?"

"Do what?"

"All that dumb girl stuff? No one else would have if you didn't make 'em."

"It wasn't dumb, Champ. We were all stiff and sore from the hard work we did yesterday, and Kara showed us how to make it better."

"You didn't do that stuff before," Champ accused.

"Well, maybe I should have. A lot of the rodeo cowboys do it, bull and bronc riders, mostly."

"But she's acting like the boss! How come you let her act like a boss?"

"I don't *let* her, son. She *is* the boss. All these cattle belong to *her*. We work for *her*."

"Well, let's work for somebody else! I don't like her!"

"I can't do that, Champ. I gave my word to Mr. Detmeyer before he died. I promised I'd help her get her cattle to New Mexico, and that's what I'm going to do. You don't want me to go back on my word, do you? What kind of man does that?"

"A man don't," Champ grumbled, "but women do! It ain't fair! We can't go back on our word, but she does hers!"

"You don't know that."

"But you said—"

"Champ, I think you may have taken some of the things I've said in the past a little too seriously. All women aren't liars and cheats, son. Some of them are pretty much like us. I was hurt and angry when I said those things about your mother, and I regret doing it. It's right to be careful, but it's wrong to judge every woman by one woman. Besides, this is business with Kara. It's different."

"You like her!" Champ accused.

"You're taking this too seriously."

"You like her!" Champ bawled, hurt and fear sharpening his voice. "You like her, and I hate her! I hate her!"

The boy shoved past his father and ran away. Kara had edged around the front of the truck, eavesdropping unabashedly, and she stepped straight into Rye's path as he made to go after the boy. "Let him go," she said gently.

Rye's face went white, then burned red. She couldn't tell if he was embarrassed or angry. "I can handle my own son, thank you very much," he rumbled.

"I just— He sounds confused," she said. Rye wouldn't look at her anymore. He made himself busy repacking toiletries in his kit. Kara swallowed, knowing she was making a mistake but unable to stop herself. "What did she do that made you hate her so much?" She didn't add, "so much that you turned her son against her." She didn't have to.

He drew up tight, hands balled into fists, shoulders hunched, jaws working. Finally he said, "It's none of your business," but he said it without rancor or heat, so that she knew he was feeling shame.

"I'm sorry. I didn't mean to pry open old wounds."

"Don't worry about it," he said, zipping the kit closed. "I'll speak to Champ. He won't be disrespectful, I won't allow it."

"That doesn't matter."

"It matters. I won't have my son behaving like some spoiled, hateful brat. Now if you'll excuse me..." He brushed past her, and she let him go, deeply saddened.

She'd known he'd been hurt; she just hadn't realized how deeply, how mortally. The poison from those old wounds had spilled over onto his son—and onto her. And probably onto any woman who got too close. No wonder he kept her at arm's length. She ought to be grateful that he did, given his—and his son's—obvious bias. God knew she had enough on her plate already. She didn't need more problems. And yet... She shook her head. No, she wouldn't think about the ifs. She didn't dare.

It went better than they had any reason to expect it would. Taking down and then restringing the wire as they left one property for another required more time than anyone wanted it to, but Shoes suggested that it really ought to be his and Bord's job from then on. Bord objected, briefly, but the logic of the plan so completely outweighed any argument he could think of that he had no choice really but to shut up and accept this new duty gracefully. Henceforth, he and Shoes would take down the wire when they had to. The drovers would take the herd through and keep them moving, and Shoes and Bord would get out the come-alongs and other tools, restringing before falling in with the caravan for the noon rendezvous.

Rye tried to keep a steadier pace that day, without so much back and forth, as much to keep from running his horse to death as for any other reason. As a result they spent some time going after breakaways. The herd was still green to the trail, but they were settling in about as well as the drovers. By lunchtime they'd come well over halfway toward that day's goal, so he gulped down beans and fried potatoes while looking over his charts and trying to decide whether to bypass the site chosen only the night before in favor of a third or call it a day early and rest up for a hard drive tomorrow. It wasn't a decision he could make alone. Much as he dreaded it, he had to talk to Kara.

He rode out with the clipboard balanced on his hip. "Got a minute?"

She neither answered nor looked at him, just reached for the clipboard. Obviously, she had been thinking along the same lines as he had. "I've had the luxury of riding over nearly every bit of the Canders Ranch. Walt and Granddad used to trade services during branding. Then Walt decided to retire."

"Your grandfather commented about it a few times," Rye confirmed. "He couldn't see retiring himself."

She smiled down at the clipboard. "Bet I know what he said." She deepened her voice and approximated her grandfather's slow drawl. "Walt's pro'bly the smarter man, but I wouldn't do no good settin' on my hands anyhow."

Rye laughed, marveling that she could make him do so even now. "Close enough."

She handed back the clipboard, saying, "If there's another campsite within distance that meets our needs, I don't know about it. We'll be better off pulling in early. The rest will do us good. We'll be making a hard drive tomorrow."

He nodded. "Okay. Dean's got something he wants to show us on the computer, anyway."

"Don't forget that Walt Canders is coming for dinner."

Rye quipped, "I'll have your mother pull out the good china."

"I was thinking more along the line of a guitar and a harmonica," she said. "He sounded intrigued on the phone. I figured we'd give him the old campfire treatment. He's been awfully generous with us, after all."

"Sounds good. I'll see to it."

She nodded and turned her horse, walking it after a cow that was ambling toward a fresh patch of grass. Rye folded the clipboard against his side, watching her move away from him with genuine regret. Why couldn't they just talk like friends? They enjoyed each other's company, now that they weren't trying to take each other's heads off with every other word. Fact was, they often thought alike, just now being no exception. If only he hadn't given in to the sexual attraction, they wouldn't be avoiding each other. But maybe it was for the best, after all, considering Chase's animosity. He'd spoken to the boy briefly that morning, but he knew that he had another long, detailed talk coming. How did he explain to an eight-year-old what he didn't completely understand anymore himself? Maybe he'd better have a talk with Shoes before he said anything else to Champ. Shoes seemed to understand some element of his son's personality that Rye himself didn't.

He did just that at first opportunity. Shoes wasn't quite as supportive as he'd hoped, though.

"What'd you expect?" his friend asked drily, sorting through a drawer in the side of his van. "You vilified Di'wana for two years. You think two of silence will undo that?"

Rye ignored the question in favor of justification. "Hell, Shoes, she cheated on me. She went with anybody who'd buy her a good time."

"You took her off the reservation, Rye, introduced her to a life she'd never known before and left her alone so you could rodeo."

"I was trying to earn a living!"

"She was just trying to live."

"She didn't have to sleep around!"

Shoes lifted an eyebrow at that. "Like you didn't before you met her?"

"*Before!*"

"Granted. But she was unsophisticated, Rye. She didn't know what she was getting into at first. Later she figured it didn't matter. Soon as you got wind of it, you were going to throw her out, and she knew it, so why try to change?"

Rye stared at his friend in confusion. "Why didn't you say any of this before?"

"Would you have listened before?"

Rye didn't know how to answer that. Frankly, he was surprised he was listening now. Not too long ago he'd have walked away in righteous indignation the moment her name was mentioned. Rye pushed away his own confusion, opting instead to focus on his boy. "How do I explain this to my son?" he asked.

Shoes closed the drawer without picking out a tool and turned to face Rye. "Maybe you don't," he said. "He may not be ready to listen."

"I ought to try, though, don't you think?"

Shoes nodded. "Oh, yes. Especially as he'll be seeing his mother before too long."

Rye went very still, waiting for the old pain to sear through him. It wasn't quite as bad as he expected, somehow. "Then you're pretty sure your uncle won't let us take the herd across the reservation unless I agree to let Di'wana see Champ?"

"Aren't you?"

Rye reached for an answer and yet shied away from it.

"Weren't you pretty sure that's how it would be when you wrote the letter?" Shoes pressed. Rye didn't answer. He didn't know how. One part of him suspected that he'd always known it would come to that, another rebelled vehemently. Shoes took pity on him. "I'll talk to the boy with you. Just don't be surprised if he doesn't hear us."

They could have saved their breath. Champ had absorbed much more of his father's anger and pain than Rye had realized. The idea of seeing the mother whom he could barely even remember infuriated him. He obviously felt threatened somehow, even though Rye and Shoes both took pains to assure him that he wouldn't be leaving his father. They would still live together, work together. Rye wasn't sure where, but they'd always found a place for themselves. They would again. Meanwhile, Granny and Papa and Uncle Jess would be happy to have them around for a time.

"But I still don't want to see *her*."

"Your mother's name is Di'wana," Shoes told him with just enough censure in his voice to make the boy bow his head, "and whatever else she is, she is still your mother. You need to see her."

Champ looked to his father. "How come, if I don't wanna?"

Rye swallowed. "Because a boy needs to know his mother."

"I know she needs to see you," Shoes told him. "She's missed you, Champ, very much."

"I don't care!"

Rye took a deep breath. "Your grandfather is an important man in the tribe, Champ. You should know him and the people. They are part of your heritage. It's a proud one, and it's time you understood something about it."

Champ turned a desperate face on his cousin. "You can teach me everything I should know!"

But Shoes shook his head. "No, Champ. I cannot. Your tie to our people is through your mother. You will have to deal with that as best you can."

Champ knuckled away angry tears, but when Rye reached out to him, he wrenched himself from his father's touch and stalked away. Rye sighed, knowing it would do no good to go after him now. Shoes clapped him on the shoulder pityingly and wandered away himself. Rye closed his eyes, regrets too numerous to count aching in his chest.

It was good to see Walt Canders again. He had aged, growing so thin that he seemed to have shrunk in on his bones, but he had the same hearty laugh and easy manner. He came early and surprised Kara by showing even Dean a few things available to them on the computer that they wouldn't have known of otherwise. Dean had set up an Internet link, and they pulled down all kinds of information about the route they had chosen and what the weather was holding in store for them. Her grandfather had done his homework well, but it was good to have their assumptions confirmed by their research. "A nineteenth-century business with twentieth-century technology," Walt pronounced it. "Best of both worlds, if you ask me."

Dayna made a special dinner in Walt's honor, remembering all his favorites: barbecue, beans, spinach wilted with hot bacon grease, biscuits spiked with cayenne and cheese. He praised her to the moon.

"A woman who looks like you and cooks that good ought to draw men like flies to honey."

"She draws them," Kara commented wryly. "She just doesn't let them hang around."

"Maybe she hasn't drawn the right one yet," Pogo muttered, and knowing looks went around the campfire.

"That's right," Dayna snapped smartly. "I haven't." And the knowing looks turned to teasing hoots.

Kara was surprised, then amused. The implication was that Pogo had an interest in her mother, but Dayna had let them all know that she wasn't interested. Still, Kara couldn't help giving Pogo a purely speculative lookover. Tall and lean with mossy green eyes, hair that had long since gone steel gray and was thinning at the crown, Pogo was of average looks, it seemed to Kara. His face was deeply tanned and lined with crow's-feet at the corners of his eyes. Yet he took pains with his appearance, shaving every morning when no one else did and parting his hair with painful precision, despite the fact that he was just going to plop a hat down on it. Dayna could do better, Kara decided, *had* done better, and she put the idea out of her mind when he volunteered to take first watch with Shoes so George could add his harmonica to the guitars that Dean and Rye pulled out.

The music proved to be a good idea. Walt loved it, and it kept Kara herself from dwelling on matters best left alone. No one noticed much when Kara left in search of a few moments privacy. Her agreement with Rye didn't seem necessary now that they were on the trail. She let herself into the mobile home without much thought about who she might find inside. It was pretty cramped, with just enough space to walk through, but no one would deny that it made all their lives much easier. She moved into the so-called living area, which was nothing more than a narrow path flanked by a built-in couch on one side and a dining booth on the other. The kitchen came next, consisting of about a yard of combined cabinet and sink opposite a tiny stove, refrigerator and a chest-type freezer. Zigging left into the almost claustrophobically narrow hall, she reached for the doorknob of the tiny bathroom, only to pause at the sound of a voice.

"She's a no-good cheat," he said, "and she left me."

Kara instinctively reached to push open the door to the single bedroom instead of the bath. Champ was on the floor, squeezed into the narrow space between the wall and the bed, Oboe at his side. He was walking two colorful superhero action figures between the patient dog's ears and up his tail to a showdown on his back.

He deepened his voice. "'She's still your mommy. You have to go see her.' No, no," he went on in his own voice. "I don't want to. She's bad! 'Prepare to fight then, boy, 'cause I say you're goin'.'" He crashed the two action figures together with many and varied sound effects. "Pow! Kushhh! Chop-chop! Ugh! Ka-pow! Aaahhh! Splat!"

Kara leaned against the doorjamb and folded her arms. "Who's winning?" Champ jumped like he'd been shot and hid the action figures behind his back. Oboe got up and came over for a pat. Kara obliged. "How you doing, boy? Having some fun with Champ, huh? Looks like fun. Sort of." She shot a look at the boy, who glared guiltily. "How come you aren't outside listening to your dad play?"

He shrugged. "Don't have to."

"Nobody said you did. I just wondered, that's all."

He shrugged again. Kara considered what she ought to say next. She didn't have much experience with youngsters—unless they had long tails, white faces, and brands on their rumps. Still, something told her this one had problems and somehow she was part of them. She licked her lips. "Listen, Champ, I'm sorry you don't like me, but you shouldn't blame your father because I'm around. He's just trying to make the best of a bad situation, you know."

Champ glared at her. "Then how come he's making me see my mom?"

Kara was lost. "What do you mean?"

"He says when we come to the reservation, I gotta go see her, even if I *don't want* to."

It clicked. "Your mother lives on the Chako reservation?"

He sent her a disgusted look. "She's a Chako Indian." Meaning, where else would she live?

"That means you're Chako, too," she pointed out.

"Half."

"That's enough to be counted part of the tribe."

"So?"

"So you don't live on the reservation. How was I supposed to know that she does?" He shrugged sullenly. Kara sighed. "Look, Champ, none of this is your father's fault. He was trying to help me because—"

"He doesn't have to help you!"

"He promised my grandfather that he would, and so he feels obligated, and frankly, Champ, I couldn't do it without him. But I didn't know when he said he could get permission for us to take the herd across the reservation that it was because of you and your mother."

The boy's chin wobbled, and his eyes filled with angry tears. "I don't wanna see her!" he said, swiping at the tears.

Her heart went out to him. "I'm sorry, Champ. I...I'll talk to your father. Maybe we can—"

"No!" he cried, lurching to his feet. "Just leave us alone! Leave us alone!" He squeezed past her roughly and pounded through the motor home, caroming off one obstacle after another until he reached the steps and ripped through the door. He'd left his superheroes behind on the floor, abandoned. As he had been abandoned? Kara bowed her head. How had this all gotten so complicated? She didn't understand enough about the situation to know how to fix it, and yet talking to Rye about it might well make matters worse. She didn't know what to do.

She still hadn't decided when Walt took his leave and everyone moved toward sleep, knowing they had a hard day coming. She decided that she wasn't sleeping next to Rye. Maybe it would make Champ feel better. She unrolled her sleeping bag between Shoes and George. Rye watched what she was doing, his hands on his hips, a question in his eyes, and she realized that he was going to force the issue if she didn't. He ought to be aware of what his son was feeling, anyway, for the boy's sake. Aware that many interested eyes were on them, she finished laying out her bed, then rose, dusted off her hands and walked straight to him.

"Can we talk?"

"I think we better."

"Um, let me get my briefcase." She headed toward his truck, hoping he would follow. He didn't disappoint her, but when she reached the truck, she simply turned and put her back to the fender. He didn't get within four feet of her.

"Okay, what's up? You forget the security precautions?"

She shook her head. "I don't think it matters much now, though. We left behind whoever killed the cattle."

"You don't know that. If somebody's trying to stop this drive—"

"You don't know that!" she retorted.

"And falling boulders?"

She shrugged. "Could've been an accident."

He gnashed his teeth at that, but he didn't argue. "I still think we ought to be careful."

"Fine. This isn't about that, though."

He brought his hands to his hips once more in an obviously impatient gesture. "Yeah?"

She took a deep breath. "I spoke with Champ this evening."

Rye grimaced. "Look, I'm sorry if he—"

She shook her head. "No. He, um, was playing with these two action figures, and one of them was supposed to be you, I think, and he was beating you up for making him go see his mother."

Rye sighed and pushed both hands over his face. "He's angry right now, but he'll get over it."

"It's because of me, isn't it? Because of the drive, I mean. They're insisting you let her see him before they'll let us cross the reservation."

He looked as though he wanted to scream. His hair had fallen forward from a natural center part and framed his upper face within two wide curves like parentheses. He swept a hand through it in frustration. "I let that be my excuse," he said roughly, "but the truth is Champ needs to see her. He needs to see that she's not the demon I painted her to be. He needs to find some common ground with her. I think I knew it a year ago or more."

"What happened, Rye?" She felt she had to know.

He trained his gaze on the ground and prepared to tell her. "I told you that Shoes came to work on my folks place outside of Durango."

"Yes."

"Well, he doesn't live completely off the reservation. Never has. He doesn't get back these days as much as he used to, but back then he went home just about every opportunity. I used to go with him. That's how I met Di'wana. She was too young, and you know how the Chako protect their children, but that didn't keep us from getting together. She was crazy to get married, wanted to live in the white world. I...I thought she was as in love as I was, so I let her talk me into eloping."

Kara gulped, unprepared for the pang that hit her. He hurried on, pushing the words out through his teeth.

"I had to make a living. I'd had some success on the rodeo circuit, so I went back to it and took her with me, but it didn't go easy. She...she didn't know how to act in my world. My friends were a pretty sophisticated lot, and she embarrassed me," he admitted, squeezing his eyes closed. "When we knew she was pregnant with Champ, I rented a little house outside Phoenix. I had lots of rodeo friends there, and it was convenient. I left her there, and I went on rodeoing. I came home as often as I could, but she was lonely. She wanted some excitement. She resented my having the freedom to come and go when she didn't. She started going out, meeting people, men mostly." He wadded his hands into fists and relaxed them. "I think she slept with everyone I knew before—" he cleared his throat "—before someone told me."

Kara crossed an arm over her stomach in a effort to still the roiling there. "Rye, I'm sorry."

He went on as if she hadn't spoken. "Champ was about four. I...I took her back to the reservation, and I left her there. Champ and I went home, and I tried to stay drunk for the better part of the next year." He shrugged wryly. "Guess I'm not an alcoholic, because it just eventually seemed to take more effort than I could put into it. But instead of trying to fix the mess I'd made of my life, I spent the next two years justifying it. I said some awful things to my son about his mother. Finally I realized I was just keeping the wound raw, and I stopped, but Champ's a kid. He understood the anger and the pain instinctively. He's having a harder time coming to terms with the idea of acceptance and..."

"Forgiveness?" she supplied gently.

His own ambivalence was demonstrated in agitation. Finally he said, "Shoes kept on trying to draw rein on me. The Chako, see, they have this notion that they're actually responsible for the people they love. In their eyes, I'm as much responsible as her, and maybe they're right. I know they're right." He put a hand to his head. "I've known it all along."

Kara looked away. This then was what made him want his distance, not just his pain but his own guilt. She didn't know how to help him with that, didn't know that she had any right to try, considering that the boy and his feelings had to take priority. She said carefully, "Maybe we can take the longer route like Plummer planned. If we make good time tomorrow, then surely we can keep on—"

"No," he said flatly. "And I'm not saying it just because I promised Plummer I'd get this herd through on time. There are some things I can't fix, some things I can't change, but there are some I can prevent. I won't let my son grow up hating all women because of my failures. We're crossing that reservation just like we planned. And he's going to see his mother, make his peace."

"What about you?" she asked softly. "Can you make your peace this way, Rye?"

He frowned and cupped a hand over his mustache, smoothing it. "I don't count in this. Champ's what matters."

She nodded, understanding those feelings. "He seems to like Mother well enough. She hasn't said anything about problems when we're out on the trail."

"He sees her as a grandmother type, like my own mother."

"So it's only me he has a problem with right now."

He flashed her a guilty, apologetic look. "I think he senses... He seems to think any woman I might be attracted to is a threat somehow."

There it was again, that *something* that was better than nothing. Even his son knew that Rye was attracted to her. That and a buck would get her a cup of coffee—most places. She wasn't certain, anymore, that she could take comfort in it. She was right to keep her distance. They both were.

"We'd better get to sleep," she said. "We've got a long day coming."

He nodded, and for one moment, his gaze held hers, rife with regret and what might have been and could never be. She couldn't bear to see it.

"Good night, Rye," she whispered, hurrying back to her lonely place in the shadows.

Chapter Nine

It was a long, torturous day, and at the end of it the drovers were exhausted. Thankfully they had the luxury of real holding pens for the night, courtesy of Bridger Hoffman, who was there along with two of his sons to meet them. Unsolicited, the Hoffman "boys," both of whom stood well over six feet, assumed night guard duties, while Bridger showed Rye how to fill the water troughs for the thirsty cattle, then the water tank on the truck. Like every other cowboy Rye had talked to, Bridger was thoroughly intrigued by the notion of a real trail drive.

"Tired as your bunch looks," he told Rye, "I'd still go with you if I could."

Rye had just about enough energy left to smile. "Watch it. I could be persuaded to trade places."

Bridger chuckled. "You wouldn't say that if you had to work with my boys every day. Between you and me, they're good hands, but they aren't much when it comes to thinking. The whole lot combined—and there are three more at home—couldn't think their way out of a piecrust with the oven getting hot."

Rye laughed. It hurt, but he couldn't help it. "I can just hear my daddy saying something like that."

"Well, there's hope, then," Bridger said, clapping Rye on the back. It nearly put him on his knees. "You better get you some hard sleep, son."

Rye nodded. "I intend to soon as I get something solid in this belly of mine."

"You'll be riding right by the house in the morning. Leave the boys off there."

"We'll give them breakfast first. Least we can do for all your generosity."

Bridger Hoffman shook his head. "Plummer Detmeyer was a good cowboy and a good friend. That's all the reason I need. He spoke highly of you and that girl of his. I have it in mind that he hoped you'd make a match."

Rye blanched. He hoped to God Plummer hadn't set up this whole thing just to get him and Kara together. That was one wish he couldn't fulfill for the old man. Not for anyone could he risk that kind of involvement again, least of all with Kara.

They quickly established a routine, pulling out soon after daybreak and staying with it until they reached the night's preselected campsite. Soon the cattle showed signs of adapting to the trail. The drovers hazed fewer wanderers and breakaways. The tough old cow they'd dubbed "Number One" had claimed uncontested leadership, no longer needing to be pulled along at the end of Kara's rope. Rye could direct their way with less difficulty, experienced now with reading Plummer's charts and using a compass. Dean was up to speed and turning out to be even more help than Rye had counted on. All in all, Kara felt they were in pretty good shape. But it was hard, gritty work, and exhaustion was a big problem. It became obvious early on that her mother was one of their greatest assets.

She took care of a myriad of details, was as good a navigator as Rye, and became adept at finding ways to get lunch to the men on the trail. Somehow she managed to keep their clothing and sleeping gear clean, finding and hitting a laundromat about every other day. Most important, camp was always ready when the drovers dragged in, dinner on the air. Her meals energized them and lifted their spirits. Only Pogo ever found fault with the woman, and it was pretty obvious why.

One night, the crew was treated to a heated argument about the merits of bug spray versus citronella candles for keeping mosquitoes and flies at bay, not that they had a problem with either. Dayna, however, liked to feel that she'd covered all the details. Pogo found the candles a safety hazard; Dayna objected to the harsher chemicals in the spray. When they'd shouted at each other enough to entertain everybody, they went off in opposite directions to grumble about each other's pigheadedness.

"Old Pog has a woman thing," Dean said, giving Kara a wink.

"Well, it won't do him any good with that woman," Kara replied confidently.

"Wouldn't be too sure of that," Shoes said. "Ask any of his ex-wives."

"Wives?" Kara echoed, accentuating the plural.

George chuckled. "Always goes after the best-looking ones, happily marries them, happily lets 'em walk off again later. They'd all come to his aid in a heartbeat if he called them. Darnedest thing I've ever seen. They all love him. They all leave him. He goes right on to the next one."

"Perhaps he just hasn't come across the right woman yet," Shoes said. "When he does, I doubt he'll let her get away."

"Well, it won't be Mom," Kara insisted, walking off into the pines toward the truck carrying her personal gear.

"I wouldn't be too sure of that," Rye said, startling her as he stepped out of the shadows.

Her heart raced lickety-split, and it irritated her. He always had this effect on her, even when he didn't come on her by surprise, but she tried hard to hide it. "That's because you didn't know my father," she said, lifting her chin.

"Never met the man," he admitted, "but your grandfather talked about him a lot."

"I'm sure he did. They weren't just father and son. They were two of a kind," she told him proudly.

Rye looked doubtful. "If you say so."

Kara was outraged. "That's a hell of an attitude! What, may I ask, do you have against my father?"

He shrugged. "Nothing, only..." He thumbed his earlobe.

"Frankly, Plum was pretty upset about the shape he left your family in. Didn't seem to me like something Plummer would do himself."

Now Kara was incensed. "What would you know about it?"

"Hey, you asked. I'm just telling it like I see it. Whatever else he was, he wasn't as careful as the old man. That's all I'm saying."

Kara bit back an angry retort, conceding only, "We were all shocked that he'd let his life insurance policy lapse, but I'm sure he had his reasons. He didn't know he was going to be accidentally shot by some hunter."

Rye cocked his head. "Some hunter? You ever talk to the guy who did it?"

She folded her arms. It was a sore point, but over time it seemed to have lost its urgency. Knowing who had done it wouldn't bring her father back, after all. "No. The woods were crawling with them, though. Probably whoever did it didn't even know it."

"Then how can you be so sure what happened?"

"What else could it be? The local authorities were satisfied it was a hunting accident. He didn't have any enemies. No one stood to gain anything by his death. Knowing who did it wouldn't make any difference."

"No?" Rye muttered. Then he seemed to have a thought. "How'd you find out there was no insurance?"

"Payne told us, of course."

"Payne." Rye shook his head disgustedly. "Did you check your father's bank records, his personal papers?"

"No reason to," she said testily. "Payne's always taken care of those things. That's Payne's area of expertise, finance."

"Did Payne even say when your father stopped making the premiums?"

"What difference does it make?"

Rye threw up his hands. "Hell, Kara, the man could be stealing you blind, for all you know!"

"That's absurd. Payne would never—"

"You don't know that!"

"It isn't any of your business, anyway!" she yelled, stomping her foot.

"Well, for once you're right," he snapped. "Forget that I ever said a word. You want to live blind? Fine. My job is to get you to New Mexico. Period."

"You do that, then, and leave my family to me!"

He held out his hands as if warding off a fate worse than death. "Believe me, I want nothing more to do with your family."

"That's a fine thing to say after everything we've done for you!"

"Nobody but Plummer ever did anything for me! Not that I have anything against your mother. It's the rest of the Detmeyers who make my skin crawl."

"Me included, no doubt!"

He opened his mouth, but then he shut it again, all the fight seeming to go out of him. When he spoke again, his voice had gone all soft and rough, velvet on corduroy. "I wish," he said, and not even anger could deafen her to the sound of desire. She blinked, and he was gone.

"It's like something out of a bad movie," she said, putting her hand to her forehead. "Who would do this?"

Rye looked at the slashed feed bags. This one couldn't be pretended away. Though not as horrific as the slaughter of the cattle, it was no less blatant. "The same person who doctored the water trough yesterday," he said flatly.

She sighed. "I guess you're right."

"You know I'm right. You didn't want to admit it yesterday, but now you have to."

"I bowed to your judgment, didn't I? I just couldn't believe it was intentional."

He pointed to the feed spilled all over the ground. "Is this intentional enough for you?"

She bit her lip and bowed her head. "Yes." Suddenly she was glaring at him, hands dug into her hips. "But that doesn't mean that it's somebody I know!" He didn't bother to point out that it didn't mean it wasn't.

"We're going back to the original plan," he said. "You go nowhere alone, and I mean without Shoes or me."

"You don't think someone on the drive could—"

"I don't think anything. But I'm not taking any chances. Suppose you can get that dog of yours to stay in camp at night? The

PLAY THE
Lucky Key Game
and ge[t]

HOW TO PLAY:

1. With a coin, carefully scratch off gold area at the right. Then check the claim chart to se[e] what we have for you — **FREE BOOKS** and a **FREE GIFT** — **ALL YOURS FREE!**

2. Send back this card and you'll receive brand-new Silhouette Special Edition® novels. These books have a cover price of $4.25 each, but they are yours to keep absolutely free.

3. There's no catch. You're under no obligation to buy anything. We charge nothing — ZERO — for your first shipment. And you don't have to make any minimum number of purchases — not even one!

4. The fact is thousands of readers enjoy receiving books by mail from the Silhouette Reader Service™ months before they're available in stores. They like the convenience of home delivery and they love our discount prices!

5. We hope that after receiving your free books you'll want to remain a subscriber. But the choice is yours — to continue or cancel, any time at all! So why not take us up on our invitation, with no risk of any kind. You'll be glad you did!

YOURS FREE!
A SURPRISE MYSTERY GIFT

We can't tell you what it is...but we're sure you'll like it! A
FREE GIFT—
just for playing the
LUCKY KEY game!

n have come to depend on his help guarding the cattle, but I
nk it's more important we have warning if someone's coming
t night."

"'ll see to it."

od. But there's one more thing. I want you close to me
e night. You hear me?"

She nodded. "But that goes both ways. You were riding on
e inside the day the boulder fell, if you remember." He said
othing to that. "I mean it, Rye."

"All right. Joined at the hip."

She relaxed. He didn't. "What else?"

He lifted his hat and swept back his hair. "I'm wondering if
should've brought Champ on this trip. I thought it would be
n experience for him, but I also thought we'd be leaving the
hreats behind."

"No one in the world could want to hurt him," she pointed
out. "Unless..."

"Unless they're striking out at me," he said. "But why?
That's what I can't figure. The only person I've hurt enough to
make them want to hurt me back is Di'wana, and she's out of
the question. No matter what I did, she'd never take it out on
our son."

"No," Kara said softly, "she'd sleep with your friends."

Pain spasmed across his face.

"I'm sorry," she whispered. "I shouldn't have said that." But
she'd wanted to hurt him, the way he was hurting her.

"It's this cattle drive," he insisted, ignoring everything else.
"Somebody wants to keep us from getting to New Mexico on
time."

"I know, I know, but that doesn't mean it's Payne."

"He still gets my vote," Rye said stubbornly.

She bowed her head. "What if I call Payne in Denver, prove
to you that he's there."

Rye tugged at his ear lobe. "Worth checking."

She'd taken to carrying the phone in a little hip pack buckled
around her waist. Unzipping it, she took out the phone, flipped
it open and punched in Payne's home phone number. A sleepy-
sounding Payne answered on the second ring.

"Hello?" He cleared his throat. "What time is it?"

Kara grinned, relief sweeping through her, and glanced at her wristwatch. "About six-fifteen. Good morning, sleepyhead." She lifted an eyebrow at Rye, who combed his mustache with his fingertips thoughtfully.

"Kara? What's wrong?"

She chuckled, hoping it didn't sound too forced, and lied through her teeth. "Not a thing. This is just the first moment I've had to get in touch."

"How's it going?" he asked. "Where are you?"

"Oh, we're just outside La Sal Junction. Right on schedule."

"Utah? You're still in Utah?"

"That's right, and will be for three or four more days."

"It's going well, then."

"Everything's fine. We're all tired, and I, for one, never want to sleep on the ground again after this, but we're managing." They chatted on for several minutes, until Rye caught her eye and impatiently tapped his wristwatch to indicate that it was growing late. He had salvaged as much of the grain as he could sweep up off the ground, having appropriated several trash bags from Dayna. Kara quickly rang off and stowed the phone. Folding her arms, she gave Rye a smug, challenging look. "Well?"

"Well what?"

She stomped her foot, a recently developed habit. "You just don't want to admit you're wrong about Payne!"

Rye leaned an elbow on the rail of the truck bed. "I'll admit that whoever put a knife in these bags had to be here to do it."

She took that for capitulation. "Then it couldn't have been Payne."

"True enough," Rye agreed. Turning, he strode off toward the remuda, pausing only to ask, "You coming? Or were you thinking of putting your feet up for the rest of the day?"

"I'm coming," she muttered, but she hesitated a moment to frown at the feed spilled on the ground. A shiver skittered up her spine. It wasn't Payne behind this; she'd stake her life on it. But if not Payne, then who?

It rained buckets for two days. Everyone lived in dusters and plastic hat bonnets, but water found its way inside them. The ground became a quagmire that no covering could withstand. Difficulties magnified. Horses came up lame. Cows went down sick or just plain exhausted. It was the worst at night. Even after the rain stopped on the third day, they were still sleeping in mud. Everyone, excluding Dayna and Champ, both of whom slept in the motor home, were teetering on the edge of exhaustion, and it told most forcefully in the snappish moods of the crew. Kara especially found herself on edge, so much so that Rye loosened the leash and suggested she ought to sleep in the motor home with Dayna and Champ. Even as the thought of a dry bed tantalized her, she vehemently rejected it.

"I'll throw my bedroll on the ground like everyone else, thank you very much. Just because I'm a woman, don't think I can't hack it out here with the rest of you!"

"Whoa!" Rye held up his hands in a gesture of surrender. "I wasn't implying you aren't tough as nails. Fact is, if someone offered me a bed inside tonight, I'd jump at it."

"Done!" Dayna said, stepping up to make herself a part of the conversation. "In point of fact, Pogo and I have discussed this recently."

"You have?" Kara and Rye asked in unison.

Dayna let that pass and went straight to the heart of the matter. "We feel that from here on out we ought to take turns sleeping in the motor home, just as we have driving the vehicles—well, all but the most boneheaded of us. That way everyone has a chance to get a good night's sleep once in a while."

Kara and Rye looked at each other. "What do you think?" he asked.

"Mom, are you sure you want to give up a nice, warm bed to sleep on the ground?"

"No, I don't want to! But I'm not selfish, and it's only fair." She grinned. "Besides, it may do me some good."

Kara could almost feel the soft, dry mattress at her back. "Rye?"

"I will if you will."

"*Please* say you will." This came from Dean, but George was nodding his head encouragingly. "That way, we can, too."

"Let's draw up a schedule," Kara said, capitulating easily.

"Uh, your mother and I already thought of that," Pogo said, stepping up next to Dayna and draping an arm across her shoulder casually. Kara had trouble keeping her mouth closed as Dayna whipped a folded sheet of paper from her jeans pocket.

"Now we figure Champ ought to stay inside, period."

Everyone agreed to that instantly.

"So," she went on, opening up the paper, "it depends on whether or not you guys can share a bed."

Dean looked at George and wrinkled his nose. "I don't know."

"Fully clothed, separate sleeping bags," George mused. "I think I can hack it." Dean nodded his agreement.

"Okay, then," Dayna announced. Reading off the paper she went on, "Rye and Champ get the big bed tonight. Kara's on the couch. Tomorrow it's Dean and George; Champ's on the couch. Next night, Shoes and Bord."

"Champ can sleep with me," Shoes volunteered. "Won't be the first time."

"Bord's on the couch then."

"That just leaves you and Pogo," Kara commented. The camp went instantly silent. Pogo lifted an eyebrow at Dayna, who calmly handed the paper to Rye, while smiling at her daughter.

"That's right, dear." Dayna lovingly patted Kara's cheek. Her eyes held a wealth of warning, a hint of apology and the underlying shine of implacable decisiveness that Kara had come to know so well as a child. She had decided that she liked Pogo, and she was sorry if Kara had a problem with it, but those were the facts. So that's why they were getting along so well all of a sudden! Good grief, they were just like her and Rye, striking sparks off each other until... Kara gulped. Pogo Smith would be sharing a bed with her mother—if he wasn't already.

Kara hoped her face retained more color than she feared it did at this moment. "W-well then, that's it." She hadn't sounded as light and offhanded as she'd meant to, but it was the best she could do, and her mother accepted it as such.

"Thank you, darling," she whispered, leaning forward to kiss Kara's cheek. Then she walked away, hand in hand, with a man who wasn't Kara's father.

Kara quickly got busy gathering her things for transfer to the motor home. The camp remained quiet, but gradually the others went back to whatever they had been doing before. Kara found plenty to do, repacking her clothes, checking charts and maps, counting and recounting the money left in the strongbox. Everyone else had turned in by the time she climbed up into the motor home and closed the door behind her. She'd tried not to notice that Dayna and Pogo were not with the others. No doubt they'd found some privacy, zipped their sleeping bags together and were at that moment...

Oddly, she couldn't form a picture of what they might be doing, and it hit her suddenly that she'd never formed that picture of her parents, either. She'd witnessed many gestures of affection between her parents, some of them pretty steamy, and she'd known they slept together, had sex—and yet she couldn't form the picture. Maybe because she'd never pictured *herself* making love, never wanted to—until lately. She glanced through the living and kitchen areas and down the narrow hall of the motor home to the bedroom door.

Rye was in there now with his son. She knew that if she just closed her eyes, she could see herself making love with Ryeland Wagner. She'd been trying not to see it for days and days now, but it had been creeping up on her all this time, and now she wondered how much longer she could hold it at bay. Suddenly that couch looked like a torture rack to her. But surely she was too tired to lie awake dwelling on matters best put out of mind.

She went to the bank of cushions built into the wall and began removing those along the back, stacking them in the seat of the dining booth. The resulting bed was wider than she'd expected, about the size of a twin bed. Her sleeping bag unrolled with space to spare. She unzipped it and sat down on the edge of the bunk. Reaching up she switched off all but one small light recessed into the wall at the head of the bed. She slipped off her boots and pulled out her shirttail, then lay down and flipped the side of the bag over her body. She folded her arms beneath her head, sighed, and closed her eyes.

He heard her come in, heard the muted clumps of her boots as she removed them. He lay in the dark, aware of his son's sleeping form beside him, the comfort of the mattress beneath him, the warmth that came merely from blocking out the wetness. A tiny night-light glowed red in the switch beside the door. His boots sat at the foot of the bed. He vowed that he would never again take the simple luxury of a bed for granted, even though he knew he would not sleep this night. The irony of the situation was not lost on him.

They had lain side by side several nights within arm's reach, and yet to him she had felt farther away then than she did now at the other end of this little house on wheels. He could feel her there in the dark, feel her distress, her unease, her awareness. It was odd how much difference a few walls made. Walls meant privacy. Privacy provided opportunities that sleeping around a campfire with five or six snoring cowboys did not. The privacy would keep him awake and, as he was being honest with himself, concern would, also. She'd been thrown by her mother's tacit announcement that she was sharing a bed with Pogo Smith. Everyone in camp had known it, of course. Everyone but Kara. And they had all wondered how she would take the news when it was finally spelled out to her.

He'd been proud of her, perverse as that was, for though the news had come as a shock, she hadn't vented any of the emotions she must have been feeling. Embarrassment. Disappointment. Disillusionment. Perhaps even betrayal. He'd wanted to take her in his arms and whisper that everything would be all right. He'd wanted to explain things that her mother should have explained, point out that nothing was chiseled in stone, reassure her that no one could ever take her beloved father's place. Those unsaid words had lodged in his throat, congealing into a doughy lump that wouldn't move. He wished he had Pogo's courage. A three-time loser, how did he manage it?

A whisper of sound brought Rye upright in bed. The skin on his arms tingled. The soles of his feet itched. He knew it was her, and the instant he heard the doorknob rattle, ever so softly, he knew she'd given up. Moving swiftly, he slid out of bed, picked up his boots, lifted his jacket from a hook on the wall and let himself out into the narrow hallway flanked by a small pantry and a dinky bath. He ran on the pads of his feet, jeans swishing as the seams rubbed. Dropping down onto the side of her bed, he pulled on his boots. Then he went to the door, opened it carefully and stepped down into the night. He caught a glimpse of her off to his left. Shrugging into his coat, he went after her.

The ground was spongy under the trees, but not too bad for walking. Still, it wasn't as easy as it should have been to find her. She seemed to have disappeared into thin, cool air. He shivered inside his coat, though in truth he felt plenty warm. It was having her out of sight, out of sense. She wasn't thinking reasonably or she wouldn't have gone off by herself. If someone was trying to get to her, this would be the moment. Urgency drove him on.

He found her a few minutes later, sitting on a rock in a small clearing, staring up at the sky. The white peaks of mountain limned the horizon. The going was rough enough, but thank God they didn't have to go over the tops of those. He kicked pinecones to make himself heard as he approached her. She didn't move so much as a muscle until he drew to a stop.

"You'd think we'd be dead to the world by now, tired as we are," she said without turning her head.

He picked up a tiny pinecone and rolled it around in his hand. "He's been dead over a year, Kara. A woman gets used to some things. She misses them. It's only natural to—"

"I know," she said on a sigh. "It's all right. I think, more than anything else, I'm jealous."

He dropped the pinecone and reached for her, pulling her off the rock and into his arms. He was shaking, frightened. He tried to make light of it. "Got a thing for Pogo Smith, do you? I'm sure if he knew—"

"No," she said against his shoulder, so solemn. "I have a thing for you." She slid her arms around his waist inside his coat and tilted back her head, gazing up at him. "I've never been with a man, Rye, never really wanted to be until now. That's funny, isn't it? I'm almost thirty years old. I've lived and worked with men all my life. I've never made love with one."

"God, Kara!" He pressed her face into the bend of his neck and folded her close. His heart was thumping like a rabbit sounding alarm, and his jeans were too tight again, so tight they hurt. He felt her tears, warm against his skin. "Don't cry, baby. Don't cry."

She turned her head, laying her cheek in the hollow above his collarbone. "It was so easy when Dad was alive," she whispered. "We worked together every day. Sometimes we had help, mostly we didn't. I never wanted to be anywhere else, never wanted to leave the ranch at all."

"What about school?"

"I didn't go. It was too far away. Mother taught me at home.

I got my high school diploma early, and we studied some college-level courses after that, but eventually I let it go to concentrate on the ranch."

"Weren't there ever any—" he had to swallow to get the word out past the lump in his throat "—boyfriends?"

"A few, but never for long. They'd come to help with round-up or just for the experience, and at first they were friendly, flirty. We'd laugh and spend time together. Sometimes we'd even walk out alone. A few even kissed me. But then we'd saddle up and get down to business, and before long I'd find myself barking orders at some greenhorn nonsense or just showing them up by doing what I've always done best. It's funny how ugly and unattractive you get when you best a man. I got sort of defensive about it."

He chuckled. "I noticed."

She smiled, but it was faint and it faded quickly. "I'd give ten years off my life," she said, "to be loved as a woman just once."

He closed his eyes, but the decision was already made. "I don't want ten years," he said, stepping back and grabbing her hand. "I just want tonight and you." He pulled her with him.

"Where are we going?"

"To hell," he said, "by way of heaven. Hurry!"

They ran, dodging around trees and rocks, sliding on pine needles over mud, and were back on the edge of camp within two minutes. He drew her to his side, lifting a finger to his mouth. She nodded, blue eyes gleaming like beacons, and he led her quickly to the door of the motor home, opened it, and pulled her up inside. He kissed her hard and shoved her toward the bunk. "Get undressed." He shot a look at the back of the hall, expecting to find just what he did. Silence, darkness. Privacy. He locked the door, then hurried through the kitchen to open the bathroom door and block the view if Champ should come out of the bedroom. Hurrying back, he dropped down onto the end of the booth and yanked off his boots. Looking up, he saw Kara watching him doubtfully. "Shuck 'em, Detmeyer, and be quick about it." He stood and peeled down to skin, then kissed her as he unbuttoned his jeans. He backed her against the edge of the bunk, his hands pulling free everything he could reach while he explored her mouth with his and her hands worked at the buttons at her wrists.

"Rye, are you sure?" she asked breathlessly, ripping her mouth from his.

For answer he lifted her flannel shirt and pulled it off over her head. Her T-shirt followed, and then he reached around her to release the catch of her bra. He was shaking so badly it took several tries, but eventually the blasted thing was swept away, and bare skin met bare, succulent skin. He sucked in his breath through his teeth and filled his hands with her. "I've never seen anything like you," he whispered between kisses. "Never felt anything like you. Never wanted anyone like this." He pushed her down on the side of the bunk and tugged her boots off one at a time. "Lie down."

She angled her long body across the bed. He lifted one foot and then the other, peeling off her socks to press his thumbs against her arches, watching as she gasped and her large, peachy nipples peaked invitingly. She got her jeans unbuttoned, and he stripped them off, leaving only her panties. Stepping back, he raked off his remaining clothing, while she lifted her hips and shoved down her sensible cotton undies, kicking them to the foot of the bed.

He opened her legs with his hands and came down between them, fitting his body to hers. Perfection. He throbbed against her. Absolute perfection. She was wet, ready. He closed his eyes and brought his forehead down to hers, working hard to get out what he had to say. "I don't have any condoms. I'll try to pull out, but I can't make any promises. I want you so much!" He opened his eyes and steeled himself for some sign that she'd changed her mind. She wound her arms around his neck and arched her back, moving against him urgently. He smiled and slid his hand down between them. "Hold on, sweetheart."

She dug her heels into the bed, lifting her pelvis. He slid inside her, shuddering as her sleek, wet tightness accepted him. She convulsed, taking him to the hilt, panting and clawing at his back. He was panting himself.

"Be still, honey, or it's all over!" he gasped, holding himself rigid.

She blew out her breath and lay her head back, eyes closed. Tears leaked out the corners.

"Aw, Kara. Don't, honey. It's not too late!"

She laughed, arching her back and sliding her luscious body against his in unmistakable demand. "It better be!"

"Hell!" He lifted above her, pulled back, and slammed into her with all the urgency and demand of his own desire. She wrapped her legs around him, rising up to meet every thrust, and in the end he had to cover her mouth with his hand, letting his own tears drip joyfully onto her breasts. By morning, heaven was still within reach.

Chapter Ten

Hell came in the form of a saddle and regret.

Actually, Kara had less trouble physically than Rye did. She hoped that the others did not notice how gingerly he sat in the saddle and how often he found it necessary to stand in his stirrups. Much more painful to her than the physical ramifications of sexual overindulgence was the way Rye began withdrawing into himself from the moment he left her bed near daylight. The attentive, inventive, amazingly generous lover reverted back to the slightly prickly, emotionally cautious and distant business partner of her experience. It was obvious to her that he regretted, at least to some extent, the breathtaking intimacies of the night before.

He hadn't fully met her gaze since checking on his sleeping son that morning before leaving the privacy of the motor home. Throughout the morning he spoke little and astutely avoided her touch. It was in some ways no more than she had expected. After all, he had offered her no promises beyond the moment. No mention of love or the future had been made. And yet she felt so profoundly changed by what they had shared that she could not believe he remained unaffected. Surely there should have been a fleeting, secretive look, a small, bemused smile, a sly, suggestive whisper, some acknowledgment of past wonders, *something*. Instead, she seemed to have ceased to exist for him.

She tried not to be hurt. She did try. But when Rye picked up his lunch, had a quick word with Bord, then rode right past her without so much as a lifted finger in greeting, her heart dropped to the pit of her stomach. It didn't help that Bord had bad news.

"We got four sick horses, Ms. Detmeyer, and something tells me it won't stop there. Never seen anything like it. Spreading like wildfire."

"Did you tell Rye?"

"Yes, ma'am. He said to run it by you."

"Where is the remuda?"

"Campsite. Want me to turn your horse in with the herd so you can ride ahead with me in the truck?"

Kara sighed. "Guess so." She dismounted, saying, "I'll just grab a sandwich while you get the saddle off."

"No problem."

She joined her mother at the other truck. "You get a look at those horses?"

Dayna nodded. "They're sick all right, but it's nothing I've ever seen. Dean was getting on the computer when we left, said he'd find the nearest vet."

Kara nodded. "Sounds like a good idea." She lifted her hat and wiped her forehead with her shirtsleeve. "Man, I hope it doesn't stall us. No rancher anywhere in the world would want us crossing his property with sick animals."

"What are you going to do?"

"I don't know. Rye will keep 'em headed to camp for now. Dean's got a cell phone. Maybe you'd better keep this one." She unzipped her fanny pack and extracted the small flip phone, handing it to her mother. "Tell Rye to wait until he hears from me before bringing them all the way in. If this is something that will affect the cattle, I don't want them anywhere near those horses."

Despite a look of surprise, Dayna nodded and slipped the phone into her shirt pocket, where it made a strange lump atop one breast. "You haven't already discussed this with Rye?"

"Rye has other things on his mind just now," Kara told her dismissively, taking a sandwich from the cold box and a prepackaged cup of soup from the other. For some reason, Kara felt compelled to kiss her mother's cheek before striding off toward the other truck, not knowing how much she'd given away.

"Poison!" Rye exclaimed. "You're telling me someone's poisoned our horse feed?"

Kara pressed her fingertips to her pounding temples. "Dr. Weitz didn't actually use that term, and he's not one hundred percent positive yet, but that's what he expects the tests to show."

"Dear God!" Rye shook his head, bringing his hands to his hips. "What treatment does he recommend?"

"Fluids, diuretics, emetics, depends on what was used. He doesn't think it's anything fatal, but we need to flush it out of the animals' systems."

"Damn!"

Kara felt close to tears, but she wasn't about to give in to them now, not in front of him, never again in front of him. Pity was not something she could take from him again. She was pretty sure, now that she'd had some time to think, that pity was behind the events of the previous evening. He'd felt sorry for her. Poor, inexperienced, unloved Kara. The least he could do was see to it that she didn't go to her grave a virgin without ever knowing what she was missing. If he'd been unusually caring and thorough, well, she supposed that was just Rye. Whatever he did, he gave it his all. As a work ethic, it was a commendable trait from which she willingly benefited. It would be boorish of her to be ungrateful now. Still, she couldn't help wishing that he'd been slightly less meticulous. She feared that Ryeland Wagner had taken her to heights that she would never again scale, no matter how many attempts she might be foolish enough to make. She tried to bend her mind around this latest catastrophe.

"Weitz says this could cost a thousand bucks before it's over," she said with a sigh, "but that's not the worst of it. Those horses are going to need time to recover, more than we can give them, I'm afraid."

Rye made an inarticulate sound. "That means abusing the few healthy mounts we've got left or staying put, which is exactly what the son of a bitch who did this wants!

Kara pinched the bridge of her nose. "I'm open to suggestions."

"Soon as I have one, I'll let you know."

Kara nodded as he turned and walked away. Her stomach roiled. Her head felt as though it might split in two. Fatigued and emotionally drained, she wanted nothing so much as she wanted a long, hot bath in a tub full of bubbles. Now if only one would magically appear. Yeah right. She'd be lucky if she could soak both feet at the same time. Not that it made any difference. Heartaches were damnably difficult to treat.

Rye fought the urge to slam a fist into the first thing he saw. Better to save it for the spineless scum who was doing this to Kara. Then, in all fairness, he'd have to stand back and let the wretch take a swing at him; God knew he'd already done more to hurt her than anyone else. He'd known he was going to the moment he'd found her sitting on that rock last night, but he couldn't have stopped if his life had depended on it. The only thing he could say in his favor was that he'd known he would be hurting himself as much as her. He just hadn't understood the nature of the pain. The term *regret* took on a whole new meaning when the regretted action tended to color the rest of your life. Looks like he'd have learned that, but nothing could have prepared him for how it felt to make love to Kara.

He kept wondering if it had really been so much better than anything else he'd ever known, or if it had just been so long that he'd forgotten. Unfortunately, he remembered only too well his disappointment with Di'wana. His only other experience had been with the "buckle bunnies," the trophy hunters among the groupies who flocked around rodeo athletes much like those who followed rock musicians. He'd known women who loudly bragged about all the champion cowboys with whom they'd slept, women who publicly discussed the superior techniques of the bronc and bull riders, saddle versus bareback, ropers as opposed to steer wrestlers. The open indulgence in such raucous sex had been heady indeed—for a while. But even in the midst of it, he'd realized that something was missing. He'd expected to find that intangible something with the woman he loved, with Di'wana. Yet, it had been many months before their sex life had developed into something approaching satisfying, and it had never, ever been anything approaching what he'd experienced last night.

Kara had blown away every concept he'd ever had about *satisfaction* in one evening. And he didn't know what to do about it. He didn't have a clue. One part of him was convinced that trying to repeat the phenomenon would be like trying to hit the lottery twice in a row. Another part wanted nothing more than to drag her into the woods, rip her clothes off and go at it like two animals in heat. But the consequences of that were utterly terrifying. If Kara were pregnant, he'd have to marry her. He couldn't do anything else. And just the idea of falling into that trap again made him sick to his stomach. He was a failure at marriage. He'd suspected it even at the time. He'd known that he wasn't making Di'wana happy, but he hadn't seemed able to do anything about it. That hadn't changed. He knew, deep down, that *he* hadn't changed. He didn't even know how to go about it.

He and Kara would both be much better off if he just stayed away from her, but that was harder to do than he'd expected, especially when she stood there patiently enduring such obvious pain and worry. He'd had to walk away to keep from taking her in his arms, but if he was going to maintain the distance he'd so carefully constructed during the day, he'd have to find some way to help her. He sat on the bumper of his truck and tried to think what to do. That's where Champ found him.

"Hi, Daddy."

"Hey, sport, what's up?"

Champ shrugged. "Dunno. The horses got sick, though."

Rye nodded. "Come here and sit with me. Tell me about your day."

Champ climbed up onto the bumper and parked himself. "I made cookies with Miss Dayna."

"Oh, yeah? Think I might get some?"

"Ever'body gets some," Champ said, as if anything else would be unthinkable.

"Great. What else did you do?"

"I played a game with Dean on the computer."

"You're getting to be a real computer whiz, aren't you?"

Champ nodded emphatically. "And I helped Bord clean the curry brushes."

"Yuck," Rye said dramatically. "I always hated doing that myself."

"It's easy!" Champ exclaimed. "You just rub 'em and rub 'em together in a bucket of soapy water, and then you rinse 'em, and you shake 'em out real good." He demonstrated how he'd shaken and shaken the brushes. "Then you just let 'em dry."

"Well, you must be a lot better curry-brush cleaner than I am."

Champ nodded matter-of-factly. "Yeah, prob'ly."

Rye laughed and ruffled the boy's thick black hair. He'd been a lousy husband, but he loved being a father. "Listen, pard, I'm sorry I haven't had much time to spend with you lately. I miss hanging out with you."

Champ screwed up his face. "Well, you know, Dad, it won't last forever, this trail drive thing. Bord says that afore long we two will be at Grandpa's and Uncle Jesse's, and we'll have all kinds of stories to tell 'em about this—" he squinted, trying to remember the exact words, finally coming up with "—historial ebent."

Rye clamped down on another laugh. "Historical event, I think is probably what he said."

Champ nodded. "Yeah. That's it. That's what Bord said."

Rye paused a moment and casually asked, "Champ, do you like Bord?"

Champ shrugged. "Sure, I like him. Uncle Jesse and Grandpa and Shoes are still my second favorite to you, though."

"Of course. They're family."

"And Dean and George and 'specially Pogo are prob'ly third, but I liked Mr. Detmeyer real good, too."

"So did I. He was a fine man."

Champ looked down at his hands. "And Dayna's not too bad. She's about as good as Miss Meryl, but she's prettier."

Rye smiled. "Yes, she is prettier." He wondered if Champ would say anything about Kara, but the boy changed the subject.

"Uncle Jesse's got a bunch of horses, don't he, Dad?"

"Yes, as a matter of fact, he does."

"That's what I told Miss Dayna when she was worrying about ours. I told her, prob'ly we'd just borrow some of Jesse's."

Suddenly Rye grabbed his son and kissed him in the middle of the forehead. "Champ, you're a genius!"

"I am?"

"You sure are! I can't believe I didn't think of it myself!"

Rye hurried back to camp and practically snatched the telephone from Dean's shirt pocket, quickly punching in the numbers while his son announced to everybody in camp that he was a genius. Minutes later Rye gave a curious Dean a thumbs-up sign. He'd solved the immediate problem.

"I really appreciate this, Jess," he said into the phone. "She's fighting for something we can both identify with. It's our way of life as much as hers. And you can be sure I'll take your advice about locking up the feed and keeping the key. The other will have to be Kara's decision, but I'll run it by her and give you a call back."

A few seconds later he broke the connection, handed the phone over to Dean and went in search of the one person from whom he most needed to keep his distance. She had showered and changed and was drying her hair with a towel. Rye grinned. "I thought of something. Actually, it was Champ."

Kara stared at him a long moment, the towel still next to her head. "I overheard something about him being a genius, not that he'd tell me, mind you."

She seemed so sad about it that Rye had to clench his hands into fists to keep from reaching out to her. "He just might have saved our bacon. See, he remembered that his uncle Jess has a neat little sideline business going. He trains horses. He's going to meet us outside Dove Creek tomorrow with half a dozen of his strongest mounts, and he's taking our sick ones back with him."

Kara gasped, dropped the towel onto her shoulder and closed her eyes. Swallowing, she said, "I'll pay him somehow, I swear it. Whatever it takes, I'll see that he's compensated."

"You just try it," Rye told her, "and Jess'll pin your ears back for you."

"I can't let him do it for nothing, Rye. It wouldn't be fair."

"Listen, I'm an easygoing fellow—"

"Yeah, right."

"Compared to my big brother."

She actually smiled. "Hard to think of you having a big brother."

He cocked his head. "Oh, no. Jess is half of everything I am, all the good. He's the best of big brothers, truly."

She looked away. "You're lucky," she said. "I would have liked to have a big brother, well, a sibling of any sort, actually. But Mom couldn't have any more after me." She suddenly turned back to him. "Payne's the closest thing I have to a big brother. That's why I can't believe he has anything to do with what's happening."

Rye bit his tongue. When the urge passed to point out that Payne had the best motive, Rye said, "There's more."

"More?"

"You won't like this, but we're doing it, anyway."

Some of the fire leaped back into those blue eyes. "Don't try to tell me—"

"Just shut up and listen a minute," he said flatly. To his surprise, she did. It made him uneasy. He wasn't used to quick capitulation from her. He shifted his weight uncomfortably. "You can pay for this if it'll make you feel better, but later when you can afford it."

"What are you talking about?"

"Jess is bringing us some feed, too, in bulk, 'cause that's how he buys it."

"Where are we going to keep it?"

He chuckled because she always asked the most salient questions. "He's bringing it in a container with a lock and a key."

Kara blinked and slid to the edge of her chair, pointing a finger at him. "I want you to keep that key on your person at all times. No one goes into that container but you. Period."

"My thoughts exactly."

She smiled lopsidedly. "That happens to us a lot. Have you noticed? We seem to think alike, strange as that sounds."

He suddenly felt the ground shifting beneath his feet and scrambled for firmer footing. "One m-more thing."

Kara sighed, then tossed back her hair, the damp tendrils curling fetchingly about her face into a pale golden halo. "All right."

He couldn't look at her anymore. "Jess wants to bring a newspaper reporter with him, someone he knows."

"Whatever for?"

He hurried to explain Jesse's thinking. "He figures there ought to be a public record of what's been going on, if for no other reason than to build a case against the saboteur once we catch him. There's a chance, too, that the publicity might scare him off, make him think twice about pulling another one of these stunts."

Kara shrugged. "Can't hurt, I suppose."

"That's what I th—uh, I mean, I told Jess you'd have to give the word on this one."

Kara nodded. After a moment she picked up her towel and began drying her hair with it again. He sat there like a lump, watching her, wishing... He couldn't even bear that. Wishes were just regrets dressed up in longing, his father always said. Rye mumbled that he'd promised Jess he'd call back after talking it over with her. She neither spoke nor looked at him before he hurried away.

They took it real slow and easy on their last day in Utah, which kept Kara from falling out of her saddle in a pathetic heap. She was exhausted from losing two nights of sleep in a row, and from the sharpness of Rye's temper, he wasn't in much better shape. The horses had been fed on grass and hay, not the high-energy oat and protein blend to which they were accustomed, and were tired from the hard day before. So it made sense to go slowly, even if it did make for a terribly long day.

Knowing that dinner would be later than usual, Dayna provided a particularly hearty lunch, but Kara still felt as though her stomach was digesting itself by the time they dragged into camp. Thank God that they had real holding pens just outside the small town of Dove Creek, Colorado. They also had ample electricity, which meant real hot water showers in the dinky bath in the motor home. Kara made darn sure that she was at the head of that line, putting off dinner until afterward despite the gnawing in the pit of her belly. Rye's brother, Jesse, was standing in the chow line next to his nephew when she picked up her plate and fell in behind. He immediately stepped aside, sweeping out his arm.

"Ladies first, ma'am."

Kara stuck out one hand. "In this outfit we're all equals, Mr. Wagner. You are Jesse Wagner?"

He swept off his silver-gray Stetson, displaying an impressive head of wavy chestnut hair. It was hard to tell without a matching mustache, but he didn't strike Kara as particularly resembling his brother. Besides being clean shaven, he was taller by a couple of inches, and his hair bore no trace of premature gray. His sparkling eyes were almost as blue as they were silver, and his well-sculpted mouth tended to quick, easy smiles that displayed strong, white teeth.

"He takes after our mother," he explained cheekily, as though having read her mind, as his big, broad hand enveloped hers.

"I see."

"A pleasure to meet you, Miss Detmeyer."

"It's Kara."

"And Jess."

Frowning, Champ tugged hard on his uncle's arm. Jess immediately dropped his gaze to his nephew's face, going from affability to rock-hard sternness in the blink of an eye. "Your father may tolerate that behavior, young man, but I won't. Now mind your manners. I'm talking to the lady, so you just bear up."

Champ bowed his head abjectly. Kara immediately sought to lessen the blow. "He didn't mean anything."

"The heck he didn't," Jesse Wagner said baldly. "He and his father have a problem with good-looking young women, and you qualify in spades."

Kara's brows went up. "Er, thank you."

He grinned, switching on the charm again with disarming abruptness. "Just telling it like it is, one of my many virtues."

Kara laughed. She couldn't help it. Jess Wagner was about as different from his careful, aloof brother as a man could be. "Generosity must be another, then. I haven't thanked you for the horses and the feed yet. You've saved my life."

Wagner shrugged his broad, thick shoulders. "Frankly, I'd have done more to get an early look at the only woman I've heard my brother praise in years."

Kara had to work to keep her jaw from dropping. That left no space or time for subtlety. "Praised how?"

Jess chuckled. "Isn't that just like a woman, always wanting the details. Let me tell you something about men, Kara, they see the big picture. Details sometimes get lost. That's what we need women for.... Well, one of the things we need women for.'' He winked. As they'd been shuffling forward in line, they now found themselves at the serving table. Dayna was there with a big smile and a huge pot of spaghetti and meatballs. Jess split a look between the two women and said, ''My, my, you Detmeyer women sure dress a place up!''

Kara hid a smile. ''Jess, allow me to introduce my mother.''

He drew back in overdone disbelief. ''No, surely she's your sister!''

Dayna rolled her eyes. ''Now that's just what we need around here, more hot air.'' Just then, Pogo appeared at her side, an arm sliding possessively about her trim waist. Dayna slung an elbow halfheartedly at his ribs, saying, ''This one could launch dirigibles.''

Jess laughed and stuck out his hand, which Pogo gripped heartily. ''I should have known, you sneaky old buzzard.'' He turned his smile on Dayna again. ''What do you women see in him?''

Dayna smiled secretively. ''Trust me, it's not visible to the eye.''

Kara felt herself blush while Jess Wagner laughed delightedly. For the first time she truly understood the innuendo. For one bleak moment she felt such intense jealousy that her stomach turned over, but then her heart swelled and she let herself be glad for her mother. If what Dayna felt with Pogo Smith was anything like what she'd felt with Rye, then Kara rejoiced. She couldn't help wondering, though, if it had been like that with her mother and father. If it had, how had Dayna borne it when he'd died?

Rye arrived before she could ponder that question further, slapping his brother on the back. ''I see you've met the Detmeyers.''

''Oh, indeed, I have, and a real pleasure, too.''

Rye addressed Kara then. ''Bord and I got the fresh horses settled and the feed out. Jess has brought us some fine mounts.''

Kara kept her gaze on the older brother, afraid she would betray her own personal misery if she looked at Rye just then. ''I've already told Jess how grateful I am. Guess I'll have to up the ante now.''

Jess chuckled and picked up the plate Dayna had filled with spaghetti. Passing it to Kara, he took her empty one and put it on the table for Dayna to serve. Champ added his, splitting avid looks between Kara and his uncle. Jess treated Kara to a particularly charming smile. "Your company through dinner is more than ample compensation." Suddenly he looked up, first at his brother, then Pogo, adding, "Er, unless someone else has staked another claim I ought to know about...."

Kara caught her breath, torn between the need to look at Rye and the desire to run. Long seconds ticked by, during which no one said a word. Finally Jess Wagner picked up his plate, placed a hand in the small of Kara's back and gently pressed, saying mildly, "Tell me all about this trail drive. Rye said something about a codicil to a will."

Kara nodded and latched on to the subject gratefully, doing her best to ignore the ache spreading throughout her chest.

The reporter showed up the next morning just as they were mounting up. Rye did his best to tamp down his temper, but watching his brother fawn all over Kara the evening before had just about exhausted his control. It didn't help that Jess had actually seemed able to put the roses back in Kara's cheeks and the flash in her eyes. She had relaxed with Jess, laughed with him, even glowed beneath the constant shower of flirtatious charm. Rye couldn't help feeling invisible, forgotten. Now here was Jess pulling Kara down off her horse—as if she couldn't dismount on her own—to introduce her to a drugstore cowboy more comfortable with pen and paper than horse and rope.

He walked his horse over to the trio shaking hands and making introductions. Drawing rein, he leaned a forearm on his saddle horn and said, "Anybody around here remember that we've got work to do?"

Kara lifted a hand in his direction. "Chad, this is Jesse's brother Rye. You might call him my good right hand. Rye, I'd like you to meet Chad Bevery. He's a reporter."

He looked more like a kid playing reporter to Rye, a blond, pretty kid. And he was staring at Kara's chest as if taking her measurements. Rye put on a false smile.

"Do tell. Well, *Chad,* your timing's bad, son. We're just about to move these cattle down the trail. Schedule's to keep and all that."

Chad flipped open his pad and busily scribbled as if trying to get down every word. Jess laid a hand on Rye's arm. "This is important, Rye. Get someone else to fill in for Kara this morning."

Rye ground his teeth. "You seem to forget who's giving the orders around here, bro. Besides, Kara can't be replaced. I need her on point."

The reporter shook his ink pen at Rye, saying excitedly, "This is so good. Two centuries collide! Sabotage on the trail. Liberated female holding her own in a man's world. Fortune at stake!" The fool was talking in headlines. Rye rolled his eyes. Jess, meanwhile, seemed intent on playing the hero.

"Tell you what," he said to Kara, placing his hands familiarly on her shoulders. "I'll take your place until the noon rendezvous. You give our boy Chad here everything he needs. All right?"

Kara nodded and patted one of his hands where it rested on her shoulder. Rye fought down the urge to kick his brother off his feet, choosing instead to wheel his horse and gallop away, barking orders left and right. Damn Jess! What the hell did he think he was doing, mauling Kara like that, countermanding his own orders, sticking his nose in where it just didn't belong! He rode to point himself, shouting, "Head's up out there! New man on the wing!" Without waiting for Jess to fall into place, he cut out Number One from the milling herd and started her down the trail at a trot. "Let's move 'em!"

The herd gave a satisfying surge forward, the drovers hawing them and slapping leather. They moved out like a gigantic, well-oiled machine, throwing up dust in their wake. Rye realized suddenly that he was going to miss this moment in the future. He was going to miss giving the order to move, miss looking forward and seeing Kara driving out the leaders, miss the sounds of his men calling and ropes snapping. Miss her. Oh, God. He'd tried not to notice where she'd laid her bedroll last night, but he knew—*knew*—that she'd slept next to Jess. What had he done, bringing the two of them together?

He concentrated on moving the herd over some rough terrain. Some of it was so rough that they had no choice but to move out into the roadway in places. Rye prepared himself for confrontation with the locals and possibly even the constabulary. To his surprise people tended to pull over to the side of the road, roll down their windows or get out of their cars, wave their hats and shout questions.

"Where you headed?"

"New Mexico!"

"Where you from?"

"Utah!"

"How many head?"

"Better'n three hundred!"

"Who-ee!"

When Kara finally joined the drive at lunch, she was full of big news. "Chad says we can drive 'em right through Cahone, says he'll take care of everything as soon as he gets back to his office."

"Is that so? And what happens if somebody decides to throw us in jail for disturbing the peace or some such?"

"I told you, he'll take care of it. If some problem should crop up, he'll call."

"Well, isn't that special," Rye crabbed.

Kara just shook her head and rode out to point, Jess falling in beside her. Before long they drew up, and Jess leaned out of the saddle like some circus rider to buss her on the cheek. Kara laughed and waved him off as he rode away. Rye swallowed gall and yelled at George to get off the blankety-blank phone and mind his business. "That Wanda's got him on a short tether," he grumbled, referring to George's intended wife.

Jess laughed, catching him off guard. Rye wheeled his horse around to face him. "What's so funny?"

"You."

"Yeah, I'm a laugh riot, especially when I'm moving three hundred head on a public roadway with an inexperienced hand."

"We did okay, seems to me. Everybody says Kara's a surprisingly good hand—"

Rye snorted. "Kara's the best hand on the crew."

Jess grinned. "Next to you, you mean."

Rye shrugged, sensing that he was being led somewhere he didn't necessarily want to go. "Guess you'll be shoving off now all the rescuing's done."

Jess grinned and said, "I like her."

"I noticed."

Jess heaved a long-suffering sigh and crossed his hands over the saddle horn. "She's not a whit like Di'wana."

Rye turned his horse. "Tell Dad I look forward to seeing him in a few days."

Jess spurred forward and grabbed Rye's reins. "Sit still, damn it! I'll let you know when I'm through with you."

Rye actually cocked his fist. "I'm not ten years old and still taking orders from you!"

"Then stop acting like it!"

It took a few moments for that to sink in, fortunately his hand got the message before his brain did and was hanging at his side by the time he realized what he'd almost done. He tugged his reins from Jesse's grasp and made a show of relaxing. "All right, I'm listening."

"I want to take Champ home with me."

"Champ?"

"Living on the trail is exciting, but it's also hard. He needs a break, and you need some slack. Besides, I'm worried about all the stuff that's been going on."

Rye nodded. What Jess said was true. He hadn't been able to spend as much time with the boy as he'd intended, anyway. Seemed there was always something needing his attention. And he had another reason for liking the idea. Jess had a way with Champ, for making him see reason. "Okay. But there's something you ought to know, something I haven't been able to prepare him for myself."

"Seeing his mother. He told me."

Rye lifted a hand to the back of his neck. "It's time."

"Past time, if you ask me."

"Which I didn't."

Jess reached across the distance between them and laid a hand on Rye's shoulder. "You're doing the right thing, Rye. I know it's hard, but if the two of you are ever going to put this behind you, you have to make your peace. Champ doesn't understand that right now, but I intend to tell him how proud I am of you for taking this step."

Rye blinked, surprised at how his brother's approval still had the power to warm him. "Thanks. I'll ride back to the lunch wagon with you to tell Champ so long."

Jess nodded. "You'll see him again in a few days."

"Yeah. Meanwhile, he can have a good time with his grand-parents and Uncle Jess."

"And you can have a good time with that hot number riding point."

Rye jerked his horse to a halt. "What the hell do you mean by that crack?"

"Give it up, Rye. She's wild about you, and you're behaving like a bad-tempered stud with his first whiff of scent. I know you've been wanting to put out my lights just for looking at her."

"You've got some nerve, you know that?"

"I just want to see you happy, Rye, for once. Even if it's only for the next week or so."

Rye was startled. "I'm happy."

Jess shook his head. "Rye, you're the unhappiest fellow I know. Just this once, take a little time for yourself. Enjoy some of the good life has to offer. Let that little gal do everything she's aching to do for you. Take it and be grateful. Please. I guarantee you, the world will seem a new place after."

Rye was speechless. Was this his big brother begging him to cut loose? After all those lectures on responsibility and sobriety? Had Kara told him something about the two of them? If so, he wanted to hear it from Kara herself.

"Think about it," Jess said, kicking his horse into a canter.

He was thinking about it. He was thinking that he could walk into any drugstore in any town along the way, buy a box of condoms and walk out again without answering to anybody. He could have Kara in his arms every night until Durango. And maybe the world would seem a new place afterward. He closed his eyes. Could he do this? Could he love Kara for now and walk away later? Would she come to him, knowing he wouldn't, couldn't stay with her beyond Durango? He only knew that he was going to find out.

Chapter Eleven

"Care if I join you?"

Kara looked up, frankly amazed, and inclined her head as Rye sat down on the ground next to her and folded his legs, depositing his plate atop his crossed ankles. He scooted closer, until their knees touched. Kara shook her head and said rather caustically, "Finally managed to place my face, did you? And only two days after *the fact*."

"I'm sorry." He spread his hands and fixed her with a direct look. "I didn't know how to act that next morning. I was afraid everyone would know, and I wasn't ready for that, not with Champ around."

"You made me feel ashamed, Rye," she told him softly.

"Oh, Lord, honey, I never intended that." He sighed and swept his hands through his hair. It was damp still from a recent shower, and the firelight and lanterns picked out the silver threads against the darker hues. "Kara," he said finally, "I've never experienced anything before like that night. I can't just write it off as a one-night stand because, even if it never happens again, I know those feelings will always be with me—and I'm hoping it will happen again. But I don't have much to offer you, sweetheart, not everything you deserve, for sure, just now, a few days.''

Painfully aware of his meaning, she stalled for time, looking around them. They were not alone. Her mother and Pogo were washing dishes over by the old truck, laughing together and bumping hips from time to time. George was eating his dinner in the back seat of the double cab, his beloved Wanda on the telephone. Shoes had finished his meal and was working lanolin into a piece of leather from atop a five-gallon bucket placed end up beside his farrier's wagon. Dean was on the computer at the table, his dinner as yet untouched, while Bord watched over his shoulder and forked pork and beans into his mouth. No one was paying the least attention to the two of them, and yet Kara felt exposed. She pretended an intense interest in her dinner plate as she asked, ''What brought this on now?''

Rye covered his knees with his hands and leaned forward, saying in a voice barely above a whisper, ''I just don't know how to stay away anymore, not since I let Champ go to Durango with my brother.''

Kara looked up abruptly. She'd known, of course, that Jess had headed back to the Wagner ranch, but Champ kept so carefully out of her path that she hadn't even missed him. ''I just assumed he was inside the motor home or something.''

''Jess asked me to let him take the boy back to the ranch with him.'' Rye licked his lips and brushed his mustache with his fingertips. ''Did you maybe say something to him, about us, I mean?''

Kara thought carefully. Had she said something to give them away? Finally she shook her head. ''No, I don't think so, certainly not intentionally.''

Rye nodded. ''I guess he knows me well enough to figure my moods by now.''

''He talked to you about us?''

''Yes.''

She didn't know what to say to that. She turned her fork over in her hand. He picked his up and speared a piece of pork. They ate silently for several minutes. Finally, she couldn't keep quiet anymore. ''What did he say?''

Rye turned a quirky, almost sad, smile on her. ''He told me

to stop being such a damned fool and let you make me happy...even if it's just for a little while.''

Kara closed her eyes, wishing she hadn't asked. She knew exactly what he was telling her, and it was not enough, but it was tempting, so very tempting. She focused on her plate again, but she couldn't make herself eat. She had a decision to make; she understood that. She was even grateful that Rye hadn't tried to make it seem as if he was offering her more than a few days—or nights, really—together. But how could she do it, knowing they had no future? Then again, she hadn't thought about the future when she had essentially begged him to make love to her before. She hadn't thought of anything but how it would feel to be with him. This was different, of course. Now she knew without any doubt that heartbreak awaited her at the end.

She shook her head. Who was she trying to fool? Her heart had been breaking from the moment she'd laid eyes on Rye Wagner. He was every cowgirl's dream, tall and lean and handsome, with that striking hair and the drooping mustache, cowboy to the bone, as natural in his spurs and chaps and work gloves as his boots and jeans and hat. He loved the life that she loved, lived for the same work, knew his business in and out. She hadn't believed, at first, that he would even notice her as a woman, but she was glad that she'd been wrong. He was a loving father, and he knew what it meant to have his own heart broken and his world destroyed. He'd made her no promises; she hadn't asked for any. She would ask for none now. If it was true that she could make him happy in some way, even for a short while, she knew she wouldn't let the opportunity get by her. She had more courage than that. Or perhaps she was just weak willed and stupid. She was surprised to find that she didn't really care which.

Her decision made, she finished her meal and got up to carry her plate to the washtub. That done, she went directly to the gear she had laid out in her usual place inside the ring of vehicles that created the boundaries of the camp. Calmly, she went down on her haunches and began gathering up her things: hat, belt, bedroll, flashlight, a magazine she'd thought to thumb through. Shoes reacted immediately.

"Where are you going?"

"I'm going to sleep outside camp tonight," she told him matter-of-factly.

"You can't do that. You're not supposed to be off by yourself. Rye told me—"

"I won't be alone," she said lightly, even though her heart was pounding, and just in case he didn't get it, she looked purposefully at Rye. He was still sitting on the ground, watching her over his shoulder. She smiled, feeling ridiculously shy all of a sudden, and pushed up to her feet, her arms full. She looked around her at all the curious faces and said loudly, "Good night."

She made for a gap between the farrier's wagon and the big horse trailer. Suddenly Rye shot up to his feet and practically threw his plate at Pogo. She paused just around the end of the motor home, listening unashamedly. She didn't have to wait long. Within seconds Shoes was asking Rye what the hell he was doing.

"None of your business," came the distracted reply.

A long pause followed, then Shoes said, "I'll be damned. Just look at the grin on your face."

Kara could almost see Rye's reaction. "I'm not grinning."

"Yeah, right."

"So what if I am?"

"I'm just not used to it, is all," Shoes said, his own smile somehow audible. "I'll be damned," he said again.

"Probably," Rye shot back. "Good night, now."

Shoes chuckled. Kara shot around the corner of the motor home and threw her stuff on the ground. She ripped off the down-filled vest she'd put on after her shower. The temperature seemed to have risen suddenly. She dropped to her knees and began ripping at the strings on her sleeping bag. Rye was there before she got it unrolled, his own arms filled as hers had been.

"Need some company?"

She lifted her gaze to his face and said quite deliberately, "Yes, if it's you."

He dropped everything he was carrying and stepped over it, coming down on his knees next to her, his hands rising to cup her face. "Stay with me to Durango. It won't be enough, but—"

She covered his mouth with her fingertips. "We won't talk of that. We have better things to do."

He smiled. She felt it against the pads of her fingers, saw it in the lift of his mustache. He sent one hand into her hair, threading his fingers through it and cupping the back of her head. With the other, he grasped the wrist of her hand and pulled it away from his mouth, first kissing her fingertips. Then his mouth was on hers, his tongue delving deeply. She looped her arms loosely about his neck. He framed her face with both hands, tilting her head to give himself better access. Finally he pulled away, settling back on his heels to smooth her hair with his hands.

"I was so afraid you wouldn't want me again," he whispered.

"I'll always want you," she said softly. "Please make love to me now."

He gulped and nodded, then began looking around for his sleeping bag. She moved away, unzipping her own bag and spreading it out. He threw his on top of it and went to work joining the zippers. She sat down and tugged off her boots. He reached for her, pulling her up to her knees, and his hands went to the snap at the top of the placket on her shirt. He pulled it apart and reached for the next, confessing, "My hands are shaking."

"Mine aren't," she said, yanking out her shirttail. She gathered up the hems of her work shirt and the undershirt she wore beneath it, pulling them up and off over her head. He followed suit, stripping to the waist as she reached around to the catch of her bra. He reached for the straps and slowly slid them down her arms. Cool air prickled her skin and hardened her nipples to stiff, round peaks. He covered them with his palms, massaging gently.

"Heavens above, girl, you take my breath away."

She closed her eyes, amazed at her own lack of embarrassment. How easily she had grown accustomed to, even greedy for, his touch. How right it felt to be here with him like this. Perhaps it wasn't right, but she couldn't let herself think of that. The time for regret would come later. She put those thoughts aside as he slid his arms around her and pulled her tight against his chest. His skin was delightfully warm and smooth and firm. His arms felt strong and hard about her. She wrapped her arms around his waist and laid her head on his shoulder. He held her for a long time, his cheek against the top of her head. She felt safe, treasured, even loved. With the fires of passion banked, it was enough just to be there with him, to feel him against her. Gradually, however, the chill night air seeped into even that warm embrace, and Kara shivered involuntarily. His hold loosened instantly.

"Let's get you into bed."

Nodding, she moved away, surprised to find that her knees were stiff from kneeling there. She let him hustle her beneath his sleeping bag, saying, "I didn't get out any pads."

"I can do without them. How about you?"

It was chilly in the bag. She rubbed her arms vigorously. "All I need is warming."

"Done," he said, quickly popping the buttons on his jeans. He shucked them and stripped off his socks, scrambling into the bag. Once there, he dragged the jeans over and reached into the pockets, spilling out foil packets. He reached for her, and she came into his arms. He rolled onto his back, pulling her on top of him. She pressed against him, feeling his hard length against the fly of her jeans. He groaned as she moved against him. "Oh, honey, did anything ever feel that good?" he asked.

"I seem to remember one or two things even better," she whispered.

He grinned up at her. "Yeah? Maybe you should remind me."

She leaned her upper body weight against him and began working open her fly, letting her hands brush him frequently just to revel in his instantaneous reactions. When she had her jeans open, he slid his hands into them, cupping her bottom and pressing her against him. She worked her body upward, so that the jeans worked down, laughing huskily as he groaned and pushed against her, momentarily thwarting his own efforts to rid her of the garment. Impatiently, he shoved and tugged while she twisted against him, until finally she kicked the jeans away. That was when he began kissing her, pulling her face down to his before roaming her body with his hands. She took as much as she could, then lifted herself upright. "Now, Rye."

"Hang on." He fumbled around and found one of the packets. She tried to help him with it. Finally, with much interesting maneuvering and gasping, they were both ready. She eased herself down onto him. As his length filled her, his hands fell away, his head tilted back, and his eyes rolled closed, his breath coming in deep gasps.

"Aw, Kara!" he said through clenched teeth, thrusting upward. "Nothing was ever this good. I've never needed anyone this much!"

She bent forward, bracing herself on her arms, until her breasts rubbed against his chest. "I'm here," she whispered. "I'm here."

They were the last coherent words either would manage for a long time.

Later, much later, they lay twined together in the slightly moist warmth of the double sleeping bag. Kara smoothed her hands across Rye's chest, her head pillowed against his shoulder, his arms loose about her. The rhythm of his heart had slowed to a strong, steady beat. His breaths came deep and easy as he slept. The tears caught her unaware, and after a few, ineffective sniffs, she let them fall, crying all at one time for the beauty of what they shared, the joy of the love she carried in her own heart, and the parting to come. He would leave her. She didn't doubt it, and nothing she could say would change it. She had only one option then, to love him with all her might while she could. The tears dried. She closed her eyes and let herself drift into the deepest, most peaceful sleep she'd ever known.

"Ryeland. Ryeland."

Rye jerked awake, several disorienting facts assailing him at once: he was wet; a strong, oily odor filled his head and made it ache; Kara stretched against him, her warm skin sliding against his and telling him that they were naked; and Shoes Kanaka was frowning down into his face. "What is it?"

"Listen to me. You're drenched in gasoline."

Rye felt the mushiness of the sleeping bag beneath his left side and pressed his fingertips against it, lifting them to his nose to sniff. It was a purely instinctive gesture. He knew Shoes was right, even though it didn't make the least sense. Kara lifted her head.

"What's going on?"

Shoes went down on his haunches, forearms balanced on his knees. "It would appear that the gas tank of the motor home has a hole in it and the gasoline drained out during the night. Your sleeping bags are soaked on this side. Rye's hair is wet with it on the back of his head. I can see it from here."

Rye's hand clenched on Kara's arm. "Are you okay?"

"I...I think so." She moved slightly. "It seems dry here."

"How 'bout your clothes?"

She turned her head. "They look okay."

Rye blinked his eyes, resisting the urge to rub them, and forced his mind around the problem at hand. "Okay, I want you to get up and get dressed."

"Small problem," she muttered.

Rye lifted his head to locate his own clothes, knowing perfectly well what "small problem" to which she alluded. "Nope, Shoes is going to get me some dry clothes, shampoo and a towel right now. Aren't you, Shoes?"

"Yep," Shoes agreed, pushing up to his full height and turning away.

"Leave 'em next to the water truck," Rye called to him as he left them.

Kara sensibly decided to drag her clothes into the sleeping bag with her and get dressed in the relative warmth there, muttering about the embarrassment of being found naked in her lover's arms. Rye let her grouse, his own mind working over this latest problem. He had no doubt that it was sabotage. Holes did not just appear in gas tanks in the middle of the night. The real questions were who and how—and did the saboteur mean to do more than merely scare them and slow them down this time? Was a careless match or spark of some sort supposed to find them before Shoes had? Kara finished dressing and knelt at his side, pushing her hair out of her way.

"Rye, you're soaked, your whole left side."

"I'm okay, slight headache, nothing major."

"We've got to get this off you."

"Hand me my jeans, will you? But keep clear of the gas."

She leaned across him and snagged his blue jeans. "They're soaked."

"It's okay. I'll only wear them to the shower." He took them from her, folded back the top sleeping bag and rose, asking as he slid into them, "How are my boots?"

She picked them up from the foot of the camp bed. "They're dry."

"Good. Now I want you to get a big plastic bag from your

mom. And tell Shoes to pour lots of soapy water on this spot. I don't want anything catching fire around here.''

''What about you?''

''I'm going to shower.''

''The water's cold. You'll freeze to death this time of morning.''

''I'll be all right as soon as I get this gasoline off me. Soak all these things in soapy water and shove them into the plastic bag. Better put on the rubber gloves your mom uses for washing dishes first.''

''I'll take care of that,'' Shoes said, coming around the end of the motor home dressed in the plastic apron he used to keep his clothing clean when working out of the farrier's wagon. He tossed a pair of moccasins at Rye's feet. ''You just get cleaned up before somebody ignites you. You can wear those to the shower.''

''Thanks.''

Rye shoved his feet into the soft shoes and tramped off toward the water truck, hearing Kara say to Shoes that she'd get the plastic bag and have the boys lug around a big bucket of soapy water.

He was shivering so hard his teeth clattered before he was satisfied that he'd washed away as much of the dangerous gasoline as possible. Kara was waiting on the other side of the makeshift tarpaulin wall with a pair of towels and his duster draped over one shoulder. She tossed a towel over his head and began rubbing his shoulders and chest with the other. He snatched up the towel that Shoes had provided and whipped it around his waist. Kara chuckled and shook her head.

''Suddenly embarrassed to let me see you naked?''

''Nope. Just don't want whoever's coming to get an eyeful.''

She turned a look over her shoulder just as Dayna and Pogo appeared from the direction of the camp. ''Are you all right?'' Dayna demanded.

''I'm fine,'' Kara said, draping her towel over Rye's shoulder.

''I will be as soon as I'm warm again,'' Rye said, shivering and using Kara's towel to mop under his arms and scrub dry his back. He bent and dried off his legs. They were awfully hairy. Did Kara mind that they were awfully hairy? Guess she didn't. She handed him his underwear as calmly as if her mother wasn't standing there with her hands on her hips watching. He snatched them and backed into the haven of the tarp, struggling into them beneath the towel. Kara shook out his dry jeans and handed them in to him, taking the towel from him. He pulled on the jeans and reached for his undershirt.

She pulled him out from beneath the tarp and put the work shirt on him herself, buttoning the front while he managed the cuffs. That done, she helped him slip into the long, sturdy coat made especially for riding horseback with its reinforced slit up the back. He stomped into his boots and rubbed his wet hair with the remaining towel. All the while, Pogo and Dayna were talking.

"Shoes says the hole was punched into the tank deliberately."

"It's a wonder the two of you are here. Whoever did it could have dropped a match, and the two of you wouldn't have known a thing apparently."

"I don't suppose we'll ever know if he just meant to delay us or if maybe Shoes chased him away before he could drop a match."

"Either way, we've got a big problem."

"Dean says we can't just have it towed into the nearest town. There's still enough gas in the tank to spark a fire or maybe even an explosion. The gas tank has to come out."

"Damn," Rye muttered.

Pogo nodded in understanding. "Dean's calling a mechanic and a tow truck now."

"Soon as that's done," Rye said, "I'm calling in the local law."

Pogo nodded again. "You'll have to handle that yourselves, you and Kara. What I want to know is if you trust the rest of us to move the herd."

Rye sighed, pushing a hand through his tangled hair. Finally he looked Pogo in the eye. "Think you can do it?"

"I know we can." He stepped closer. "Don't let him win. Whoever the hell it is, I say we don't let him win. Let's keep this herd moving!"

"All right," Rye said. "You're in charge now. Get 'em on the trail, but be careful. Whoever's doing this means business."

Pogo whipped his gaze back and forth, then stepped closer. "If it's anybody here," Pogo said softly, "it's Bord Harris."

"We don't have any proof of that," Dayna added urgently, "and not for lack of trying."

"You're telling me you've been watching Bord?" Rye said, and both Pogo and Dayna nodded. "Where'd he sleep last night?"

Pogo made a face. "In the motor home—with us."

"He might have slipped out," Dayna said, "but if so, he was awful quiet about it, and frankly I don't think he could manage it."

Rye sighed. "Okay. Well, keep an eye on him, anyway. I sure can't believe it's one of the others. I've known them all for years."

"I can't believe it's a stranger," Kara said. "Oboe would've barked at a stranger."

"Maybe it wasn't a stranger," Rye said. "Maybe it was someone from outside but someone the dog knows."

Kara looked shaken by that. Dayna said, "I don't think it matters right now. Seems to me that all we can do is keep our eyes open and keep moving."

"My thoughts exactly," Pogo said.

"You're right. Kara and I will catch up with you as soon as we can," Rye said.

Pogo grinned, winked and clapped Rye on the shoulder. Dayna split a wary look between Kara and Rye, then put her arms around her daughter and kissed her on the cheek. "Take care of each other," she said worriedly before hurrying away at Pogo's side.

Kara slid an arm around Rye's waist. He returned the favor by slinging an arm across her shoulders. "Guess she knows, huh?"

"I'd think everyone does. We weren't exactly subtle."

He nodded and said, "I'm assuming it's all right with you."

She turned against him and lifted her face to his. "It's all right with me. It always will be."

He hugged her tight, hoping she was being honest with him. He hated to think about leaving her hurting or, God forbid, ashamed. He hated to think about leaving her at all, but he knew it would come to that. The days when he could justify trying to make something like this work were long behind him. But there was no point dwelling on that now. Right now they were together, a team. He dropped a kiss on her crown. "We've got work to do, honey." Arm in arm they went to it.

They saw the herd off, Rye shouting orders at his crew until they were well out of hearing range. Then they both had phone calls to make. Rye called the law back in Utah and the local brand. Afterward Kara rang up Chad Bevery, the reporter to whom Jesse had introduced her. Chad said something about broadening the scope of the coverage, but only after Kara had given him the details first. The tow truck and mechanic showed up soon enough. Meanwhile Dayna and Borden started leapfrogging the vehicles ahead to the next campsite.

Rye put on a pair of greasy coveralls much too small for him, borrowed from the mechanic, and crawled underneath the motor home to have a look himself. A pair of sheriff's deputies showed up about the time he crawled out again. "So how's it look?" one of them asked.

"It's definitely a deliberate puncture."

"What're you going to do?"

Rye nodded toward the mechanic and tow truck driver as he peeled off the coveralls. "They've ordered another tank, but it'll be tomorrow before it gets to us. Soon as the old tank's out, we'll tow the motor home into town. They say we can spend the night in front of the shop. They've got electricity and even a water hookup for us."

"That's good, then. Want to tell us about everything that's been going on?"

Rye nodded and filled them in. He'd been doing a lot of that lately. After they'd gone, Kara asked, "Anybody say what this is going to cost?"

"I'm afraid to ask."

"We'll know soon enough, I suppose. Don't worry. It'll work out."

"I suppose so. Meanwhile there are benefits."

"Benefits?"

She grinned at him. "A real bed, for instance, all night long."

"Have I ever told you how much I love the way your mind works?"

She laughed. It occurred to him suddenly that it was another thing he loved about her—one of many.

The mechanic finally got the tank out, and the crippled motor home was hoisted up onto the tow truck. They rode all packed together in the cab of the tow truck. Rye didn't mind. Kara rode sitting on his lap. In town they had plenty of help getting the motor home in place and set up for occupancy. Indeed, the whole town seemed to have turned out, along with some fellow with a microphone, which he shoved into Kara's face the instant she set foot on the ground.

"Ms. Detmeyer! Ms. Detmeyer! Chad Bevery of the Mountain Times is reporting that your operation has been sabotaged. Is this true?"

"Well, yes, actually."

"So this historic trail drive is stalled?"

Rye stepped in then. "By no means. No spineless, lily-livered coward who skulks around in the dead of night is going to stop this trail drive. We've got the cattle moving even as we speak."

"But is a skeleton crew able to—"

"Our crew are seasoned, capable drovers," Rye said pointedly. "They're a couple hands short right now, but our animals are broken to the trail, and this latest little stunt shouldn't keep Kara and me out of the saddle longer than a day, two at the most. We'll make the deadline."

The reporter started talking about the codicil to Plummer's will, but as he seemed to be speaking mainly to himself, Rye and Kara abandoned him. They had too much to do with the hours remaining to them that afternoon to worry about some independent reporter, but it was smart of him to record everything rather than try to write it all down. First order of business was to locate a laundromat. They were shown to a single heavy-duty washer and dryer lodged in an outdoor stall behind the local car wash. They elected to use the car wash first, laying out the gasoline-drenched sleeping bags and clothing and chasing them across the concrete floor at the end of a high-pressure hose. It took two hours to put the stuff through the washer and dryer. Afterward, they wandered down to the local grocery to pick up some necessities. It was on their way back that an elderly cowboy named Hud Tenery, bowlegged from his years spent on horseback, hailed them and offered to buy their dinner, refusing to take no for an answer.

Dinner at the only place in town turned out to be ribs, fried chicken nuggets, onion rings, baked beans and salad, accompa-

nied by pitchers full of beer. They were minor celebrities, thanks
to Chad Bevery. Every cowboy and wanna-be for miles around
seemed to have turned out to buy them drinks and ask questions
about the drive. The questions became pretty pointed after a
while. What did they need most? Could they use a couple more
hands? Was their route a secret? Rye could see no reason not to
answer honestly, especially the questions concerning their route.
The more eyes watching them the better. Everybody was interested and friendly. It actually turned into a pretty good time,
almost a party. When someone dropped a quarter into the juke-
box and punched in an old standby Western tune, Kara was instantly inundated with offers to dance, but she merely put on a
smile and said, "Thanks, fellas, but I don't dance with anyone
but the guy who brought me."

"In that case," Rye said, pushing back his chair and standing,
"this dance must be mine."

Smiling into his eyes, she put her hands in his. He pulled her
up and into his arms. Tables were shoved back so they had their
own private dance floor. Kara closed her eyes and laid her head
on his shoulder. He thought he'd bust his buttons, he was that
proud to partner her. He pushed away thoughts of the future,
focusing instead on the bed that awaited them back at the motor
home.

He made sure that bed didn't wait too long, and the loving
that followed was everything he'd come to expect and more.

Later, when he lay with Kara snug against him, his thoughts
turned, oddly enough, to Plummer Detmeyer. If the old man had
been matchmaking, he'd been more right than he knew. Kara
was everything Rye had ever imagined in a woman, and it would
have been grand to be part of the old man's family, but that
didn't change the realities of the situation. Rye knew he was no
fit husband for a woman like Kara, or any woman, most likely.
Moreover, there was the situation with Champ. He hadn't realized until Kara had been thrust into their lives how very insecure
his son was and how much responsibility he himself bore for
that. Champ wasn't ready for a stepmother and might never be.
Rye wasn't ready for a wife. However much he would have liked
to please the old man, he just couldn't. It wouldn't be fair, least

of all to Kara. He knew she thought she loved him, but she didn't really know him, not the Rye he became once the legalities were observed.

Only to Durango. She was only his until Durango.

Chapter Twelve

Morning brought an uneasiness that Kara had not expected. Alone here in the little motor home, it seemed somehow as if they were playing house like children who did not yet fully grasp what such relationships required. It felt odd to wake with nothing more pressing on her mind than getting breakfast. She wondered how the drive was doing, but it was Rye who snatched up the telephone and called George to be certain, even at a distance, that all was going as it should. Rather than pleased, he seemed a little deflated that the crew and the herd could manage without them. At least there had been no more instances of sabotage—yet.

Kara scraped back her hair into a damp ponytail and made breakfast, rolling soft tortillas around eggs scrambled with bits of sausage, onion, peppers and cheese, while Rye made coffee strong enough to walk unaided. They lingered over the meal, uncertain quite what to do with themselves until, with a sigh, Kara brought out a calculator and the strongbox.

Even after they had each emptied their wallets, the picture looked grim. Rye rubbed his hands over his face, smoothing his mustache and tugging at his ear. Kara smiled, recognizing the signs of deep thought in him. Finally he said, "I can borrow some money from Jess."

Kara shook her head. "I can't let you do that. Unless..."

He lifted a brow at her. "What? Maybe you'd rather let old Payne make you a loan?"

She didn't have to think long to reject that idea. Even if Payne wasn't behind the sabotage—and she couldn't quite convince herself that he was—it wouldn't be fair to ask him to actively contribute to his own loss. Besides, she liked her original idea better. She tried to state it mildly. "You could always buy into the operation."

"Buy into your ranch?" he said with chilling surprise. "I don't think so."

"Why not?"

"That's a Detmeyer operation."

She bit her lip to keep from suggesting that it could remain Detmeyer land in the larger sense if the two of them married. Instead she said, "Well, it will just have to be a Detmeyer-Wagner operation."

He shook his head again and swept a hand through his hair. He needed a haircut, she noted, or maybe he was thinking of growing his hair long like Shoes. She smiled at the thought, trying to picture Rye with long hair in that fascinating weave of color shot through with silver. When he grumbled that he thought he'd shave his head, she burst into laughter.

"What?"

"I was just picturing you with long hair."

He shuddered. "Think I'll see if there's a barber around this one-horse town."

She smiled. "I could cut it if I had some scissors."

"I keep a small pair for grooming my mustache in my kit," he said hopefully.

So she cut his hair, trimmed it, actually, pretending at intervals to snip his ear or cut away huge chunks. He was peering at his reflection in the bathroom mirror, smoothing the cut with his fingertips and looking pleased, when someone outside pounded on the door. They went together to see who it was.

Thankfully, the new gasoline tank had arrived, and the mechanic was ready to get to work on it. Kara and Rye vacated the motor home immediately, taking refuge in the grimy little office

of the two-pump gasoline station attached to the shop. A small
television occupied one corner of a battered old desk covered
with grease-smudged papers in various pastel hues. Rye
scratched his chin. "I think I saw a satellite dish out there, didn't
I?"

"You don't suppose it's there for this, do you?" she asked,
pointing at the dusty set. He shrugged and flicked it on.

"Let's see."

A dazzling array of programming flashed before them with the
simple turn of a dial, not much of it worth watching in Kara's
estimation. It was on one of the morning magazine shows that
she saw her own face, though it was a reporter's voice that she
heard. Rye's hand froze on the dial.

"Good grief!"

"I don't believe this!"

"That guy was a TV reporter?"

They instantly shushed each other and turned up the volume.

"So it is that a historic event harking back to the fondly held
legends of the past is placed at risk by a person or persons un-
known. As their hardy forebears faced drought and hostile op-
position, marauders and starving Native Americans, barbwire and
the harsh brutality of life on the frontier, so our valiant crew of
modern-day cowboys face failure at the hands of unseen oppo-
nents with all the deadly convenience of the modern world at
their disposal. Will they make it, this band of tough men and one
strong, capable woman, or is the era of the trail drive dead and
closed for all time? And just what have we all lost if that is so?
Horace Vega Shiles, Channel Ninety-Nine, Sky Creek, Colorado."

The camera returned to the homey, trendy main set and the
show's snappy and polished host and hostess, who made cooing,
concerned sounds about the fate of the trail drive and hit again
the fact that a—gasp—*woman* was the owner of the herd and
part of the crew. In the midst of it, Kara and Rye stared at one
another, mouths ajar, for about ten seconds, then burst into
stunned laughter.

"National television! Holy Cow!"

"I cannot believe this!"

Rye seized her by the upper arms. "This is good. Honey, this is good. The more attention the better, I say. He'll have to think twice before attacking us again.''

She looked deeply into his eyes. ''You're convinced it's Payne, aren't you?''

He really wanted to lie to her, but he never had yet, and he wasn't about to start now. ''I'm afraid so. He's the one who stands to gain the most, Kara, the only one I can see, anyway.''

''It's not just because you don't like him?''

Rye grimaced. ''I don't think so. Something in my gut tells me it's him.''

Kara wished she hadn't asked. Payne, more brother than cousin. She thought of all those idyllic months they'd shared growing up, of all the teasing and petty arguments, the grudging respect that had grown to deep affection and even admiration. They were different. She'd always known they were different, but he did love her; she'd always known that, too. And yet he was the one with the most to gain. She closed her eyes. *Oh, Lord, don't let it be Payne.*

''Look,'' Rye said, pulling her into his arms. ''All that matters now is that whoever is doing it doesn't succeed. The news coverage will help. He, they, have to know by now that everyone's watching.''

''Think we ought to call the herd again? They won't know about the national coverage until somebody tells them.''

''That's right.''

He whipped out the cell phone and dialed up George. While he explained all about the morning news program, Kara sat on the edge of the desk and smiled at him. She smoothed her hands over his chest and down his sides, admiring the way he was built. He nudged her knees apart and stood between them, still talking to George. He slid an arm across her shoulders, sliding his hand down her back. She sighed with great contentment. It was wonderful to be close to him like this, to openly touch and be touched with such affection. He flipped off the phone and stuck it into his back pocket before bringing both arms around her.

''Heavens, girl,'' he said, laying his forehead against hers. ''You sure know how to make me want you.''

''Do I?'' She smiled at him dreamily. ''You're the only man I've ever made want me.''

''I doubt that. You just don't see how the others look at you.''

"I don't care how anyone looks at me but you."

He took a deep breath. "I'd like to make love to you in the daytime," he said huskily. "In a patch of warm sunshine somewhere with blue sky overhead."

"And a soft, clean bed," she added drily.

He groaned. "I hope I never have to sleep on the ground again when this is over," he said in agreement.

"Maybe we could move the bed out of the motor home into the vacant lot out back," she quipped.

He shook his head. "It's built in." He looked to the desk. "That's a prodigious pile of paper there," he said consideringly. She laughed, which encouraged him to come up with even more far-fetched ideas, such as building her a bed of used tires and grease rags or sneaking into a booth in the corner of the little café where they'd dined the night before. She teasingly suggested the back seat of a car. "But only a 1970 model or older," he said with a straight face. "I'd break my back in one of these newer jobs."

They were still teasing each other with tantalizing and downright silly possibilities when old Hud Tenery pulled up out front in his pickup. Rye looked questioningly at Kara before stepping away. Tenery got out and came inside, sweeping off his hat as if in the presence of royalty. "Miss Detmeyer. Mr. Wagner."

Rye offered the old cowboy his hand. "Tenery."

After the handshake, Tenery kneaded the brim of his hat until Kara feared it would disintegrate. Finally, he said, "Ya'll see that program this morning?"

Rye smiled and folded his arms. "We saw it. Couldn't believe it, but we saw it."

Tenery nodded and went on in his gravelly voice. "A bunch of folks saw it, and some of us have been talking."

"About?"

Tenery licked his lips. "It's been a hard year for stockmen," he said. "Some are just barely holding on. Me, now, I'm retired. Oh, I run a few head now and again just for the pleasure of it, but I butchered my cows rather than give 'em away last year, and the thing is, I've got some feed just moldering in my barn. I'd be pleased if you'd take it off my hands, free of charge."

Rye looked at Kara in surprise. "That's awfully generous of you, Mr. Tenery," she began, "but—"

"Shucks, ma'am, it's nothing. Better it go to you than to ruin, and I'm not the only one that feels that way." He whipped a sheet of paper from his shirt pocket. "Now, you said last night that the herd'll be bedding down at the Hetherton Sales Barn 'bout ten miles past Manco, isn't that right?"

"That's right."

"Well, this here is a list of what'll be there when your bunch rolls in for the night."

He handed over the paper. Kara shared it with Rye, and together they read over the list, their eyes growing large. It was everything they'd need to see them through to New Mexico and more. She could even replace the feed Jesse had given them! Tenery was talking as they read.

"We sorta come up with this idea last night after you left, but we didn't really plan nothing, you know, till this morning. I guess everybody hereabouts watches that show, so we were all calling one another, hoping to help out. My whole party line was gabbing at once! Anyway, we'd be obliged if you'd let us do this, and you might as well say yes because all that stuff's gonna be there anyhow. Couldn't stop it now if I wanted to."

Kara was too overcome to speak, so it fell to Rye to step forward and offer his hand one more time, saying, "Mr. Tenery, we can't thank you enough, all of you. We never dreamed folks would take our troubles to heart like this."

"Hell, son, we all figure we've got some stake in this, too. Some of us won't be tending our own stock anymore, but we can still see that the real lifeblood of the ranching business don't go the way of the family farm. Least we'll know that you young pair will be keeping on down in the Chama Valley."

Kara sent Rye a loaded look, which he deflected neatly. "We'll make this drive, Mr. Tenery, I swear. We'll make it on time with all the cattle we need to meet the terms of the will, whatever it takes."

The old man grinned. "Glory be," he said, "if I was a decade or two younger, I'd saddle me a horse and go with you!"

Rye chuckled, but something caught Kara's eye. She pointed past Hud Tenery out the window at two men in full gear galloping their horses right down the center of what passed for Main Street toward them. Hud glanced over his shoulder.

"That'd be Wesley Randal and Charlie Choate, good cowboys

both, though Wes, he sells insurance now and Charlie—that'd be the one with the beard—he's a trucker." He sent Rye a confidential look, adding, "Charlie's wife, she left him, took the kids and went back to Idaho, so he drives a run between here and there to look in on the kids now and again." He shrugged. "Ain't a bad life for a single man. Wesley, now, he's got a pretty wife and two little girls cute as buttons. Twins. Named them both Elizabeth—calls one Beth and the other Betty. Can't tell 'em apart for nothin'."

Kara didn't know if he meant that their father couldn't tell them apart or if he, Tenery, couldn't, but she didn't suppose it mattered and was too bemused to ask.

"Are they coming here?" Rye asked, disbelief ringing in his voice.

Tenery looked at him. "Oh, yeah. Some fellow heard you say to that reporter yesterday that you was a couple hands short, so a bunch of the guys got together and drew straws to see who was gonna get to go and work for you."

"But, Mr. Tenery," Kara said, "we can't afford to pay them."

"Pay 'em!" he said in shock. "Why, honey, they're probably gonna offer to pay you!"

"Pay—" Kara choked at the notion. "B-but they can't do that! Why, it's hard, dirty work, sleeping on the ground, cold showers."

"Food's good," Rye mumbled hopefully.

"No TV," Kara went on. "Riding all day. It rains, too. Man, I hate it when it rains!"

"There's music," Rye said. "Dean even wears earphones on horseback."

"Bugs and vermin." Kara shuddered. "And you won't believe how stuff wears out!"

"Still, there's something to be said for sitting around a campfire at night," Rye pointed out. "And we could post extra guards."

"Guard duty!" Kara said, rolling her eyes. "It's boring and it's cold and all you want to do is sleep, even if it is on the ground." She shook her head and bit her lip. Rye had a pleading look about him. She thought what it would mean to have extra hands to share the work. "Well, I couldn't possibly charge them," she said flatly. "It wouldn't be—"

Rye put his hand over her mouth, explaining, "But we can darn sure feed them. You tell them, would you, Mr. Tenery? Tell them just how it is, and if they still want to go, well—"

Kara pulled his hand from her mouth and exclaimed, "We'll take them!"

Tenery chuckled and rubbed his hands together. "I'd go myself, I purely would! But I wouldn't be no help to you." He held out gnarled hands, adding, "Arthritis." Shaking his head, he went out to greet the two cowboys riding up. Their eagerness showed on their faces as they dismounted.

"I can't believe this!" Rye said, watching the conversation progress. He shook the paper still in his hand at the cowboys listening intently to Hud Tenery's explanation of what they could expect. "Honey, do you know what this means?"

"It means we're going to make it," she said excitedly. "God bless them all, we are going to make it!"

He swept her up into his arms and threw back his head, laughing. "Lady, you are magic! Pure magic!" Eyes sparkling, he kissed her hard on the mouth. Then he sobered. "You didn't really think we'd fail before now, did you?"

"Not a bit of it," she told him, looking straight into his eyes. "You're a winner, Rye Wagner. I knew that about you the very first time I laid eyes on you, and that you're arrogant as all get-out." He just grinned and kissed her again.

"I swear," Rye said into the telephone, "it was like something out of an old Western. These two come riding up through the middle of town all geared out for the trail. I half expected six-guns slung low on the hip, and actually, one of them—that'd be Charlie Choate—is packing a rifle. I assured him there wouldn't be any call to use it, but you never know."

"We can sure use the help, though," Pogo said. Then he paused and added, "Hey, Rye, you don't think there's anything suspicious about this, do you? I mean, they couldn't have been set on us or anything?"

The thought had occurred, but Rye had satisfied himself that it wasn't so. "They drew straws for the jobs, Pogo. Hud Tenery held them in his own fist while they drew. I think we just sort of captured their imaginations, you know?"

"Hell, Rye, why do you think I'm here? When do you suppose any of us will ever have an opportunity to experience something like this again?"

"I suppose. But you haven't had the organizing or the worry of it."

"It's a big job, for sure," Pogo allowed, "but you're a big man, Rye. You and Kara have done right fine together. Seems like you two make a pretty good team."

Rye clamped his jaws shut. They made a good team, all right. When it came to sex or work, they were better than just good together, but beyond that, he just didn't know. Actually, he did know. He knew that beyond those two things, he'd find some way to screw it up. Just the suggestion that he and Kara ought to be a permanent thing lifted the hair on the back of his neck and brought the very real urge to run fast in the opposite direction. And at the same time the idea of ending it was eating him alive.

"Rye? Rye, are you there?"

"Yeah, I'm here, but you know what, you've got work to do, so I won't keep you. I just wanted you to know that Charlie and Wes will be joining you, and that you're to put them to work, and also that it'll be tomorrow afternoon before Kara and I can catch up to you. Something about connectors. Anyway, we'll spend one more night here and catch up with you by lunch tomorrow. Anything comes up, you know how to reach us."

"Sure enough, boss. Take it easy. You two deserve a break."

"See you tomorrow."

He pushed the Off button on the phone and flipped it closed. One more night. Tomorrow night they would spend at the ranch south of Durango, and after that, Chance would be with them again. One more night. Just one. He felt an odd pain in the vicinity of his chest, a tightness that made him want to cough and pound a fist against his breastbone. Kara bumped open the door with her hip and came inside, carrying two large containers of fountain drinks.

"This cola is so good," she said, sipping from one straw. Then she stopped and looked at the hand he'd unwittingly pressed against the center of his chest. "What's the matter, hon? Something wrong?"

He dropped his hand. "Oh, no. Pogo's really pleased about

the new guys, especially since we'll be here one more night. I told him we'd be in the saddle by tomorrow afternoon. If we could afford to pull another hand away from the drive right now, I'd have someone come get us. With two new men we could always send somebody back for the motor home.''

''Unfortunately, that's not an option. Guess we could have somebody come tonight after the herd's bedded down, but I know they'll all be tired, and we should be back with them before lunch tomorrow, anyway.'' She slipped up onto the corner of the desk. Leaning forward, she placed his drink in front of him. ''I should've stayed with them. You could've handled this alone.''

''Glad you didn't,'' he said softly.

She smiled. ''Me, too. Tomorrow night we'll be at your family's ranch.''

He couldn't quite look her. ''Yeah.''

She straightened and sipped her cola. ''So tell me about it, your folks' ranch, I mean.''

He reached for his drink, sucked down several gulps so cold they hurt and launched into a detailed description, beginning with the ranch's location south of the city of Durango. ''It's not in the mountains, but they're there, you know, regal and beautiful, a perfect backdrop. Then there's the Animas River to the west. It moves, that river, sometimes like gangbusters. Fishing's great. Pasture's real good, too. They have to do some haying in winter, but not so much as you'd think, you know?''

''Sounds kind of like Chama, but without the mountains. Summers are great, really green and rich. And the winters are cold, plenty of snow, that sort of thing, but not so bad as around here. I love it.''

Rye nodded. ''Sounds like home.''

''What about the house?'' she asked.

''Big old two-story thing. Dad built the original ground floor himself. Then later they had the upstairs added on. Mom has this thing about green on white, so they put on white siding a few years ago, and the shingles and shutters are all green.'' He went on to describe the deep front porch that was stacked with cordwood in the winter and the red rock fireplace, one in the living room, one in the master bedroom, which was habitually the coldest room in the house. He talked about his mother's big, homey kitchen and how hard it was getting for her to manage with her arthritis so bad. "My brother's wife, Kay, was a real help to her," he said.

Kara was surprised. "I didn't know Jess was married."

"She died. It was a freak accident. They went out for a late dinner one summer evening to this place out on the mountain road, and a storm came rolling down on them. Thunder and lightning, sheets of rain. It was real intense, lasted an hour or more. Lightning struck a transmitter, but nobody minded too much. They just lit the candles on the tables, and that made it more romantic. They were the first ones to leave, and Kay took her shoes off because, she said, the ground was wet and she didn't want to ruin them. Jess always said it was more that she couldn't resist a good mud puddle. He offered to carry her, but she wanted to walk. He was wearing boots with rubber soles himself. Anyway, it was dark out, so they couldn't see.... They just didn't know that lines were down all over the parking lot. She stepped barefoot into a little bitty puddle, and a jolt of electricity knocked her about twenty feet. They said she died instantly. Jess got a good shock himself when he went down on his knees to try to help her, but it was dryer there, so that and the rubber soles on his boots saved him. Ambulance driver told me that he had to pry their hands apart, though. Jess had grabbed her, and then he either couldn't or wouldn't let go again."

Kara's eyes were full of tears, though he'd told the story in the frank, unemotional way he'd learned to long ago. She swallowed hard and took a deep breath. "When was that?"

"Eight, nine, no, by golly, I guess it's ten years ago next summer now. I was twenty-three. So she would've been twenty-five, and Jesse was twenty-eight."

"And he never remarried."

He shook his head. "Naw, guess he didn't have the heart for it after that. There's a woman in Durango, I understand, but Jess is real discreet. Must not be very serious. He's been seeing her four or five years, I'm told."

"And you've never met her?"

He shook his head. "Nor the folks, either, and if it was serious, you can bet she'd have been introduced to Mom by now. Besides, he occasionally dates, not too often, but occasionally. He says at his age they're all too young or divorced and needing help with another man's kids. Not that he wouldn't make a good father or that he'd object to a ready-made family if there wasn't another man in the picture somewhere. He likes to take a hand with Champ now and again, and I'm glad to let him. It's hard, raisin' a kid on your own.''

Kara sighed. "Life gets awful complicated, doesn't it?"

Rye nodded. "Yeah. Even for Jesse, and he's a real uncomplicated sort of guy.''

"You're not," Kara said matter-of-factly.

"Guess not," he admitted. "Most of the time, *I* can't even figure me out. You'd think brothers would be more alike.''

"Just look at my dad and Uncle Smitty, though," she said. "They had even less in common than you and Jesse. You'd think they'd been raised in different households, in different parts of the country, even. Smitty grew up on the Utah spread same as Daddy, but he has no feeling for the life at all, and Dad, well, you couldn't separate him from it. It was part of him.''

"Like you," Rye said.

"Like me.''

She held his gaze for a long time, and he knew that she was telling him this was something strong they had in common, but there remained something stronger still, something that made him aware of his own body in ways he'd never been aware before, something that made him crave the feel of her, made him long to have her next to him. It scared him. He didn't want this need that she'd awakened in him. And he had Champ to consider. His son always would come first. He couldn't let her become so important to him that he'd risk Champ's emotional well-being, too. How the hell was he supposed to stop these feelings, though? He hadn't found any way yet. But he would, even if it meant just digging down and enduring. He'd endured worse, after all.

Hadn't he?

Chapter Thirteen

She had the feeling that he was trying to make it last, trying to store up memories to hold them through the worst of what was coming. Already she could feel him steeling himself to walk away, to endure the regrets and recriminations with which he would heap himself when it ended. She couldn't help him. She wanted to. Perversely, she wanted to make it easier for him to walk away from her, but only because she didn't want him to hurt, didn't want to add to the well of pain that he so carefully tended inside of him, because she loved him. In the end, it all came down to that simple fact. She loved Ryeland Wagner, loved him with a fullness and completeness at which she could only marvel. The pity of it was that for Rye it wasn't enough.

She thought sometimes that she could hate Di'wana Wagner.

But not tonight. Tonight was about squeezing the most out of every moment they had left.

They borrowed a radio from the mechanic and tuned in the local station, amused and amazed to find that the trail drive was a favorite subject for comment by the listeners who called in to request songs and dedications. The only spot in the motor home big enough to dance in was the space meant as a kitchen, and even there they could only hold one another and sway to the music, shuffling their feet in a tight, never-ending circle. The fact that they did it naked, wet from a long, hot shower together in the claustrophobically small bath, more than made up for the lack of ambience. Who needed ambience when there was so much slick, wet skin on bodies that fitted so nicely together? Who needed room when closeness proved so rewarding?

They danced until their bodies dried and then until the little puddles of water that dripped on the floor dried, as well. When Kara could no longer deny the necessity of combing through her damp hair, they went on to another, altogether surprising form of stimulation. She wouldn't have believed that having her hair slowly and gently brushed by a naked man cradling her between his thighs could be so blazingly erotic. Somehow her hair seemed to get longer by the yard as he stroked surely and rhythmically through it, and she felt every glide of the brush throughout her whole body until even her bones seemed to crackle with electricity. When at last he dropped the brush to the sofa and pulled her back against his chest, sliding his hands around to cup and lift her breasts, she was near to shattering, every nerve ending hypersensitive, and yet, at the very same time, she felt a languid contentment completely at odds with the situation.

She laid her head back on his shoulder and closed her eyes, giving herself up to the incredible sensations wrought by his hands on her body. They never moved from her breasts, never faltered or hesitated in their skillful, gentle ministrations. She reveled in the gradual swelling, the pooling of heat, the correlating tautness and melting in parts of her body as yet untouched. Still, the climax caught her by surprise. One moment she was arching her back, instinctively begging for more, and the next she was falling off a cliff somewhere, darkness shattering with wave upon wave of explosive color.

She was aware of moving to the bedroom, of where his hands went and what his mouth did. She devoted herself to repaying every sensation received with one given, and yet she never quite recovered herself. From that first moment of explosion onward he kept her spinning, tumbling, soaring, plummeting. Time after time he led her to the edge and urged her, pushed her, flung her over it. She wept at the sweetness, screamed in joyful turmoil, clawed and clung and sobbed and sighed, and with every touch, every whisper, every glance and movement, she loved him more, until her whole being expanded with it, grew and changed and reinvented itself. She was stronger, deeper, wiser, more selfless. Complete.

She loved completely, and nothing could ever take that away. No pain, no separation, no thought, no word, no deed could render completion less. The agonized looks that occasionally flickered across his face to be quickly replaced by a calm, indulgent smile told her that she could not truly spare him. Rye's emotional turmoil was his own product, the result, yes, of past betrayal but also of present determination not to allow himself to truly love again. She grieved for him, but did not try to tell herself that she could change him. How could she love him and want him different? Instead, she tried to trust that the man she loved would prove singularly unable to let real love pass him by. And if he did not? Well, she would love him still, unreservedly, even unconditionally. She didn't know how to love any other way.

They were on the road earlier than they had expected. Also unexpected was the mechanic's refusal to accept payment for his labor. They got out for the price of the parts. Rye marveled. Even burdened with the overwhelming tasks of logistics and organization, a part of him had relished the notion of the drive, and he had recognized the same in his friends, but he had somehow gotten lost in the gritty, day-to-day battle to pull this thing off. The romance of the trail ride, in effect, had become his reality, so much so that he had almost forgotten that the romance was real. It did him good to see that so many others had gotten caught up in it with him. Still, it continued to amaze him.

When they passed the Hetherton Sales Barn outside Manco and saw that a huge banner had been draped across the front wishing them good luck and Godspeed, he found himself turning around and going back. The moment the motor home rolled into the parking lot, a man came out of a small door marked Office and hurried to intercept them. Rye brought the vehicle to a halt and popped open the door. The large, pleasant-looking, middle-aged man stepped up inside.

"Sorry, folks, they're already gone." He pointed out the windshield. "They drove 'em down that slope there and around that point, heading southeast. Best chance of catching sight of them again is around Hesperus off 140."

"Music to my ears," Rye said, grinning and sticking out his hand as he left the driver's seat. Kara came forward, too, smiling. "I'm Ryeland Wagner, and this is Kara Detmeyer. You must be Al Hetherton."

Hetherton grinned and grabbed hold of Rye's hand, pumping it enthusiastically. He nodded at Kara. "Ma'am. Wagner. Gosh, it's good to meet you two. That's quite an operation you got going there."

"I want to thank you for allowing us use of your pens," Rye said, "and for your obvious support."

"My pleasure, sir. Honest to God, I was tickled to do it."

"Everyone's been so good to us," Kara said, positively glowing. She'd been looking like that all morning now, and it unnerved Rye a bit. Last night was the end, didn't she know that?

"Not everyone," Hetherton said, shaking his head, "not from what I hear." He switched his gaze to Rye. "You got any idea who's trying to stop you?"

Rye didn't know quite what to say to that. "We're not ready to level charges, if that's what you mean."

"But you got an idea," Hetherton surmised.

Kara said smoothly, "We're not going to worry about that, frankly. We're just going to concentrate on getting home on time. Once we're there, it won't matter anymore."

Rye could see that she'd made up her mind about this. Even if it was her oily cousin, and even though she didn't mean to let him win, she didn't mean to make him pay, either. Well, Rye wasn't so charitable. Whoever was doing this to Kara was not going to escape responsibility. Rye would make it his personal mission to see to it. But Kara didn't need to know that.

"We have to be on our way, Mr. Hetherton," he said. "We've spent too much time away from the herd as it is, but we did want to say thanks."

"Sure, sure. Glad you stopped by. Give my best to your mother, Miss Detmeyer. She treated me to some mighty fine cooking."

Kara laughed. "Yes, she's becoming quite famous for that."

"You take care now. So long." He made to step down to the ground, but Rye halted him with an uplifted hand.

"Uh, you seemed to think before that we were—oh, I don't know—casual observers, maybe spectators, looking for the drive. Have you had some of that this morning?"

"Some?" Al Hetherton chortled. "Son, you wouldn't believe what's been going on around here. This parking lot was full this morning when your boys moved those beeves out, and I must say, they put on quite a show. There was cheering when that Pogo fellow gave the go-ahead. Folks been stopping by ever since, hoping to get a bead on 'em. I swear, you could sell tickets."

Rye shook his head, grinning wide. "I never dreamed we'd catch the fancy of so many folks."

"Well, this being the last day—"

"The last day?" Kara echoed.

"That's what the news is saying. Apparently nobody will be allowed to follow you onto the reservation."

Rye looked at Kara, then back to Hetherton. "Where'd they get that information?"

Hetherton shrugged. "Guess somebody talked to the Indians."

Rye didn't like the sound of that. What if the media attention worked against them with the tribal government? But that was another worry he'd keep to himself for the moment. "Yeah, that must be it. Well, thanks again, Mr. Hetherton. You have a good day."

Hetherton stepped off the vehicle backward. Rye reclaimed his seat and put the transmission in gear before giving Hetherton a final wave and closing the door. Once on the road again, Kara took out the flip phone and called the crew to verify the rendezvous near Hesperus. Her mother, Borden Harris, Dean and George were already on site and preparing lunch. They were not, as her mother put it, alone.

"You mean you have company?"

"Sugar, just wait until you get here."

Thankfully, they didn't have to wait too long. Sedately walking cattle took hours to cross rough terrain; vehicles required minutes to travel smooth roads. Those smooth roads were now clogged with uncustomary traffic, however, and as they drew nearer the rendezvous point, it became obvious where all that traffic was going. The narrow road was dangerously lined with parked cars around which the browning grass had been trampled. An outcropping of rock on one side of the roadway hid the bowl-like pasture beyond from view, but as soon as they passed it, they both gasped. The pasture was teeming with vehicles and people. There would hardly be room for the cattle.

"Dear heaven!" Kara gasped.

"I do not believe this." It was becoming his pet phrase. He shook his head and began looking for a way to get to the ring of vehicles that were their own. It wasn't possible. Finally, in sheer desperation, they crowded the motor home onto a spot of grass and got out to begin weaving their way to the temporary campsite. Dayna met them halfway there.

"Rye, you've got to do something! It's chaos. They only want to watch, but it's getting out of hand. I'm afraid the police will come!"

"Maybe they should," Rye said worriedly. He tugged on his earlobe, then said suddenly, "Let's find Dean."

It didn't take long to accomplish that feat. Prying him away from a gaggle of curious onlookers was something else.

"If this don't beat all," Dean said, finally making a polite escape. He looked harried and nervous. "What're we gonna do with 'em all?"

"That's what I want to talk to you about. I need a telephone number."

"What's that?"

"Nonemergency number for the local police authority. We've got to have some help out here."

Dean nodded, and said, "We're getting to be regulars with the law dogs. I'll set up the Internet link."

Rye turned to Kara. "Honey, see if your mom needs help getting lunch together, and tell George to meet me at the remuda. We're going to mount up and take a stab at crowd control."

Nodding, she hurried off. George showed up about the time Rye slung his saddle onto the back of the big bay known as Bets. "Hey, pard, how's it been?"

"Wild," George said. "Dean'll be ready for you in another minute or two."

Rye bent and grasped the girth. "I'll ride over as soon as I get this big boy saddled. Pick a fresh mount. I'm going to need your help.''

George hurried to the back of the truck where their tack was stowed and picked up his own saddle, which was handily near the end. Rye finished and mounted up, telling George to join him and Dean as soon as he was ready. Then he rode into the center of the vehicle ring, where Dean was plunking away on the computer balanced atop his knees.

''Okay, okay, here's the number I think you're going to need.''

Rye flipped out the cellular phone and punched in the numbers as Dean read them off to him. A woman answered on the third ring. Rye explained precisely and clearly who and where he was and had the distinct feeling that she recognized his name right off. He asked to speak with the senior officer and was informed that he was doing so. He wasted no time describing the situation.

''We're amazed and appreciative, but I'm worried someone's going to get hurt when those cattle show up. I've got a buddy and myself mounted, and I was figuring to ride out and tell these folks, polite as I can, to get back, but there's the matter of traffic, too. I mean, it's just a circus out here, and I've got three hundred head of cattle on the way, not to mention riders.'' He was much relieved when Chief Cantu promised to get right out there with a couple of volunteers. Meanwhile, he had her permission to push back the crowd. George had already shown up, having saddled a placid piebald. Rye turned off the phone and looked to Dean. ''Good work, bud. Now get on a horse and come help us move these people before they get trampled.''

''Will do.''

Rye turned his horse toward the women who were working apace. ''Ladies, we're going to try to quell a little chaos. When I see Bord, I'll send him over to help you get lunch together.''

''Thanks, Rye,'' Dayna called, too busy to do more than glance in his direction. Kara, however, took the time to stop and look up into his face. She said nothing, but he felt jolted just the same. She was changed somehow. It was as if that serenity had taken root in her. She was in charge, fully composed, while he himself felt fractured and confused. It irritated him, though he wasn't quite sure why. Shouldn't she be sad or something? He was going to have to explain to her again that Durango was the end of it, and he resented having to do it. He jerked away and walked his horse through the maze of vehicles parked around their makeshift camp.

People were, thankfully, cooperative. He knew from experience that a man on horseback somehow represented authority to those on foot, and when he began explaining that they were putting themselves in danger, they willingly withdrew back up the slope toward the rocky outcropping.

Bord found him, along with a fellow so skinny that he looked like a stick figure wearing a poorly fitted cowboy hat. "Hey, Rye, this fellow here wants a word with you."

"Make it quick. I've got stock coming."

"Yassir," the man drawled, "that's what I was thinking. You got nowhere to pen 'em, though, and your fellers are s'posed to eat their lunch here. 'At right?"

"Right."

"So, see, I got to thinkin' on your problem, an' I can help."

Rye tamped down his impatience and leaned a forearm on the saddle horn. "You ever ridden herd on a bunch of cows used to moving?"

The man shook his head. "Naw. But, me and the boys used to meet out on the range on a Sunday afternoon and rope in a corral made of cars."

"Cars!"

"We'd measure off and pull our trucks 'round the perimeter, see. We'd even make a chute that way and use a rope barrier as a gate."

Rye looked around him at the vehicles crammed into such a small space, then back at the stick man. "Cowboy, you may be a genius."

The fellow tipped back his hat and grinned, displaying tobacco-stained teeth. "My thinker works right fine, if I do say so m'self."

Rye chuckled. "The thing is, though, somebody's car might get dented."

"Never happened but once or twice on us," he said. "Feller fell off his horse onto the hood of a car one time. Cows just naturally shy away from barriers. Tell you what, though, we'll just ask for volunteers with old junkers like me."

Rye pushed back his hat. "What's your name, mister?"

"Ellis Jenkins."

"Think you can ramrod this operation for me, Ellis?"

The skinny cowboy hitched up his jeans. "No problem."

"I can't promise you anything but a damned fine lunch."

Jenkins padded his concave middle. "You got yourself a deal, but I'm warning you, I can eat my own weight at a sitting."

Rye figured that couldn't be too bad. After all, how much did bones weigh? "Saddle him a horse, Bord, then see what you can do to help the women. Oh, and be sure to tell them we'll be one more for lunch."

Borden and Ellis trotted off in the direction of the remuda. Rye turned his horse and began calling out to people to move on back. Within half an hour, Chief Julia Cantu, two volunteer policemen and a convenience store arrived. An enterprising sort, the local grocer had quickly loaded a pickup truck with iced drinks and snacks.

"I didn't imagine you'd want to feed them," Chief Cantu explained in her lilting Spanish accent. She was a surprisingly young, attractive woman with flashing black eyes.

"No, ma'am."

She nodded toward the meadow below where a handful of autos were already parked. "Those the vehicles you want moved?"

Rye grinned and explained what was going on. Chief Cantu removed her beige cowboy hat, revealing a wealth of rich brown hair twisted up on top of her head. "Looks like you've got everything under control."

"It's the aftermath that concerns me," Rye told her. "Once everybody starts pulling out of here, it's going to be a royal traffic jam."

Cantu sighed. "Well, guess the boys and I will just have to hang around until the show's over."

"In that case," Rye said, "I insist on giving you lunch, though the cook may shoot me when I tell her."

Julia Cantu laughed. "As long as I don't have to arrest him until after lunch."

"Her," Rye said, "and she's some cook, let me tell you. Walk on over with me. Maybe the sight of that badge will make her keep her hands off the firearms." He swung down off the horse and together they walked over to the noon camp.

Dayna was frying sweet-potato cubes, while Kara grilled sourdough bread and Bord Harris sliced roast beef. Rye made the introductions, particularly noting the way Kara's eyes flared slightly at the sight of Julia Cantu's well-filled uniform. Rye couldn't help a surge of satisfaction.

Despite his dire predictions, Dayna took the addition of three more mouths to feed in stride. "Just don't think I can manage that crowd out there."

"Actually," Julia said, "I brought a vendor with me." She craned her neck and twisted around, trying to get a view of the goody truck.

"Looks like he's doing land-office business," Rye said, straining upward to look over the vehicles parked slightly downslope around them.

Julia Cantu sighed. "Wish I was tall. The hat helps, but not much, especially when I have to haul in some drunk, lard-belly, chauvinist-type."

Rye was wondering how long it would be before the herd arrived. He resisted the impulse to check his watch, figuring it would be rude. "That must be a challenge for you," he said, trying to sound interested.

She shrugged. "Doesn't happen often, fortunately."

He nodded and said, "Well, I'd better see how that car corral is coming."

Kara turned from her work, then. "Bord told us about Ellis Jenkins and his idea. Says he's from Texas, west of the Pecos. Thank him for me."

"You can thank him yourself at lunch," Rye said.

She nodded and turned away again, looking a little hurt. Well, she was finally facing the facts, he told himself. So why wasn't he relieved? He resisted the urge to walk over and slide an arm around her waist, giving her a squeeze. Instead, he turned toward the horse he'd tethered to the farrier's wagon. Suddenly Dean rode in at a gallop, hauling up so short that his horse gave a little hop.

"Holy—"

"Rye, come quick. It's George."

"What happened?"

"Saddle came off! Bad spill!"

Rye jerked forward again, yanking free the tether and vaulting into the saddle as Julia Cantu cried, "Wait for me!"

He didn't take time to think about it, just kicked one foot free of the stirrup and leaned down a hand. She grabbed it and climbed aboard. They were moving before she got settled, so she threw an arm around his waist. They were there within seconds. George lay on the ground, a crowd of people around him. Someone had his horse by the bridle, and several people were crouched down around the saddle. Someone else reached for Rye's horse, leaving Rye free to leap down from the saddle and shove his way to George, Chief Julia Cantu at his back.

"Nobody touch that saddle!" Cantu yelled.

Rye went down on one knee beside George, who was struggling to sit up and moaning.

"Whoa, there! Let's get a look at you before you go moving around."

"I'm all right," George groaned. "It's just my arm."

Rye saw a small patch of blood on his sleeve but chose to ignore it for the moment, running his hands over George's legs and ribs first. People were talking.

"One of the volunteer cops went for a medical kit."

"He was knocked out for a minute or so."

"Saddle just fell off, like it came apart."

"Somebody ought to call an ambulance."

Rye fished out the flip phone and handed it off without even bothering to see into whose hands he was putting it. "I'll call the local doc first," Julia Cantu said. "He can get here a lot faster than the ambulance out of Durango."

"Do it," Rye said, and rammed a hand into a pocket, pulling out his small, well-used pocket knife. He flicked open the blade and reached for George's sleeve. "Step back everybody. George, old buddy, this has gotta come off."

George licked his lips and nodded. Rye carefully inserted the tip of the blade into the heavy fabric of the shirt and slid it upward through the cuff and all the way to the shoulder seam. George hissed in his breath but made no other sound. He looked over the white tip of the bone sticking out of his arm with almost detached interest. Other people made sounds of disgust or sympathy. Rye heard Julia Cantu say to someone on the phone, "Compound fracture."

The volunteer returned then, hauling a med kit with both hands. Rye waved people out of the way. The guy was red in the face from lugging that enormous kit. He dropped down beside George and opened up the metal box. "Nasty break you got there, cowboy. How you feeling otherwise?"

"I'll live."

"Doc says to check for shock," Julia announced.

The deputy was looking under George's eyelids. "Pupils are normal." He felt for George's pulse.

"Any abdominal or back pain?"

George shook his head. "Naw, I landed on my head and elbow."

"Pulse is good." The deputy took out a stethoscope and a blood pressure cuff.

"What happened, George?" Rye asked.

"I don't know. Some kids were chasing around the edge of the crowd and I was going over to warn them not to do that when the cattle started into the valley, but I never got there. Saddle seemed to just let go."

Julia Cantu laid a hand on Rye's shoulder and handed back his phone, saying, "Doc's calling the ambulance himself. He's on the way." The deputy was piling pads of gauze over the wound to keep it clean. "Let's take a look at that saddle," she said to Rye.

Rye nodded and patted George's shoulder. "You just lie there." Rye stood and let Cantu lead him toward the saddle. A group of men were crouched down beside it, talking softly among themselves. As they drew near, one of them looked up and said apologetically, "We turned it over, ma'am, before you got here."

Julia went down on her knees. The girth, composed of several rows of soft, tightly braided cotton cording, lay on the ground, telling an eloquent story. Julia Cantu looked at Rye. He didn't need her to say that it had been cut. The slice had been made straight across on the underside, almost all the way through, leaving the weakened strands to fray and eventually come apart.

"Your saboteur," Cantu said flatly.

Rye grit his teeth. "I want a word with my wrangler."

"Fine," Cantu said. "Soon as I'm done with him. Where is he?"

"Helping make lunch."

"You stay with your man for now," she told him. "I tend to do better on my own." She batted her thick black eyelashes at him, saying, "After all, who would be intimidated by little old me?"

One of the men listening snickered. Cantu cut him a deadly glance. "Sorry, Chief," he said, "but nobody around here believes that anymore."

"He's not from around here," Cantu reminded him coolly.

Someone else said, "Doc's coming."

Rye turned and spotted a young, balding, athletically fit man making his way through the crowd, the ubiquitous black bag in tow.

"You stay with your friend," Cantu said again. "We'll chat after."

Rye agreed reluctantly and went back to George. The doctor shook Rye's hand briefly then got down to business, doing again all the things the deputy had done while calmly questioning George. "The ambulance is on its way," he said finally. "We'll want an X ray of that break before we set it." He lifted away the gauze pads. "Don't think it'll require surgery, but I'll know more later. Right now, I just want to make you comfortable before we attempt to move you." He questioned George about allergies to medications and removed a syringe from his black bag. When he'd injected George in the upper arm, he again covered the wound and requested an isolation board, which the deputy already had waiting.

"They're coming!" somebody shouted.

Rye looked up. "The herd or the ambulance?"

"Both!"

At almost that same moment, he heard the wail of an ambulance in the distance and the low bawling of a cow. Great, that's all he needed. "George, I've got to ride out and warn the herd."

George smiled. "Don't worry 'bout me." Obviously he was feeling better already.

"We'll be taking him in to the hospital," the doctor said. "He'll be there at least four or five hours, but I don't think he'll have to stay the night."

"I'll get there soon as I can," Rye told George.

"Don't worry 'bout me," George said again, seeming a little drunk.

Rye smiled. "Okay, buddy. Take it easy."

"Don't worry 'bout me," George said once more, and then he added with something very near a giggle, "Wanda's gonna be happy to have me home early anyhow."

Rye went off feeling both relief and slow, intense rage. He didn't have much time to dwell on this latest catastrophe, however, with everything happening at once like this. He had all he could do for the whole afternoon, and he did it at top speed, wanting to get the herd onto his family's ranch as quickly as possible so he could see his son and get to the hospital for George.

Cantu questioned Bord Harris and several others, but nothing definite came of it. George had both put away his gear the night before and saddled his own horse today, but Bord admitted checking everything out before he turned in for the night. The other guys recalled George putting away his saddle, and one or two of them had seen Bord checking everything over, but there was nothing suspicious about that as he was the wrangler. No one had seen anything else that might shed light on the situation. All had seemed quiet and normal the evening before. Other than having two extra pairs of hands and an audience when they'd headed out that morning, nothing out of the ordinary had taken place at all. Rye wanted to beat someone until he told all, clearing up every nagging doubt and suspicion, but he had no object for his rage.

So instead, he drove the herd and the entire crew harder than he ever had before. As a result they still had plenty of daylight left when they met Jess at the gate on the western edge of the Wagner property. As the crow flew, the distance between the noon camp and the Wagner ranch was negligible, but traveling over open country was another story. It had been necessary to swing the herd around the worst of the rough, rocky outcroppings that comprised the foothills of the Rockies, adding miles to the trip. Jess was clearly disturbed by the latest news, but he maintained that affable, disarming manner of his, making Rye feel all the more like a grouchy bear roused too early from an uneasy hibernation.

Since they expected to spend one, maybe two days here, the

cattle were taken to a lush, forty-acre pasture near the house. Jess had brought in water troughs and filled them. Rye ordered the cattle hayed in an effort to save as much of the dry, brittle fall grass as possible and rode off to greet his parents, who had driven the half mile or so from the house.

He dismounted, feeling the pull in his groin after only two and a half days out of the saddle, and led the horse forward, opening his arms. His parents rushed forward. "Mom! Dad!"

"You're too thin, Rye!" were his mother's first words as she hugged him. He just laughed.

"I have it on good authority there were no fat cowboys on the trail. How are you?"

His petite mother's slate gray hair and gnarled hands told their own story. His dad didn't look much different than he had eight months ago, still hale and hearty, but his sweet mother was aging rapidly. It brought a lump to Rye's throat. Sarah Wagner denied that her arthritis had significantly worsened, but the troubled look in Haney's indulgent eye put the lie to it.

"I been telling her to go to Denver to the arthritis clinic there, but she don't pay me no more mind than she ever did," he complained good-naturedly.

"And who would take care of you two?" Sarah demanded. It was obviously an old argument.

"I can cook," Jesse said defensively.

Sarah snorted at that, saying to Rye, "He can cook anything that comes in a can."

Rye chuckled. "Now don't get me in the middle of this. I've got all the battle I can handle at the moment." Seeing his mother's troubled eyes, he immediately softened that by asking, "Where's Champ? I know you've been spoiling him rotten and he's loved every minute of it, but I sure have missed him."

That brought nothing but tense silence. Haney backed off and put his hands in his pockets, bowing his head. Sarah tightened the arm she still had wrapped about her younger son's waist but said nothing. It was Jesse who finally cleared his throat, took a deep breath and put the cap on the day.

"Champ is with his mother."

Chapter Fourteen

Kara leaned her forearms against the weathered wood that was the top rung of the fence that ran around the homey Wagner ranch house and inhaled the soft, cool morning air. "I understand what you're feeling, Rye. I really do. But I'm sure Jesse and your parents wouldn't have agreed to take Champ to the reservation if they didn't believe wholeheartedly that it was the best thing to do for everyone."

"The best thing!" he exclaimed, throwing up his hands, completely forgetting that he'd intended to do the same thing himself. "How can it be the best thing? He hates his mother! Even he knows what she is, what she did to us!"

"But she *is* his mother," Kara pointed out patiently. "You said yourself that he needs her, that he has to start learning to forgive and love her, to accept her love in return."

Rye scowled. "I didn't say that...exactly."

"But it's what you meant."

Rye muttered, "They should have consulted me first. It was my decision to make."

"Yes, it was, and you'd already made it, really, so why expend all this energy being angry now?"

"He's been out there with her for two days and two nights, Kara," Rye said hoarsely. "What if he wants to come home? What if he's thinking I abandoned him like she did? What if he's *more* angry instead of less?"

Kara held back a sigh, feeling wholly inadequate to help him with this but very much needing to, especially as both his brother and his mother had suggested that she give it a try. Neither of them had had much luck getting through to him last night. The evening had turned into outright hostility followed by simmering resentment. Rye had refused his family's invitation to spend the night in his old room, but neither had he come anywhere near her. She had lain awake late into the night, trying to reach out to him with her heart, only to find that his resentment had solidified by morning and was tinged now with the scent of fear. Suddenly she realized that he was most afraid of losing his son.

"Even if he is upset," Kara told him reasonably, "he won't blame you, Rye. You weren't even here when the matter arose."

"I'm his father, Kara," he retorted derisively, implying that she couldn't possibly know what Champ would think or do. "Of course he'll blame me."

Kara ignored the twinge of pain his tone produced, saying softly, "I'm not a parent, it's true, but I was a kid, Rye, just like everyone else, and I remember how I felt and what I thought. Champ can't be that different."

"Your mother didn't sleep with half of Arizona. Your parents didn't scream and yell every time they happened to be in the same room. Your father never threw you and your things into a truck and drove away while your mother screamed filthy names at him."

She winced. "No, the screaming matches in my family were generally between my father and his brother, and they sometimes didn't leave it at that. We had more than one family holiday ruined by bare-knuckled brawls. And then there would be these long, frozen silences after my mother tried to reason with my father. There are no perfect families, Rye. We all have to learn to deal with strife and disappointment. Just give Champ a little credit, will you? Seems to me he's a bright, sensitive boy. He'll listen, eventually, to whatever you have to say to help him understand why he needs to know his mother."

Rye lifted a hand to the back of his neck. The brim of his hat shadowed his eyes. "I hope so. But there's one other aspect of this that you haven't considered. If Champ has been less than receptive to his mother's overtures, then Di'wana just might be petty enough to try to get her father to influence the tribal council to deny us permission to cross the reservation."

He was right; she hadn't considered that, but then, her priorities seemed to have shifted somewhat. She filled her lungs with clean, shining air. "Well, if that happens we'll...we'll just have to think of something else."

"What else? We can't pay the fees set by the Navajos and the Utes."

"We'll go north and drop down through the Jicarilla Apache reservation."

"North? Are you nuts? Those mountains are vicious. They'll cost us time we don't have, that's if they don't swallow up the whole damned herd!"

"Then we'll fail," Kara said gently. "That's been a possibility from the beginning."

Rye was appalled. It showed clearly in every line of his posture, in the set of his mouth and the hands that rose slowly to plant themselves on either side of his slender hips.

Kara smiled apologetically. "I know," she told him, "but I do realize now that the ranch isn't everything. At any rate, we can't cross a bridge until we come to it, and I refuse to *anticipate* failure. It will have to be forced on me."

Rye seemed to ponder that, left hand tugging at his earlobe again.

Kara laughed softly. "You're going to wind up looking like those African tribesmen who stretch their earlobes so they hang down onto their shoulders. Only you're going to have one dangling lobe instead of two."

He actually smiled at that and dropped his hand. "Old habit."

"I noticed. Now then, do you think I could go with you to the reservation? I do have quite a large stake in this, as you've pointed out."

She could tell that he didn't want her to go, but he finally nodded. "Okay. We leave in fifteen minutes. I'm going to go borrow my brother's truck keys."

"I'll let Mom know and be sure Pogo hays the cattle."

Nodding again, he walked away. Kara turned and hung her

elbows on the top of the fence, watching him. He was the most
beautiful man. If only he would let go of his pain and allow
himself to trust again, if only he would allow himself to love
her, open himself to her love. She didn't say it would happen,
didn't promise herself the moon when she had already touched
the stars, but it couldn't hurt to hope. It was what came after
hope was gone that she dreaded.

The radio blared a rocking country tune that made Kara's head
ache and seemed to set Rye's nerves on edge, but she knew that
he wasn't going to turn down the volume. He kept the volume
cranked in order to prevent conversation, not that she had anything to say. She had come along strictly to get a look at
Di'wana, but she wasn't going to tell him that.

They drove southeast and then due south. Within forty minutes
they came to the first No Trespassing sign. Nearly an hour more
passed before they topped a low rise and descended again into
a leafy vale that held four small, rough buildings, each placed in
the corner of a low mud-wall square. Built of flat stones tightly
stacked and fitted together, each boasted a single door covered
with heavy, brightly colored rugs woven by hand into precise
geometric patterns. The roof of each perfectly square hut was
constructed of long, knobby tree branches, stripped of leaves and
fitted together as tightly as the stone walls they topped. The
knobby poles overhung the front of each house, creating a sheltered place to sit and watch the sun rise and descend. In the
center of the space created by the huts and wall stood a delicate-
looking shelter, open on all four sides and roofed with the
knobby poles. Beneath it sat a communal adobe oven and a fire
pit rimmed with rock. Mats and rugs were placed around the
perimeter, and the bare ground around them had been raked in
careful lines and patterns.

Kara knew that everything held spiritual significance for the
Chako, from the placement and shape of each hut to that of the
cooking center, the height of the enclosure wall and the patterns
raked into the ground and woven into the colorful mats and rugs.
The Chako believed that everything existent, what might roughly
be called the universe, consisted of four equally important and
strong elements: all life (animal and human), the skies, the earth,

and all death. Each element was ruled by myriads of capricious spirits varying in size, capabilities and personalities. In addition, they believed that life and death were doorways through which all temporal spirits moved into and out of numerous realities, some lovely and compelling, some hideous and torturous. Traditional Chako life was governed by the appeasement and/or cultivation of the spirits that controlled the elements of existence.

Around the residential square, a circle had been drawn with a chalky red powder. Rye drew the pickup to a halt outside the circle, turned down the radio and put the transmission in Park.

"Now what?" Kara asked after a few seconds.

"We wait," Rye said tersely.

Eventually a tall, stooped figure pushed aside the door covering and stepped outside. He paused beneath the overhang, made a sign with his hands, then came slowly forward. Despite the vivid white of his long hair, he was a strong man with broad shoulders, long limbs and a wide, solid body clothed in a long-sleeved tunic in a faded print, softly belted at the waist over baggy, dark-colored leggings. On his feet he wore tall, fringed moccasins laced all the way to the knee. He walked in long, rolling strides, coming to a stop just inside the rim of the red circle. He peered into the truck, seemed to satisfy himself on some question and nodded.

Raising a hand in greeting, he said, "Ryeland Wagner, welcome, and your woman as well."

Only then did Rye kill the engine and reach for the door handle. "Stay behind me," he said to Kara. "Be sure to step over the ceremonial circle in the same place I do, and don't speak unless you're spoken to. We can't afford to offend anyone."

She nodded, fully aware that the more traditional Chako were governed by a complex variety of social rules. Rye got out of the truck and stood across from the other man. Kara walked around the rear of the truck to stand directly behind him.

"Hello, Man Father," Rye said.

"Hello, Ryeland. Is this the woman who is rich in cows and owns a valley for them?"

"Yes, Man Father, it is. Her name is Kara."

"I have heard of you," Man Father said, without looking at her. "My grandson tells me you are more man than woman, but

I think he is mistaken. He is, after all, only a child without knowledge of the world or his mother's people."

Kara didn't know what to say to that, but Rye made a motion with his fingers as if to elicit something from her. She licked her lips and said the first thing that came into her head, "It's nice to meet you, Mr. Man Father." She winced at the *mister.* He merely nodded.

"Won't you come into the circle and sit in the shade?"

"Thank you," Rye said, stepping over the red circle. "What's the significance of this, Man Father?"

"Protection," Man Father answered succinctly.

Kara followed practically on Rye's heels. They were shown to low drumlike seats beneath the shelter on the front of the nearest hut. Kara noted with some bemusement that her seat was lower than those of the men. Man Father sat with his forearms balanced atop his knees and studied Rye pointedly. Rye sat impassively, his palms resting flat upon his thighs. Finally Man Father spoke again, but this time his words were the clipped, singsong of the Chako language. Immediately, a tall, slender Chako woman emerged from the house. A quick glance at Rye's twitching jaw muscles confirmed for Kara that this was Di'wana, and her heart dropped to her soles.

The woman was, to put it mildly, breathtaking. Her thick, blue-black hair hung almost to her waist, framing slender shoulders and a softly rounded face with full lips, a strong, straight nose and enormous, exotic eyes, brown-black and set in her head like almond-shaped onyx with the inside corners tilted slightly downward. The long-sleeved red tunic that she wore belted at an impossibly small waist over a full yellow and orange skirt did nothing to downplay the fullness of her breasts or the slender roundness of her hips. She wore the traditional moccasins laced to the knee beneath the ankle-length skirt, but Kara was certain that her legs were as long and shapely as the most successful fashion model's. No wonder Rye couldn't get over her! She was perfect.

Di'wana came forward, but no farther than Man Father's back. "Hello, Ryeland. You are well?"

He nodded tersely, never lifting his gaze higher than Man Father's face. Kara waited for him to ask for Champ, but he merely sat, his hands gripping his thighs hard enough to leave bruises. Finally Di'wana said, "I should introduce my husband to you," and with that she turned and hurried back to the door of the hut. Stepping back, she held aside the blanket covering the door. An extremely tall, broad man ducked through the opening and calmly walked across the packed dirt of the shelter floor and took a seat at Man Father's side. He studied Rye for a moment, completely ignoring Kara. Then he stuck out his hand.

Rye seemed momentarily taken aback, but then his hand came out and gripped the other man's. Di'wana glided forward and laid her hands on her husband's shoulders, introducing him by one of the complex fourteen or fifteen syllable words in which the Chako seemed to delight. His smile showed white against his round, flat face, and he said, "You may call me Crow Brother."

Rye withdrew his hand slowly. "Thank you."

"Is this your woman, Ryeland Wagner, this pretty blonde?"

Kara was surprised. He hadn't seemed to notice her at all and did not move his gaze to her now. Rye seemed to be giving his reply inordinate thought. Finally he said, "She is my partner."

Crow Brother nodded as if Rye had confirmed his assumption. "I owe you a debt, Ryeland Wagner. You took from us a willful girl with eyes for only the white man's world and returned to me a fit Chako wife to make a husband proud. I regret the pain it caused you, but I am grateful, nonetheless."

Kara could see that Rye was thoroughly stunned. His hands slid up and down his thighs, and though his gaze stayed glued to Crow Brother's face, Kara knew that his mind was whizzing from one thought to another without quite making sense of any of them. Abruptly he said sarcastically, "Glad I could be of service. If I'd known I was on-the-job-training, I'd have tried a little harder."

A small moaning sound made Kara look at Di'wana. She had a hand clamped over her mouth, but tears rolled down her face unimpeded. Kara surprised herself by wanting desperately to go to the other woman and put her arms around her. Crow Brother bowed his head, then looked up again. He looked at and spoke to Rye, but Kara had the feeling that he was speaking directly to her.

"She weeps not only for the pain she has caused but for the need to make her peace in this reality before the bad feelings can follow her to the next."

Kara was confused, but Rye jerked as if he'd been poked. His spine stiffened, and for the first time his gaze actually switched briefly to his ex-wife. He turned deliberately to Man Father, whose face was frozen implacably. Man Father didn't even return his gaze.

"H-has she seen a doctor?" Rye asked tightly, angrily. "A real doctor, I mean."

Something flickered behind Man Father's eyes. "Yes. Crow Brother would not let anything that might be of benefit go untried. I told him that it was no use, for I read the truth in the omens, but he is her husband and he treasures her."

Rye gulped at that. He was shaking. Kara lifted a hand and laid it against the small of his back. He began taking deep, quick breaths. "How... Wh-what..."

Crow Brother calmly said, "She has a cancer in her brain that cannot be touched. It is a problem, a weakness, among our people. You should have your son checked from time to time. It isn't that common, but—"

Suddenly Rye shot to his feet. "Where is Champ? Does he know?"

Kara felt her own tears spill over her cheeks. She didn't remember standing with him, but she still had her hand on his back. Di'wana came forward then, her gaze targeting Rye, pleading with him.

"He understands," she said breathlessly. Crow Brother rose and turned away, moving past her toward the door. Suddenly Rye gave a small cry and lifted his arms, and Di'wana flew into them. Kara heard sobbing and only belatedly realized that it was her own. She saw Rye hug Di'wana and wondered how she ought to feel about that. She wondered how Crow Brother felt about it, but when she found him, he was standing at the doorway, holding aside the covering, and Champ was standing before him in traditional Chako garb, watching his father hug his mother, and Kara found that she couldn't look at anyone else. Crow Brother gave the boy a little push, and Champ started forward with dragging feet, only to throw himself against his parents.

Rye sniffed and wiped his eyes on his shirtsleeves before pressing a hand to the boy's back. He looked down and ruffled his son's hair, saying, "I've missed you, cowpoke. You okay?"

Champ nodded against his father's leg and turned up his face. "Missed you, too," he said, "but I think I should stay here."

Before Rye could reply, Di'wana went down on her knees and placed her hands at Champ's waist. "Your place is with your father, especially now. I have always known it, and you must know it, too."

"But I want to stay with you," Champ said, winding his arms around her neck and hugging her.

"If you stay with me," Di'wana said, "you will make it difficult for me to go through to the next world. Your sadness will follow me into it. Your father needs you, and you need him. I want to know you are together."

Champ nodded reluctantly, lifted his head and wiped his eyes. He looked up at his father, explaining solemnly, "Man Father says dying is like going through a door to another world, and that she'll be happy there if nothing bad from this one follows her."

"Man Father is right," Rye said. He switched his gaze to Di'wana's face. "And now nothing bad will follow her."

Di'wana rose to her feet, subtly shifting Champ close to his father's side. For the first time she looked quite pointedly at Kara. She seemed to be trying to tell Kara something. Kara wasn't quite certain what it was, but she nodded, anyway. Crow Brother came forward then and slipped an arm around Di'wana's waist, pulling her back against him. She laid her head back against his shoulder, and a very visible contentment settled over her. She had made her peace with this world. Whatever unfinished business had been left between her and Rye, it was settled now. Kara could only hope that Rye would find that same peace soon.

Man Father had gotten to his feet. He bent and reached behind his seat, lifting a small bundle tied in Chako cloth. He handed the bundle to Champ, a slight smile curving his mouth. "I would like to see my grandson again one day before too long. He is of both worlds, white and Chako. He should know both."

Rye nodded and said thickly, "You can send word to my brother Jesse. We'll make arrangements to get Champ to you whenever you like."

Man Father laid a hand on Rye's shoulder. "Thank you," he said simply. "You must go now."

"Yes." Rye turned Champ toward the pickup. Kara fell in

behind him. Man Father walked at Rye's side, Champ between them. No one said a word, but as they drew near the red circle Rye paused and looked back over his shoulder one last time. Di'wana stood with her eyes closed, one hand against her husband's neck, her cheek pressed to his, swaying gently side to side. Kara thought she hummed something soft and low, or was that Crow Brother? Slowly Di'wana's eyes opened, and she smiled at them. Then her eyes drifted closed again in absolute serenity. Rye stared a moment longer, then he turned back and stepped over the red line of the circle. Champ crossed next to him and Kara right behind him, but Man Father stood on the other side.

"You will have your answer from the council tomorrow morning."

Rye nodded and opened the door to the truck. Champ tossed his bundle inside, then turned to wave at his mother. Di'wana waved back. Kara wasn't sure, but she thought she caught the sheen of fresh tears in Di'wana's eyes. She turned away, hurrying around to let herself into the truck on the passenger side. Man Father lifted a hand in farewell.

Rye slipped behind the wheel. He closed the door and reached for the ignition key. The old chief stood with his hands loose at his sides as Rye started the truck, put it in gear and backed it around. Champ got up on his knees to look out the back window as they pulled away.

"It wasn't like I thought it'd be," he said, and Kara saw Rye's hands tighten on the steering wheel.

"I'm sorry, son. I'm sorry about your mother."

Champ nodded and turned around, sliding down into the seat.

"Put on your seat belt," Rye said, "both of you."

Kara helped Champ buckle his belt and then buckled her own. Champ leaned his head against his father's shoulder. After a while he said thoughtfully, "You're not still mad at her, are you, Dad?"

Rye cleared his throat. "No, I'm not still mad at her."

Champ nodded as if that answer was exactly what he'd expected and said, "I'm not, either."

Rye lifted an arm and draped it around his son. Champ snuggled against him. Kara wanted desperately to put her arms around them both, but Champ's past animosity stopped her. True, he seemed accepting enough of her presence at the moment, but it was almost as if he was unaware of her. Her hand wandered toward Rye's where it rested on the seat next to Champ's hip. To her immense gratification, as soon as her hand drew near, Rye grasped it. She closed her eyes and concentrated on pouring every ounce of her love into that hand. She felt his pain and confusion, felt his helplessness toward his son. There was nothing to say, nothing to do. All she had to give him, both of them, was what she felt. All she could do was love with her whole heart and hope that somehow it would help.

It was very late when Rye came to her. She woke from a restless, troubled sleep to find him crouched there beside her, his hand stroking her cheek. The moon had set. She couldn't see his face in the heavy darkness, but she knew his expression, felt his deep need. She clutched his hand and said softly, "I thought you'd be staying at the house with Champ."

"I thought so, too, but I couldn't sleep."

"I'm sorry," she whispered, lifting her hand to his face. She felt his jaw flex as he swallowed and knew what he was going to ask.

"Will you come with me? You don't have to. I shouldn't even ask. I promised myself I wouldn't, but—"

She pressed her fingertips over his mouth and sat up. He handed her boots to her. She pushed out of the sleeping bag and tugged them on, then stood and threw her arms around his neck as he came up beside her. He caught her to him, holding tight. "Oh, Kara!" he whispered.

"Shh!" She dipped down and caught up her sleeping bag with one hand. Together they slipped out of camp and into the shadows. They tossed the bag on the ground beneath a lone tree spreading its branches downslope of the big gray barn nearest the house. The ground had been beaten by countless feet, hooves and tires to a soft powder. Kara sat down on the sleeping bag and pulled Rye down beside her. He pulled her head onto his shoulder and for a long while simply sat there with his arms around her.

"It's so strange," he said. "I've hated Di'wana for so long,

literally hated her. I don't have an explanation for the grief I fee
now.''

"Sometimes hate is just another side of love, Rye. You love
each other. You hurt each other. You hated each other. Now you
have to make your peace, and I think it's understandable tha
you'd suffer some grief in doing so, even if she wasn't ill.''

"I can't believe she's dying," he said, his voice thick. ''Some
part of me wants to believe it's a lie, but I know it's not.''

"How is Champ?" she asked after a moment.

Rye sighed. "I don't know. He seems to understand, and he
seems to have come to terms with everything, but I can't help
wishing they'd given me some choice in what he would be told
and when.''

She nodded. "He's your son, after all.''

"Yes, but hers, too.''

He lay back on the narrow sleeping bag, pulling her down on
top of him. She kissed his chin and tucked her head beneath it
"Can I ask you a question?''

"If you want. Can't promise I'll be able to answer it.''

"Wasn't there a time when it was good between you and
Di'wana? Can't you concentrate on that now?''

"Not really," he said after a time. "I think we were both
disappointed from the very beginning.''

She folded her arms across his chest and parked her chin on
them. "What do you mean?''

He pushed a hand through his hair. "Frankly, I thought—
because of her looks, I guess—that she'd be the hottest thing that
ever crawled into my bed. But she wasn't.''

Kara slid off him and sat up. "You're telling me that you
were disappointed in the *sex?*''

"It wasn't just that," he said, rolling onto his side and prop-
ping his head on his elbow, "but it was part of it. For her, too.
Somehow it was...embarrassing." He sat up suddenly. "Holy
heavens! She was my *wife,* for pity's sake. Making love to her
was like...making love to my sister!" He said it with disgust.
"We both knew we'd made a mistake, but we were stuck. She'd
given up her family, her people, to go with me. I couldn't just
send her back, so I made up my mind to make it work. I had
lots of opportunities out on the road to cheat, but I wouldn't. I
couldn't.''

"So eventually she was the one to cheat," Kara said softly, "and set you both free."

His head jerked up. "I h-hadn't thought of it like that."

"Of course you wouldn't," she said. "You were committed to making the marriage work, however reluctantly. She took that decision out of your hands by making it impossible for you to stay together. It must have seemed to you that she threw your best efforts back in your face."

"That's exactly how it seemed," he said absently.

Kara folded her legs into a more comfortable position. "I think you wanted to make her happy, Rye," she told him, "and you thought the only way to do that was to marry her, but you were never meant to marry."

"It's funny, isn't it? We were both so convinced back then that she could never be happy as a traditional Chako, but that's exactly what it took."

"Be glad she found out before it was too late—for both your sakes."

He nodded, and his hand stole up her arm to her shoulder and down again, brushing her breasts. "I thought it would be with her," he said softly, "the way it is with you."

Kara smiled, her breath catching in her throat. "How is it with me, Rye?"

His hand moved upward again to her face and into her hair. "Magic," he said. "White-hot magic."

She tilted her head, trapping his hand between her ear and her shoulder. She kissed the inside of his wrist.

"I shouldn't have started with you, Kara," he said. "I don't know how to stop now."

"Don't think about it," she whispered. "Just let me love you."

He bent his head and pressed his mouth to hers. As one they rocked up onto their knees and began undressing each other between kisses both quick and lingering. A long while later they lay entwined inside the single sleeping bag, each aware that this loving was different. This time they had each received as much as given, taking what was needed, offering the same, until both were satisfied, filled, soothed.

Rye kissed the top of her head. "I have to get back to the house before Champ wakes."

She nodded. "I should get back to camp, too."

"I wish I knew what to expect of Champ right now. He's had a huge shock. He's gotten to know his mother and lost her in the space of a few days. I can't quite make sense of any of this myself yet, so how can I expect him to?"

"I know." She hugged him, then determinedly sat up. She wasn't going to think that this might be their last time together. She'd thought that before. No use going through that again. She reached for her clothes. He folded his hands beneath his head and watched her.

"You're beautiful," he said as she slipped into her bra.

She smiled. "If I am, it's because you make me feel that way."

"I love you, Kara," he said then, and she felt her heart crack open. She didn't dare turn to look at him, couldn't bear to see the apology she sensed in his tone. "I can't say that it changes anything," he whispered, "but you deserve to know."

She nodded, gulped back tears and made herself slip into her panties. Standing, she shook out her jeans and stepped into them. She snatched up her shirt and threw it on, angry. "Oh, yes, it changes everything!" she exclaimed, unable to hold it in any longer. "Everything!" She turned on him then. "Do you know what you are, Ryeland Wagner? You're a coward! So you've been hurt. Well, it doesn't make you special. *Everyone's* been hurt one way or another. At least Di'wana has the courage to let herself love and be loved again. She won't take her mistakes and her regrets to the grave with her!"

He sat up, draping his forearms across his knees. "I know," he admitted. "You're right. But Di'wana had something to go back to, Kara. I'm stuck with who and what I am. It'd be easier if I *didn't* love you!"

"Not for me," she said. "And walking away is still easier for you than trying to make it work!"

"I lose either way!" he yelled. "Whether I go or whether I stay and fail!"

"Then stay and succeed!" she said. "I'm willing to take the chance that we can make it work!"

He didn't have to say that he was not. The expression on his face said it all.

"Oh, Rye," she said. "I didn't feel this sad for Di'wana!"

She grabbed her socks and her boots and ran barefoot back to camp.

Chapter Fifteen

Official permission to cross the reservation came that morning
in the form of a hand-lettered document with a feathered seal
attached.

"Suitable for framing," Sarah Wagner murmured, fingering
the heavy, handmade paper.

"I'll bet there aren't more than half a dozen in existence,"
Jess added.

"Three in my lifetime that I'm aware of," Shoes confirmed.
He had been obviously distressed by the news of his cousin's
illness, but kept very much to himself. He split a look between
Rye and Kara. "My uncle reveres one or both of you."

"It wouldn't be me," Kara muttered. "I didn't do or say anything."

"I'm sure you impressed him favorably," Shoes said with a
little smile.

Kara wanted to think so, but it didn't really matter. Nothing
much did, really, not now. She had believed that the ranch was
everything to her, the most important thing in her life. She knew
better now. Things shouldn't be that important, couldn't once
you'd loved someone, really loved them. Why couldn't Rye see

that loving someone and being with them was the most important thing in the world? He should have, after yesterday. He even admitted that he loved her, but he'd convinced himself that he was a failure at marriage, and he wouldn't even give them a chance.

"We'd better get moving," Rye said from his vantage point on the back of a horse.

"Be careful, son," Sarah Wagner said, reaching up to hug him as he bent low.

"I will, Mom. Be sure George gets off okay, and tell him I'll be in touch."

"George will be fine," his father said. "Wanda's on her way to get him now, and that's the best medicine there is for a man in love."

Rye said nothing to that, just nodded noncommittally.

"You're sure you want Champ to go along?" Jess asked one more time.

Rye nodded. "He's had a shock, Jess. I want him with me. I'm sure we'll be safe as long as we're on the reservation. No one from outside can easily get to us, and anyone from inside is bound to realize the danger of discovery is heightened now."

"And we have the news crew," Kara added.

Rye made a face, but Kara still believed she had done the right thing by insisting that the film team be allowed to go along when they'd shown up early that morning, even before the Chako messenger. A team of four men with two cameras, they'd come in their own expensive, four-wheel-drive vehicle complete with satellite hookup, prepared to rough it right alongside the drovers and willing to pay their own way in return for documenting the final days of the drive for some program they were planning about the modern cowboy. It wouldn't be daily news coverage, but they'd promised to announce the project immediately on national television so at least the saboteur would know someone was watching. The star reporter, Bradley Warnke, was a national celebrity and had survived live coverage of the Saudi conflict as well as a climb up Mount Everest. A trail drive should be child's play compared to that.

Truthfully, Kara hoped that Rye's apparent disgruntlement was centered more on the way tall, dark and ruggedly attractive Warnke had stared pointedly at her chest than the nuisance of having cameras around. She'd wanted to slug the guy, but more importantly, so had Rye, if the look on his face had been anything to go by.

"Daylight's burning," Rye reminded them irritably, and wheeled his mount to ride to the point.

Kara thrust the Chako document at Shoes. "Give that to Mom for safekeeping, will you?"

"Sure."

Kara smiled apologetically at the Wagners. "Thanks so much for everything."

"Our pleasure," Sarah Wagner said, and the Wagner men nodded in agreement.

"Be careful, Kara," Jess called as Kara hurried toward her horse.

Kara tossed a smile over her shoulder. "I will! Thanks again."

They waved as she cantered her mount toward the front of the herd.

Rye had dropped a loop on the lead cow just in case some time on the loose had blunted the instinct to follow the mounted rider, so it was Kara who gave the signal, standing in her stirrups and flicking the end of her rope at the rear end of the nearest cow, yelling, "Let's mo-ove!"

The start lacked the smoothness of those in days past. One clump after another balked, so Kara rode around, twirling that rope over her head and snapping it at the balkers, while the drovers hazed and prodded them along. It was a good quarter-hour before the herd coalesced, but eventually they were back in mode, moving as a single, if somewhat sluggish, body. Kara was surprised to see the camera crew keeping track of her in the distance, the driver expertly picking his way past ravines and outcroppings while the cameraman hung out the window, camera steady on his shoulder. She didn't have much time to think about it. As usual, the work demanded her attention, and she was agreeably surprised when she spied the lunch wagon in the distance.

Bradley Warnke made himself amenable during the break, complimenting her abilities and shooting questions at her with the same suave ease. Rye seemed to take offense just because Warnke made her laugh from time to time, so much so that the break was cut short and she found herself in the saddle again before the last sip of soup hit her stomach. She put aside the nger and hopelessness of the morning and allowed herself to smile at the evidence of Rye's jealousy. The smile had given way to exhaustion by the time the campsite came into view, nestled in the convergence of three sandy hills and a natural spring.

"Walk 'em through thirty or forty at a time," Rye ordered the men, "then drag out salt blocks and a water trough and hay 'em after the last ones have tasted the spring."

Shoes and Bord had already strung a wire on two sides of a makeshift enclosure. They would string a third and use vehicles on the fourth side, throwing down their bedrolls nearby. A single rider on horseback would be sufficient guard for the night, but there would be precious little privacy on the now treeless terrain. In a single day they'd gone from an alpine setting to near desert.

Warnke staked a claim on Kara's attention the moment her boots hit the ground and maintained it right up to the moment she stepped into the shower.

"Do you mind?" she asked in exasperation, tossing a towel over her shoulder and reaching for the edge of the tarpaulin enclosure.

"If he doesn't," Rye said, coming around the front end of the water truck, "I do."

Kara just lifted an eyebrow and slipped inside, where she quickly stripped down to her smile. Well, at least he knew how she'd felt with Officer Cantu making herself too agreeable to him. Cleaned up and shivering cold, she took her hairbrush and a fresh towel to the fireside, where she began to get warm and dry her hair. Bradley Warnke came over with an expensive, fur-lined parka, which he draped over her shoulders, saying, "You look like you can use this."

She spared him a glance. "Thanks."

He crouched down beside her chair. "What's with Wagner? He seems to want to keep me away from you, but when I asked if he had a prior claim, he just walked away."

Kara smiled apologetically. Movement at the corner of her eye snagged her attention, and she turned her head to find Rye frowning at her from the dinner line. She looked him square in the eye. "Well," she said to the reporter, being sure her voice carried beyond him, "it's like this. I'm in love with Rye, but he has this problem with commitment. So I guess you could say we're kind of in limbo.''

Warnke's black eyebrows almost became part of his hairline. ''The lady's honest, I'll give her that,'' he said, rising to his feet. With a smile and a slight bow, he walked away.

Kara let her gaze flit over Rye and the others standing in line to eat, suddenly uncomfortable with so public a declaration, and then she saw Champ, standing next to one of the serving tables, one elbow hooked over the edge, his head cocked quizzically, a frown drawing his brows together and the corners of his mouth down. Kara caught her breath. Her gaze zipped to Rye apologetically, but Rye was studying his son, fingers slowly stroking his mustache. Kara got up from her chair, left the parka there and hurried away, aware that several pairs of eyes followed her. But not Rye's. Rye Wagner had eyes only for his son in that moment.

Rye lifted the saddle into place and reached for the girth. He didn't really much feel like riding night guard, but he figured he might as well. He wasn't likely to get much sleep this night, anyway. Besides, it was only fair.

''Rye, I'm sorry.''

Straightening, he turned to face Kara, one hand on the saddle horn. ''I didn't hear you come up.''

''I've been standing in the shadows working up my courage.''

He shook his head. ''No need for that.''

''I shouldn't have made such a public declaration.''

He shrugged, still surprised by the initial rush of joy he'd felt at her words. ''Doesn't matter. We've been carrying on pretty publicly. Everyone knows you wouldn't if you didn't have feelings.''

''Everyone but Champ,'' she said miserably.

He didn't know what to say to that, so he got busy tightening the girth instead.

''How is he?'' she asked, her voice rich with concern.

''I don't know,'' Rye answered truthfully. ''He seems... I don't know. *Older,* somehow.''

''He must be so very confused,'' she said, ''meeting his mother for the first time that he can remember, experiencing her culture, learning she's dying. Then hearing me blurt out my feelings like that.''

"It's odd," he told her. "He seems, well, calm." He tucked away the ends of the girth strap and lowered the stirrup, turning to face her once more. "Just a little while ago we were talking, and he made this statement that if anything should happen to me, there were a lot of people to take care of him. I promised him nothing was going to happen to me, but the really odd thing is that he made this list of people who care about him. You know, he named my folks and Jess and Shoes and Man Father...and your mother...and Crow Brother.''

Kara was as surprised as he had been by those last two. "Well," she said thoughtfully, "he's spent an awful lot of time with Mom on this trip. She's great with kids and truly fond of him. He's bound to pick up on that.''

"And Crow Brother?" Rye asked.

Kara blinked. "He must've made quite an impression."

"Actually," Rye said, trying to make it sound light, "Champ says Crow Brother is like another dad, because Crow Brother's married to his mother."

"Rye, you have to know that Champ adores you. He'd never choose anyone else over you. He—''

"I know. I know. It just kind of took me by surprise. I mean, it's just been the two of us, really, and, well, Shoes and Jess. He's never seemed to think of them as—''

"Shoes is his mother's cousin. Jess is his uncle. He's always known where to put them. Crow Brother is someone new, not related by blood. And he *is* married to Champ's mother. It makes sense to assign him a, ah, parental role."

Rye nodded, quite sure he wasn't fooling her at all. "Yeah, you're right. Absolutely."

She reached a hand out to him. "Rye, don't be hurt. Champ loves you. I—''

He didn't mean to do it. He'd promised himself that he wouldn't. It was best, after what had happened that morning, to keep his distance. He just didn't know how to stay away. It was the most natural thing in the world to step forward and take her into his arms. His body seemed to know that, even if his head didn't, and it acted on its own without even giving his head a chance to warn him.

"Kara, sweetheart, what am I going to do with you?" he asked against the crown of her head. Her hair felt clean and soft against his chin and lips. She smelled of woman and wood smoke, sunshine and earth.

"Don't decide now," she told him. "We have time, a few days, anyway. Wait until you see the ranch. Wait until—"

He covered her mouth with his, not wanting to tell her that nothing had changed for them. It was selfish, damned selfish, but he couldn't let go yet. Not yet.

She wrapped her arms around him and, as always, gave as good as she got. It was so hard to break that kiss and step back.

"I have to ride night guard, honey."

"I know."

He looked around them, knowing this was as private as it was going to get out here for now. "There's no place to go tonight, no place private enough to—"

"I know. It's all right. Maybe it's even best."

He cupped her face in his hands. "You can lay your bedroll next to mine, anyway."

She smiled. "Okay. Promise me you'll turn in right after your shift and get some rest."

"Promise."

She looked deeply into his eyes and said, "I love you, Ryeland Wagner."

He didn't want to say it, but he couldn't help it. "I love you, too. I do. I love you."

She closed her eyes as if to hold those words of his inside her. He wanted to cuss—or cry. God knew the kindest, fairest thing he could do was to stay the hell away from her. Why couldn't he do it?

She pressed a kiss into the palm of his hand and backed away, smiling, and so incredibly beautiful it hurt to look at her. With a happy little wave, she left him. He put his hands to his hips and tried to breathe deeply, but it didn't help. He felt like the biggest heel alive, because he knew he was going to hurt her. Bad.

Rolling rises gave way to flat nothing broken only by the barren, dramatic mesas pictured in so many old Westerns. It was a fit place for a crew of now scruffy cowboys and a slow-moving herd of beeves. According to Bradley Warnke, one almost expected a band of Indians to come screaming around a flat-topped mountain of rock, the cavalry hot on their heels, or a train of covered wagons to circle for camp. All Rye expected was disaster.

He expected to be sunburned by day and frozen to the bone at night, and at any moment he expected Champ to fly at Kara, fists whirling, demanding that she stay away from his father, or for Kara to demand a guarantee for the future, a public declaration of his own feelings, maybe even a marriage proposal. It wasn't out of the realm of possibility that one of the other men might call him out for the way he'd treated Kara, or ought to treat Kara. He had a feeling that even Dayna was on the verge of asking him what his intentions were, and his greatest fear was that he'd make promises he couldn't keep just to see that smile on Kara's face a little longer. He was almost glad that he couldn't make love to her just now. Almost.

On one hand he craved that girl with an all-consuming hunger that both surprised and frightened him. On the other he knew that denying himself the joy of her body was the only way, the only hope he had, of making a clean break when they got to New Mexico.

Actually they crossed into New Mexico late on the second day, and by the third night were camping on the very edge of the Jicarilla Apache reservation. They'd paid a fee for the right to cross, and so were duly met the next morning by a representative of the tribe, a small handsome woman with an authoritative manner and a keen sense of business. She spread an aerial map on the hood of her truck and pointed out the approved campsites, just so there would be no misunderstanding. Both sites boasted pens and abundant water sources. She looked over the receipt for fees paid that Kara presented her, promised someone would check in with them each night and shook hands all around before taking her leave.

"That's what I call efficiency," Shoes said, admiration ringing in his voice. Rye traded a surprised look with Kara and dismissed the matter. He had cattle to move.

About midmorning it became pretty obvious that the Apaches had garnered for themselves one of the most lush, beautiful spots on the face of the earth. The desert and all its majesty disappeared into forested vales cut with babbling brooks and still, blue lakes, tall grasses and birdsong. The men bathed that night in a spring-fed pond so clear it was like glass and cold enough to shatter their chattering teeth, while the women kept to the motor home for long, hot showers and privacy. They woke shivering the next morning, and Rye watched in horror as snow clouds banked in the east. Surely to God they hadn't come this far to lose at the last moment because of a freak snowstorm. He practically tossed the boys into their saddles, gnashing his teeth over the inconvenience of dodging around cameras and a microphone-wielding Warnke trying to capture the moment for posterity. Only Kara, with a serene fatalism totally out of character for her, remained calm.

They were locked into their schedule, thanks to the deal they'd made with the Jicarilla Apaches, but in truth it wouldn't have made much difference—and Rye wanted this remaining time with her badly enough to risk it all, anyway, even if they were confined to stolen kisses and whispered regrets. It wasn't necessary any longer, and they both knew it, but by silent agreement, they resisted the impulse to slip off together and make love. For him it would be too fraught with the feeling of goodbye; he'd had some of that already, and he didn't think he could bear more. Not yet.

Thankfully the sky held, the snow clouds stacking like the Tower of Babel reaching for the heavens. A cold wind sent them all scurrying for heavy coats and dusters. Even the camera crew broke out the hats and knit caps. They left the reservation about midmorning that next day and polished off gallons of hot soup and coffee during lunch break at a roadside park. Night would find them within thirteen miles of their goal, but mere minutes from camp they passed through a narrow gorge cut between two low rocky walls, and that's where the first shot spat dirt right beneath the belly of Rye's horse.

Just for an instant everyone and everything seemed to freeze. Then another loud crack sent a bullet flying, and Rye felt it whiz by his hat. All hell broke loose. Even as Rye spurred his tired horse, Kara screamed his name, cows bawled, eyes rolled, and they had themselves a stampede. He was pretty sure there were more shots fired, but with his every brain cell locked on Kara and the possibility of her getting caught beneath the slashing hooves of the cattle ramming themselves through the narrow gorge, he couldn't say for sure how many shots. He tried to get to her, but she was ahead of him, trying to ride against the flow toward him. Thankfully, her horse had better sense. Fighting its way around, it carried her through the narrow opening with the cattle and out of sight.

Rye spurred his poor bay mercilessly, desperate to get through the opening and find Kara. Then suddenly he was through. Horrified, he watched Kara desperately trying to contain the cattle, to prevent them from surging up and out of the narrow gorge and disappearing in two dozen directions. He yelled at her to let them go, but even as the words tore out of his throat he knew that she couldn't hear him and wouldn't have obeyed if she could've. He thought of the gun that was probably even then trained on them, but he couldn't spare time to worry about it. First things first, and at the top of his emergency agenda was getting to Kara before her frantic horse fell and took her down into the path of the crazed cattle.

He yanked his horse up onto the steep, sandy wall of the gorge and raked its flanks mercilessly. That animal was all go. It climbed, slid and climbed some more, all the while lunging forward. Suddenly Charlie Choate was there at his side and then right behind him. Handling his horse with one hand, he flapped his hat with the other, hazing the cattle back down into the ravine. By golly, they just might keep them yet! Rye leaned forward in the saddle, giving his horse rein, and it took off like lightning. He got to Kara, putting himself between her and where he expected the next shots to come from. In the process, he headed off several cows bent on wild-eyed freedom.

A glance ahead of them yielded the welcome sight of riders flying low in the saddle toward them. He recognized Shoes and Bord at a glance. The other he assumed was Wes Randal. He was suddenly glad beyond words that they'd taken on those two extra cowboys, his heart pounded with gratitude when Wes dropped a loop, pretty as you please, on that lead cow, dragging her around to turn the herd. Bord and Shoes shook out their own loops, and Kara let one fly, too. Rye was almost too weak with relief to do any good, but somehow he managed to lasso himself a bawler and bring it to heel, while Charlie and Dean used their ropes like whips. In seconds the herd had turned and was milling in a noisy circle. Moments later it stopped entirely, shaggy hides heaving.

Shoes rode up to Rye and Kara. "We heard shots."

"They were aimed at Rye!" Kara exclaimed angrily, and it was then that Rye realized Pogo and Dean had taken up spots behind him. Any shots aimed at him now would have to go through them. The hair lifted on the back of his neck.

"We've got to get out of here."

"We're going as a unit then," Kara said, "you in the middle of us, even if it means leaving these damned cows to fend for themselves."

Rye looked around him at the closed, determined faces of the best of friends and the woman he loved. He gulped down a lump in his throat. "Let's move 'em into camp, then."

Shoes gave a nod of satisfaction and smoothly assumed control. "Dean, Wes get on those flanks. Pogo, you and Charlie take drag. Rye, you're with Kara and me on point, and I mean trading stirrups."

Rye nodded toward Kara. "I don't want her on the outside. The shots came from those rocks there."

"Kara, you're riding inside, then," Shoes said, "and don't give me no lip."

She lifted her eyebrows, but moved inside as she was told. They rode to the point, real slow and easy, Rye in the center, Kara on his right, Shoes left and slightly behind, so close that his mount could have bitten Rye's leg without so much as turning its head. The film crew had parked their vehicle at the top of the rise just outside camp, and a cameraman was standing on the roof, his lens sweeping the rocks to the north and behind them. Rye was suddenly thankful they hadn't turned away the reporter and his crew, even if Warnke was too glamorous for his own good.

"Anything happens," he told Kara, "I want you to ride for that news truck with all you've got."

She slid a look at him. "Those shots weren't aimed at me, Rye. You've always been the target! And I was too worried about getting the damned cattle to the ranch on time that I didn't stop to consider, even after that rock nearly flattened you!"

He wanted to drag her off her horse onto his lap, but he didn't dare. Those shots had been aimed at him, all right, and nowhere else. Still, he argued. "We don't know that. No one has any reason to target me."

"Unless they're smart enough to realize that killing you is the one thing that will stop me," she said bitterly.

He was shocked to hear her say it. For a moment he didn't know how to reply, but then he knew he wasn't going to let her give up no matter what. "You happen to know who the local law is around here?"

She nodded. "I'm willing to bet Mom's already got the sheriff on the phone."

"These Detmeyer women are sharp," Shoes commented, grinning at Rye.

"Damn straight."

Kara leaned back in the saddle a few degrees. "That Jicarilla Apache babe wasn't exactly dull."

Shoes grinned wide. "No, ma'am." He rubbed his chin. "I'm thinking maybe I ought to hang around these parts for a while."

Rye was too astounded to come up with a pithy remark or any remark at all, for that matter. He just gaped at Shoes, sure he hadn't heard right. Shoes lifted his shoulders in a shrug. "What? You think I can only find happiness with a Chako, or don't you think I like girls?"

"I hadn't exactly thought about it. I just—"

"You just figured that if you got your fingers burned, mine naturally stung, too," Shoes said. "Well, I'll tell you something. The idea that my cousin is dying makes me think maybe I shouldn't be hanging around waiting for you to grow a brain." He leaned forward to look at Kara, adding, "I don't know. Maybe we ought to paint a target on his chest and send him in the other direction."

"That's not funny," Kara said softly.

"You hear me laughing?" Shoes came back sharply.

Rye wondered if he was in shock, or if maybe Shoes was. Or was that anger he saw tightening his usually inscrutable friend's jaw? They rode right behind the news truck and straight into camp. Bradley Warnke was following them on foot with a microphone.

"Kara! Mizz Detmeyer! Mr. Wagner! Those were gunshots we heard, weren't they?"

Rye wheeled his horse. "Yeah, they were shots. Somebody tried to aerate my hide. Now get the hell out of the way! We're bringing the herd right into camp!" He waved an arm at Pogo, signaling him to bring them on in, while Kara yelled at her mother, Champ and the camera crew to get out of the way.

"Get that table down!" Rye yelled. "Spread these trucks and block the open spaces. Put out that fire!" Even as he shouted the order, he was dismounting to take care of it himself, while Kara and Shoes put themselves into breaks between the vehicles. "I want rope strung! Use the tables to block spaces, if you have to!"

It was pure chaos for several minutes, but in the end, they had the herd inside the loose circle of vehicles, which meant making camp *outside*. Kara protested that arrangement, but Rye wasn't about to lose the herd at this point.

"We'll set up on the east side. The shots came from the northwest."

"That doesn't mean he won't circle around!" Kara argued. "Look around you, Rye. He's got plenty of cover to choose from."

"Those rocks on the east are too close," he said dismissively. "He won't want to risk showing his face."

"If he does," one of the newsmen said, his camera still perched on his shoulder, "he'll be seen around the world. Bradley's ordered a satellite hookup, and we're on standby."

"Good for Bradley," Rye muttered, turning his attention elsewhere. "Get those water troughs out! No showers! It all goes to the cattle. And drop some hay! We don't want them spooky. Bord, I want that remuda on the southeast corner, and hobble 'em! I'll be damned if I'll lose a single mount."

Rye ignored the looks traded amongst the others and handed his horse off to Bord. He meant for Champ to stay inside the motor home. He didn't even want the boy standing in the door or opening the windows, but he glanced in that direction and caught sight of his son skipping around the end of the motor home, outside of the circle. On the northeast. Rye took off running. "Champ!" The instant he showed himself, he heard the crack of a rifle.

Instinctively he hit the ground, then popped up again and took off in the opposite direction, leading the shots away, he hoped, from his son. Shots peppered the ground around him. He ran for all he was worth, felt a burn across the back of his neck and fell. He hit the ground rolling, then scrambled beneath his truck. A cameraman had climbed into the bed, and he could hear Bradley Warnke expounding on "the event unfolding before our very eyes!"

"Got him!" someone else yelled.

But most confusing of all, Kara was on her belly in the dirt, staring at him from the other side of the truck, shouting his name as tears streamed down her face, and Pogo was lying on top of her, as if holding her down.

"Rye! Rye! You're bleeding!"

"Where's Champ?" he yelled, putting a hand to the back of his neck. It came away wet. "Champ!" he yelled again. The sounds of sirens in the distance did nothing to calm his fears. Terror unlike anything he'd ever known made his head swim and the world go white.

Chapter Sixteen

The sport utility vehicle slid to a stop in a cloud of dust, its siren dying away, lights flashing amber, red and blue. The driver's window slid down, a cowboy hat came off, and a dark head poked out of the opened window.

"We got a report of shots fired! What's going on?"

Everybody started talking at once. Pogo and Kara got up. Rye crawled across the ground beneath the truck and out on the opposite side from which he'd entered. It was utter chaos, cattle bawling and milling, people all trying to tell the story at the same time. Rye had just one thought.

"Where's Champ? Champ? Champ!" He was shouting at the top of his lungs.

Suddenly Shoes thrust the boy forward. "I've got him!"

Rye nearly collapsed with relief. "Thank God!"

"Oboe knocked him down, and I was able to drag him back inside the circle."

"D-D-Daddy?"

Rye swept the boy up and crushed him against his chest, staggering. "You okay, son?"

Champ nodded his head, but then he looked up and lifted the

arm he'd flung about his father's neck. The inside of his wrist was wet with blood. Sheer panic contorted his face. "Dad! Dad?"

Rye staggered back against the side of the truck, bracing himself. "It's all right, son. I'm all right. It's just a scratch."

Disbelief still lent a wildness to the boy's dark eyes. Suddenly tears welled and spilled over. He shoved his face into the curve of his father's neck and sobbed. Rye just hugged him tight and kept repeating that he was all right. *Dear God, if anything had happened to this boy,* Rye thought, knowing he'd never forgive himself. Suddenly he remembered seeing Kara belly down in the dirt, tears streaming down her face. Had a bullet hit her? He glanced around, Champ in his arms, frantic once more. "Kara! Kara, dear God!"

"I'm here!" His worried gaze found her shoving at the rump of a bawling cow that had wandered between them. Rye hurled himself at her. They met with a full-body slam that would have knocked them both off their feet if not for the arms that clamped them together, Champ between them on one side. "Rye, Rye, I thought you were dead!"

"Are you okay? Were you hit?"

"You're bleeding!"

"Are you okay?" He practically shouted it at her.

She pulled back, gulping and nodding her head. "Yes, but you're still bleeding!"

He felt weak with relief. "Thank God! If anything had happened to either one of you..." He let the thought trail away and closed his eyes. They popped right back open again. "He's still out there! Where's that sheriff?"

"He's talking to everybody," Kara said, trying to get a look at the wound on the back of his neck without leaving the curve of his arm. "There's an ambulance on the way."

Even as he protested the need of such, the back of his neck started to sting like all get-out. His knees felt as if they might buckle. "I better sit down," he mumbled, head spinning as Champ was taken from his arms and Kara led him swiftly forward. She gave him a shove, and he sat down hard on the rear bumper of his own truck. Automatically he lifted a hand to the back of his neck. "Ow!"

"Let me look at that," Kara said, pulling his head forward

slightly. "Heavens, it dug a groove right through your hair! It's not bleeding so much now, though. My God, Rye, another inch or two and he'd have taken your head off!"

Rye lifted his gaze to find her standing close in front of him, Champ parked on her hip like a big, overgrown baby. Something about that made him smile. He wondered if Champ even realized he had both arms around her neck.

"You think it's funny?" she said, sounding angry all at once.

He reached up and settled a hand at the indentation of her waist on the side where his son did not hang. "No, I don't think it's funny. I'm just so glad..." His throat clogged up, and he couldn't go on, couldn't tell her how glad he was that the two people he loved most in this world were all right and that he was here with them. A tall man wearing khakis and a cowboy hat appeared at Kara's side.

"Mr. Wagner?"

Rye switched his gaze. "Yes. Thank you for coming when you did."

The man stuck out his hand. "It's Sheriff Hernandez, and as to that, we're pure lucky I was close by. I'm told you're wounded."

Rye shook his hand. "Just a scratch, really. Not that whoever was behind the bullet wasn't aiming for more."

Hernandez craned a look at the back of Rye's neck. "Don't look too bad. Bet it smarts, though."

"Some," Rye admitted.

The sheriff squinted at the rocky hill from where the shots had come. "I've radioed some men to look for our shooter. Meanwhile, this reporter over here says he's got him on tape. I was wondering if you could take a look, maybe identify our culprit. It'll mean walking over to their vehicle."

Rye stood determinedly. "You bet."

Champ slid down from Kara's hip and took his father's hand. Kara wrapped an arm around Rye's waist as if to support him. He draped an arm about her shoulders. They all walked over to a space between the farrier's wagon and the back end of one of the horse trailers. The expensive four-wheel drive had been pulled close to the farrier's wagon, the tailgate open. One of the camera crew sat with a computer keyboard on his lap, a stack of equipment, including a monitor, beside him. Images whooshed by on the monitor in a blurry stream. Then the crewman hit a button, and the images slowed. He hit another one, and the image froze. Rye could just make out the shape of a man's head between two boulders. The cameraman typed rapidly, occasionally highlighting spots on the screen by rubbing the tip of his finger on a small sensor on the keyboard. Suddenly the image flickered into sharpness. Kara gasped. "Damn him!" Rye swore.

"You recognize him?" the sheriff asked hopefully.

"I recognize him," Kara whispered.

Rye tightened his arm around her shoulders. "Honey, I'm sorry."

She slid both arms around his waist. "You tried to tell me." She looked at the sheriff and told him shakily, "That's Payne Detmeyer, my cousin."

The sheriff whipped out a small pad of paper and an ink pen to take down a full description, address, telephone numbers, everything they could come up with.

Rye transferred his arm to her waist as she answered the sheriff's questions. She was trying to remember Payne's fiancée's name when Wesley Randall trotted up.

"Boss," he said, addressing Rye, "I thought you'd want to know. The wrangler took off soon as the shooting started again. Just climbed on a horse and lit out."

"Well, I guess that tells us the rest of it," Rye commented bitterly. To the sheriff he added, "We've been experiencing some harassment. Sabotage, I call it, meant to slow us down, keep us from making our deadline." The sheriff had heard about their troubles and the reason for the drive.

Kara said softly, "I guess Payne must've hired Borden to keep us from getting these cattle to my ranch on time."

"And when it didn't work," the sheriff mused, "he got desperate, took matters into his own hands." He turned a page in his notepad and began asking questions about Borden Harris. It was Rye who answered this time. Before they were done, the place was crawling with police of one sort or another and an ambulance with a volunteer crew.

Rye allowed himself to be led to the ambulance for treatment. When he refused to allow himself to be transported to a hospital, the EMT took care of the wound himself, shaving Rye's hairline a little higher and stitching the wound closed. His neck was stiff and every movement of his head made the wound pull and sting, but other than a pounding headache, that was the worst of it.

Somehow camp got made, dinner got cooked, all the questions got answered and the chores got tended before dark. Neither Payne nor Borden had been found, but the sheriff was confident they would be. Rye stubbornly refused to let himself be taken into protective custody even though it was obvious that he was Payne's target, so the sheriff assigned a couple of men to watch over the drive until the fugitives were caught or the drive reached the safety of the ranch, whichever came first. Kara bullied Rye into taking analgesics and eating his dinner, then practically dragged him into the motor home. Because his wound couldn't be gotten wet, a shower was out of the question, so Kara gave him a sponge bath, which he enjoyed inordinately. But then she shoved him into bed, pulled the covers up to his chin and instructed him to go to sleep. He didn't see how he could. Yet his eyelids drifted closed and wouldn't seem to lift again.

So he slept after all, very deeply, so deeply that when he finally woke again, it was to full daylight and the bouncing of the mobile home as it moved across rough terrain. His head ached dully, but not as much as the night before. He got up, dressed and went in search of sustenance and answers. Both were close at hand. While Champ carefully warmed Rye's breakfast in the microwave, Dayna explained that Kara had insisted he be allowed to sleep as long as he wanted. Escorted by one of the sheriff's deputies, who was mounted on horseback and carrying a rifle, Kara had started the herd herself. Dayna had delayed departure from last night's campsite as long as possible, but she explained that if she wasn't on-site for the noon rendezvous and ready to get to work by ten-thirty, lunch would be late, hence they were on the move. Rye sat down at the table and let Champ proudly take care of him. He polished off the biscuits, ham and eggs, and nursed a second cup of coffee, while the boy watched.

The phone rang, and since Dayna was carrying it, she answered, reporting moments later that Borden Harris had been apprehended and confessed all. It was only a matter of time, according to the sheriff, before they had Payne in custody, as well. Less than an hour later, Rye answered the phone himself and welcomed with relief and satisfaction the news that Payne had been arrested in Colorado. It was over. Nothing but miles stood between them and the ranch.

By the time the crew came in for lunch, Rye was waiting on horseback. Kara tried to argue him out of joining the drive, but he wasn't about to miss this. Tonight they would turn the herd loose on Detmeyer land once more. Rye knew it would be magnificent property. They had passed once again into lush countryside. The grass was thick as carpet on the rolling hillsides topped with timber displaying a rich variety of golds mingled with the evergreens. Land like this could support three times the number of cattle per acre as the Utah property had, and Rye was glad for Kara.

This was what they'd strived for, never mind the growing sadness that seemed to lodge beneath his breastbone like a fist. They had won. It was all over but the final drive. He regretted that he hadn't been able to spend last night with Kara, but maybe it was better this way. He wouldn't let himself think about it. Before dark they'd be on the ranch, Kara's ranch, free and clear. And after that he supposed he and Champ would return to his family, at least until he got his feet beneath him once again and decided what to do with himself. He knew he had decisions to make about the future, but somehow he couldn't make himself think about them. Just now he was going to take control of the herd and crew one more time. The last time.

Kara wanted to both laugh and cry as she watched the cattle spilling through the gate onto Detmeyer property, her property, hers alone. Oboe nipped at their heels, his barks sounding happy and somehow smug, as if he knew he was a hero for what he'd done yesterday. She wanted to feel triumphant, victorious. She should, yet she couldn't seem to shake the sadness that came with knowing Payne had tried to kill the man she loved in order to keep this from happening. But even that was better than the thought of Rye leaving—leaving her. When she'd started this drive, she'd believed that making the ranch viable again was everything she needed to be happy. Now she knew better. She'd give up this place if only Rye would give her his heart.

Several of the men unsaddled their horses and turned them out with the cattle. Oboe seemed to take it as his personal mission to harass them until they kicked up their heels at him and cantered away so that he could follow, barking merrily. Only Charlie and Wes, along with Kara and Rye, chose to ride the remaining mile and a quarter to the house. The others climbed aboard various vehicles and made the trip quickly. When the riders reached the bottom of the long, meandering drive, Kara was surprised to find a welcoming committee. She said hellos and gave smiles to several of the locals, mostly friends of her late father's. They'd heard about the drive and its ''difficulties'' and just wanted to let her know how glad they were to have the Detmeyers back where they belonged.

Rex Hardin, an outfitter and guide, who had been a particular friend of her father's, stepped up to offer a hand to Rye, saying, ''You must be Wagner. Saw you on TV. Guess old Plummer knew what he was about, choosing you for this job.''

''Thanks. I'd like to think so.''

''S'pose you'll be staying on now that the Utah ranch is gone,'' Hardin went on. ''Just wanted to give you a welcome.''

To Kara's dismay, Rye merely smiled weakly and mumbled that it was awful nice of them, before turning his head away. She knew he was going, so why couldn't she just accept it? Why did she have to hope even when she knew it was useless? Doing her best to look pleased, she thanked everyone for coming out and promised she'd have them all up to the house for a celebration before long.

''Sheriff's up there,'' Rex informed her. ''If everything's not all right, you just let us know now.''

''I will, Rex. Thanks again.''

Hardin opened the pass gate, for the horses wouldn't cross the widely spaced pipes of the cattle guard that bridged the drainage ditch cut into the drive. Kara and the others rode through and aimed their horses up the hill. When they topped the rise, she naturally paused to relish the sight before her. The big log house sat in the middle of a shallow green bowl, sheltered on every side by the autumn blaze of tall trees and a few evergreens. The ground in front of the deep porch was carpeted with fallen leaves and needles. Soon snow would blanket the hills around it, the air so clear and cold that it would almost sparkle in the sunshine. Kara wanted Rye to see it like that as well as painted in the shades of summer, from bright yellow-green to the rich hue so deep it was almost blue. Sadly she knew he probably would not.

They rode down into the shallow valley and gave their horses to Shoes, who waited patiently in the shadow of the porch. Wes and Charlie promised to help him rub them down and turn them out. Kara and Rye went into the house, finding the others sitting over cups of coffee in the big, modern kitchen. It was a strangely somber group. Her mother didn't even look at her, her hands gripping Pogo's on top of the table.

The sheriff had hard news for them, and he repeated it now for Kara's benefit. "Payne's told us everything. It was an agreement between father and son. Apparently there have been some bad investments. I understand they've been holding on by the skin of their teeth, pilfering what they could from the ranching business, even pocketing the money that was supposed to pay your father's life insurance premiums."

Kara gasped.

"Apparently the bank is on the verge of collapse."

Kara shook her head, speechless, unable to quite grasp it.

"A plan was set in motion some time ago," the sheriff said uncomfortably. "It started, I believe, with the murder of your father."

Pain such as Kara had never known doubled her over, a hand going to her chest. "You don't mean— They didn't— Oh, my God!"

"The agreement was that Smith would take care of his brother and Payne would take care of you," Hernandez went on reluctantly.

Kara couldn't believe it. "You're telling me that Uncle Smith shot my father?"

"And pushed Payne to hold up his end of the bargain to get rid of you. Payne apparently couldn't do it. He says he argued that it would look too suspicious so quickly following your father's death. Then they waited a little longer, hoping the market would improve. When your grandfather died and the will revealed the codicil, they couldn't wait anymore. Payne says he still might not have tried to stop you, but he was afraid that the woman he wants to marry wouldn't have him if she found out he was broke. For what it's worth, Payne tried to keep you out of it, focusing instead on Rye and delaying the drive."

Kara was sick, violently so. She just barely stumbled out the door and off the back porch before her stomach gave up its contents. It was Rye who came after her. He brought her a glass of water to rinse her mouth and smoothed back the hair that clung damply to her cheeks, and then he just held her while tears slid down her face.

"This was supposed to be a happy time," Kara whispered against his shoulder.

"I know, honey. I know."

What else was there to say? Her father was still dead. Rye was still leaving. The idea that Payne hadn't wanted to hurt her held no comfort at all, because instead he'd hurt those she loved, and that was even worse. Dusk had fallen before she once again felt strong enough to face the others. She was surprised when they went inside to find Dayna cooking supper, with Pogo hovering at her elbow. Her face was splotched with the tears she, too, had shed, but Kara knew from the tilt of her chin and the squareness of her shoulders that she was doggedly meeting life head-on, as always.

"You all right, baby?" she asked gently.

Kara nodded. "Do I have time for a hot soak in the tub before dinner?"

"Absolutely."

"Take all the time you want," Pogo added. "I don't think anyone's got much appetite right now, anyway."

Kara gave his arm a squeeze in thanks as she moved by him. She was glad that he was there for her mother. Only now was Kara beginning to understand the depth of loneliness her mother must have endured during the past year and more.

Rye wanted to check on Champ, so Kara showed him the room Dayna had given the boy, then went off to take the bath she'd been yearning for. The others were packed in, three to a room, or sharing the motor home with Dean, but at least everyone would have a real bed tonight. Somehow her own bed did not seem as inviting as it might have. She dropped her clothes on it and walked into the bathroom.

It was good to soak in her own tub in her own bathroom, and by the time the water had become uncomfortably cooled, her outlook had lightened somewhat. Her father had been gone many months now. Some part of her would grieve him always, and she would never forgive Smith and Payne for what they'd done, but that couldn't be changed. It was all in the past. Dayna was apparently making a future for herself with Pogo. Somehow Kara had to forge a future of her own. She didn't know how she was going to do it, but she was determined that she would. She went in to dinner with more appetite than she had expected.

It was a bittersweet time. Come morning, the group would break up after weeks of functioning as a team. Dean was leaving at first light to drive the motor home back to his family in Utah. Kara couldn't thank him enough for all he'd done for her.

"Oh, heck," he said, "I wouldn't have missed it. I'll be glad to get home to my family, though. A man learns to be thankful for what he's got, you know?"

Kara knew exactly what he meant. Everyone at the big plank table knew.

Wesley Randall's wife would be picking up Wes, Charlie and their horses. They'd likely be gone early tomorrow, too. Shoes was in no hurry, he said. He still intended to stop at the Jicarilla Apache reservation on his way home and have a little chat with the tribal rep who'd met them on their way in.

Pogo stated baldly that he wasn't going anywhere anytime soon. It was Shoes who possessed the courage to ask Rye what his plans were. Rye cleared his throat and pushed a green bean around his plate with his fork. "I suppose Champ and I will leave pretty early. We'll bunk in with my folks for a time. Then, well, we'll see."

Everyone at the table, including Rye, avoided Kara's gaze after that. She told herself that it was up to her to put everyone at ease. "I wish George was here," she heard herself saying brightly, too brightly. "I'll have to give him a call, see how he's mending, let him know how grateful I—" Her voice broke then. She swallowed down the remaining words, forced a smile and calmly got up from the table. "Good night, everyone. Sleep well."

The unnatural silence that followed her from the room stayed with her for a long time.

With Champ sleeping soundly, Rye let himself out the screen door onto the front porch as quietly as he could. The thing needed a good oiling to stop it from squeaking. He'd noticed a few other things that needed tending, too, but it wasn't his place to mention them. Besides, all in all, the place was in pretty good shape. Hell, it was the next thing to paradise. He loved the rustic opulence of the house, the high-beamed ceilings, the gleaming wood floors layered with rugs, the big rock fireplaces and massive double-paned windows. But it was the land that sparked envy in his heart. He'd never seen such lush, beautiful pasture, such lovely vistas, not this far south. It was a stockman's paradise. But it wasn't for him.

Shoes was talking about running a trail drive for paying customers between this place and Jesse's in Colorado. He felt sure that he and Rye together could work out contracts with the tribes allowing them to cross the reservations regularly. He wanted to find a couple of old covered wagons and give the tourists a real authentic taste of the past. It was a good idea, a thoroughly workable one—for anyone but Rye. He could never bear seeing Kara on even a semiregular basis if they weren't together. More to the point, he couldn't begin to stay away from her given proximity; he'd already proven that.

It was just hopeless. But then he was hopeless, wasn't he? Wasn't that what he'd been trying to tell Kara all along? Wasn't that exactly why he couldn't stay? He turned into the darkness and leaned a shoulder against a post, willing the familiar resignation to fill him. He almost had it when the door creaked open at his back, and footsteps carried an all-too-wanted presence to his side. She slipped her hand into his.

"Will you come with me?"

He knew he should say no, but how many times had she gone with him, willingly giving herself, loving even against the odds? He couldn't say no. It was beyond him. He couldn't walk into that house and bed down alone knowing she was here, wanting him. He gripped her hand in his. "Yes."

She led him off into the night and around the house, up the slope to a place beneath the trees where she had spread their open sleeping bags. "I wanted this last night," she said, "but I didn't want to make memories in the house that I couldn't live with later."

His throat closed. He couldn't have said anything even if he could have found the words. So he did what seemed best between them and kissed her. She cupped her hands over his shoulders and came to him so sweetly that she made his teeth ache. Yet he sensed that she meant to take from him tonight, and he was glad. After a long while she broke away and laid her cheek against his shoulder.

"You know, that first night," she said, "that was for me. I wanted to give to you what I'd given to no other man—what no other man had seemed to want—because I wanted to bind you to me somehow, make you love me. Instead I realized how much I love you, and everything changed after that." She lifted her head, her eyes shining up into his, a reflection of moonbeams. "You needed me, and I wanted to be there for you. It didn't matter that you would leave. I couldn't bear to see you wanting, needing, what you couldn't have."

He squeezed his eyes shut and lowered his head, burying his face in the curve of her shoulder. The skin of her neck was soft and fragrant. He knew how it would taste, knew how every part of her would taste. He felt her breasts against his chest, the jut of her shoulder blades beneath his hands, her feet staggered with his. She would shiver and moan when he brushed her skin with his lips and mustache, arch her back and cry out when he sucked her nipple, and tomorrow she would have tiny, reddish abrasions where he had loved her with his mouth, but she wouldn't complain. He loved that she treasured those small signs of his love-making. He'd never even thought about it with any other woman. He thought about it now, with the soft cloud of her hair brushing his temple. Her shampoo smelled of strawberries. He knew how it would feel to be inside of her and wanted it desperately, as desperately as he ever had.

"I don't know how to help you now, Rye," she said gently. "I don't know what you need anymore. I only know that I need you tonight. I need you to love me. Just once more."

He put his hands in her hair and turned her head slightly so that he could lick the sensitive skin behind her ear. She shivered, and he set his teeth in her earlobe, tugging and heating the hollow with his breath, tickling it with his mustache.

It was a fierce tenderness, a calculated wildness, a deliberate loss of control deliberately prolonged, stretched to its limits and beyond. In the end, he was utterly drained in every way, a tired husk without feeling or thought. Dawn found him without even the energy or presence of mind to ask what she was doing when she silently got up, dressed and walked away. He watched her all the way down the slope to the house, her pace determined, even, shoulders squared, the tangle of her hair swinging between her shoulder blades. Oboe appeared and fell in beside her. Every few steps her hand would come up and brush across her cheeks as if she was wiping away tears until finally she disappeared into the house through the back door. Only later did he understand that he probably would never see her again.

He lay there an hour or more. Dean came out of the motor home and went into the house, then returned and drove away. An extended-cab pickup pulling a horse trailer topped the rise, and a woman with red hair got out of it. Long minutes later Shoes came out and walked to the barn, returning with Wes and Charlie's horses, which he loaded into the trailer. Sometime later Wes and Charlie came out with the redheaded woman, got into the truck and drove away, waving to someone standing on the front porch. After that it was quiet again.

Finally Rye managed to get himself up and pull on his clothes. A heaviness weighed on him, something more than loss of sleep and physical exertion, something huge and formless that he couldn't identify let alone fight. Leaving the sleeping bags where they were, he walked down the slope, around the house and in through the front door. He heard Champ talking to someone in the kitchen, smelled breakfast. He went directly to the room where his and Champ's things waited. He packed and straightened up, made the bed, opened the curtains and stood staring through the window at nothing while footsteps came and went in the hall. Water ran in the bath across the way, then stopped. Doors opened and closed. Finally it was quiet.

Rye carried his and Champ's gear out to the truck parked beneath a tree near the front drive and loaded it. Shoes would have to take the borrowed horses back to Jess, he decided, seized by a sudden haste that he couldn't stop to analyze. He had to get out of there. Now. He wanted to run, forget everything, the truck, the gear, even Champ, just walk away. Fast.

He hurried back into the house. His palms were damp, and he had to force himself to go into the kitchen. Dayna and Pogo sat at the table with Champ, nursing cups of coffee and listening to the boy's chatter. Breakfast had been cleared away. Dayna started to get up. He shook his head. "Thanks, but I don't want anything." She sat back down again. "Son, it's time we were going. Run on to the bathroom. Right now. Be quick about it and be sure to wash your hands."

For a moment Champ just stared at him. Rye had the sudden, overwhelming fear that his son was going to balk, then with a shrug the boy got up and left the room. Rye gripped the back of his empty chair with both hands. Why did he feel as if he was going to explode?

"Want a cup of coffee?" Pogo asked.

Rye shook his head, his gaze trained on his feet. He really was going to explode if he didn't get out of here.

Pogo said, very deliberately, "Congratulate us, Rye. Dayna and I are going to get married."

Something in Rye went off with a bang. "God Almighty! Don't you ever learn?" He threw up his hands, knowing it wasn't any of his business but unable to shut his mouth. "What is this now, Pogo, four? You've been married and divorced *three times,* for pity's sake! What makes you think this will be any different?"

"*I* make him think that," Dayna said. Getting calmly to her feet, she walked to the inlaid brick countertop and poured herself a refill before turning to look at him. "He'll stay if I have to chain him to a tree, because I don't quit. No one in this family quits."

"His track record—"

"He's not a quitter, Rye, not at heart."

"Then how do you explain—"

"It's natural to quit on somebody who quits on you," she said, "but I won't, no matter what. That's what it takes. I know."

"How could you? No one ever quit on you!"

"You think Law and I didn't have our problems?" she asked. "Honey, let me tell you, we fought like wildcats at times. We hurt each other. We cried and we screamed and we swallowed our pride until we couldn't swallow our spit, but we didn't quit. And it was worth it, more than worth it. I imagine your parents feel the same. Why a smart boy like you can't see it, I don't know."

"I'm not like them," Rye said through his teeth.

"Maybe not, but you're no quitter, either."

"I quit before!"

"You were quit on. But Kara's not like that. And you won't even give her a chance."

Champ slipped back into the room just then, eyes wide because of the raised voices. Rye grabbed him by the shoulder and turned him toward the dining room door, practically shoving him through it in his haste to escape. Dayna and Pogo came after them.

"She would've taken a bullet for you," Dayna said loudly.

His feet stopped working, leaving him stranded halfway across the room. It took a moment to get them started again.

"When those bullets were flying," Dayna went on, "and you were out there dodging them, she tried to go over the truck to get to you."

A chill went down his spine, but he kept walking, turning off the images of a wounded Kara that had scared the life out of him before.

"She'd have thrown herself on top of you if Pogo hadn't stopped her."

His feet faltered and would have betrayed him again, but he was ready for that and forced them to speed up across the big, airy living room, sweeping Champ along with him.

"She fought him, Rye. He had to tackle her, throw her down on the ground and hold her down."

He burst through the front door, screen slamming back against the rough log wall, with the picture in his mind of Kara, facedown in the dirt, Pogo on top of her, tears streaming down her face.

"That's how much she loves you, Rye."

He swung Champ up into his arms as he stepped off the porch, afraid he'd knock the boy down in his panic. He came up on the truck so fast it startled him, so that he had to back off slightly to get the driver's door open. He literally tossed the boy inside and climbed in practically on top of him.

"Daddy?"

"Buckle your seat belt."

Champ moved across the seat but stayed on his knees, looking out the back. Rye started the engine and stomped the gas. The big double-cab pickup banked around the curve, then tore up the slight slope and in seconds crested it. Rye let out a breath of relief, perfectly aware that this was a cowardly act, that he was running as hard as he could. The truck threw up dust behind it. Champ turned around and slid down into his seat, reaching for his safety belt. The truck bumped roughly over a drive that needed grading, bucking and lurching. Rye saw the cattle guard and beside it the little gate that one of Kara's friends had opened for them the evening before. Freedom lay just on the other side of it, safety. He could almost feel the roughness of the crossing, hear the accordion scrape of tires on spaced pipe, feel the relief that would engulf him. And then another sort of panic seized him. Without really knowing why, he jammed his foot down on the brake and sat there disbelievingly. It was right there, the last step, the end of it, the fresh beginning. Another fresh beginning. On his own. Alone. A great sadness hit him. He didn't want to live alone.

But he had Champ. He was forgetting Champ. His hands were gripping the steering wheel hard enough to snap it off, he made himself relax and looked at his son, realizing with a shock that he was eight years old. He'd grown even in these past few weeks. Just yesterday he'd been a slobbering little lump of blubber with less personality than an apple, and now he sat there staring at him with big black eyes that had seen and understood too much. For the first time Rye fully faced the fact that his son would grow up, become a man with a life of his own, needs of his own, needs a father couldn't fulfill. One day Champ would meet a woman, a special woman, and even if she turned out to be a quitter, even if she chewed him up inside and left him in pieces, Rye knew that he would want Champ to have her. He would always want Champ to have his heart's desire, always want to give what he needed.

You needed me, and I wanted to be there for you. I couldn't bear to see you wanting what you couldn't have.

The sound that came out of his mouth shamed him so much that he managed to blink back the sudden swell of tears. Determinedly he shifted his foot to the gas pedal. But that was it. Try as he might, he couldn't push down that pedal. He put his foot back on the brake and leaned his forehead against the steering wheel.

"I can't do it." Champ didn't say a word. Rye swallowed hard and licked his lips, working up his courage to face his son again. "I can't do it, Champ. I can't leave her. I don't know why, but I just can't."

Champ folded his arms and knocked his feet together, staring off through the windshield. Suddenly he turned a sly look on his father and asked, "Could you leave me?"

"Never! Never ever," Rye vowed. "Whatever happens, I'll never leave you, not for good. One day you'll leave me, though, move out on your own, make your own life."

"But that's not the same," Champ said.

"No, it's not."

"Well, if you can't leave me and you can't leave her..." Champ said, assuming that the correlation was obvious, even to his thickheaded father. And it was. He loved her, and he wasn't going to stop.

"You're right."

Rye sat there a moment longer, staring at that gate and the road beyond it, then he put the transmission into Reverse and turned the truck around. The weight that had been pressing on him since daylight lifted, but as they topped the rise, his heart started to pound ominously. He wouldn't blame her if she threw him out after this. But she wouldn't do it. Dayna was right. There was no quit in Kara Detmeyer, no quit at all. He didn't deserve a woman like her, but if she didn't know that already, she never would, or, God help her, she was determined to love him anyway. He was selfish enough not to care which it was, so long as it was.

Dayna and Pogo were still on the porch. Dayna lurched to the door and opened it, apparently shouting inside. By the time he brought the barreling truck to a dusty stop squarely in front of the house, Kara was there and Shoes, too, a wide grin on his face. Rye threw the transmission into Park and yanked open the door. He got out and started walking. Then Kara stepped down off the porch, moving tentatively toward him, and he was running again, but this time *to* love, not away from it, even though it was running toward him full tilt now. They collided and locked arms, both talking at once.

"I couldn't go! I couldn't!"

"Thank God! Oh, thank God!"

"I'm not even a good coward! I couldn't get over the damned cattle guard!"

"I love you! It means nothing without you! The ranch means nothing!"

"I love you, Kara. I need you. I want to be with you always."

"Will Champ—" she began, but he squeezed her so tight that he cut off the rest of the words.

"Hell, Champ has better sense than I have! He didn't want to go to begin with. He knows there isn't any other choice. He knows I couldn't leave you any more than I could leave him, because you're both a part of me, because I love you." He held her away a little then and let her know that he really got it, he truly understood what he was doing and why. "I can't bear to see either one of you wanting what you can't have, so I guess I'll just have to spend the rest of my life making sure you get what you need."

Kara laughed—a watery, happy sound—and threw her arms around his neck. There was other laughter, but they didn't hear it, other happiness besides their own, but they didn't feel it. In that moment love left no room for anything else. It filled up their hearts and spilled over into their lives, coloring their hopes as it flowed, converting them into strange and wonderful new realities, the stuff of marriage and partnership and family and a place where both belonged, a place where dreams come true for every cowgirl—and every cowboy.

* * * * *

Be sure to catch the latest Silhouette Romance by Arlene James called A BRIDE TO HONOR, coming November 1998—don't miss it!

Silhouette Books is delighted to alert you
to a brand-new MacGregor story from
Nora Roberts, coming in October 1998,
from Silhouette Special Edition. Look for

THE WINNING HAND

and find out how a small-town
librarian wins the heart of elusive,
wealthy and darkly handsome
Robert ''Mac'' Blade.

Here's a sneak preview of

THE WINNING HAND....

The Winning Hand

There was something wonderfully smooth under her cheek. Silk, satin, Darcy thought dimly. She'd always loved the feel of silk. Once she'd spent nearly her entire paycheck on a silk blouse, creamy white with gold, heart shaped buttons. She'd had to skip lunch for two weeks, but it had been worth it every time she slipped that silk over her skin.

She sighed, remembering it.

"Come on, all the way out."

"What?" She blinked her eyes open, focused on a slant of light from a jeweled lamp.

"Here, try this." Mac slipped a hand under her head, lifted it, and put a glass of water to her lips.

"What?"

"You're repeating yourself. Drink some water."

"Okay." She sipped obediently, studying the tanned, long-fingered hand that held the glass. She was on a bed, she realized now, a huge bed with a silky cover. There was a mirrored ceiling over her head. "Oh my." Warily, she shifted her gaze until she saw his face.

He set the glass aside, then sat on the edge of the bed, noting with amusement that she scooted over slightly to keep more distance between them. "Mac Blade. I run this place."

"Darcy. I'm Darcy Wallace. Why am I here?"

"It seemed better than leaving you sprawled on the floor of the casino. You fainted."

"I did?" Mortified, she closed her eyes again. "Yes, I guess I did. I'm sorry."

"It's not an atypical reaction to winning close to two million dollars."

Her eyes popped open, her hand grabbed at her throat. "I'm sorry. I'm still a little confused. Did you say I won almost two million dollars?"

"You put the money in, you pulled the lever, you hit." There wasn't an ounce of color in her cheeks, he noted, and thought she looked like a bruised fairy. "Do you want to see a doctor?"

"No, I'm just...I'm okay. I can't think. My head's spinning."

"Take your time." Instinctively, he plumped up the pillows behind her and eased her back.

"I had nine dollars and thirty-seven cents when I got here."

"Well, now you have $1 800 088.37."

"Oh. Oh." Shattered, she put her hands over her face and burst into tears.

There were too many women in his life for Mac to be uncomfortable with female tears. He sat where he was and let her sob it out.

"I'm sorry." She wiped her hands at her somehow charmingly dirty face. "I'm not like this. Really. I can't take it in." She accepted the handkerchief he offered and blew her nose. "I don't know what to do."

"Let's start with the basics. Why don't you take a hot bath, try to relax, get your bearings. There's a robe in the closet."

She cleared her throat. However kind he was being, she was still alone with him, a perfect stranger, in a very opulent and sensual bedroom. "I appreciate it. But I should get a room. If I could have a small advance on the money, I can find a hotel."

"Something wrong with this one?"

"This what?"

"This hotel," he said. "This room."

"No, nothing. It's beautiful."

"Then make yourself comfortable. Your room's been comped for the duration of your stay—"

"What? Excuse me?" She sat up a little straighter. "I can have this room? I can just...stay here?"

"It's the usual procedure for high rollers." He smiled again, making her heart bump. "You qualify."

"I get all this for free because I won money from you?"

His grin was quick, and just a little wolfish. "I want the chance to win some of it back."

Lord, he was beautiful. Like the hero of a novel. That thought rolled around in her jumbled brain. "That seems only fair. Thank you so much, Mr. Blade."

"Welcome to Las Vegas, Ms. Wallace," he said and turned toward a sweep of open stairs that led to the living area.

She watched him cross an ocean of Oriental carpet. "Mr. Blade?"

"Yes?" He turned and glanced up.

"What will I do with all that money?"

He flashed that grin again. "You'll think of something."

When the doors closed behind him, Darcy gave into her buckling knees and sat on the floor. She hugged herself hard, rocking back and forth. If this was some dream, some hallucination brought on by stress or sunstroke, she hoped it never cleared away.

She hadn't just escaped her life, she realized. She'd been liberated.

Take 2 bestselling love stories FREE

Plus get a FREE surprise gift!

Special Limited-Time Offer

Mail to Silhouette Reader Service™

3010 Walden Avenue
P.O. Box 1867
Buffalo, N.Y. 14240-1867

YES! Please send me 2 free Silhouette Special Edition® novels and my free surprise gift. Then send me 6 brand-new novels every month, which I will receive months before they appear in bookstores. Bill me at the low price of $3.57 each plus 25¢ delivery and applicable sales tax, if any.* That's the complete price, and a saving of over 10% off the cover prices—quite a bargain! I understand that accepting the books and gift places me under no obligation ever to buy any books. I can always return a shipment and cancel at any time. Even if I never buy another book from Silhouette, the 2 free books and the surprise gift are mine to keep forever.

235 SEN CH7W

Name	(PLEASE PRINT)	
Address		Apt. No.
City	State	Zip

This offer is limited to one order per household and not valid to present Silhouette Special Edition® subscribers. *Terms and prices are subject to change without notice. Sales tax applicable in N.Y.

USPED-98

©1990 Harlequin Enterprises Limited

#1 *New York Times* bestselling author

NORA ROBERTS

Presents a brand-new book in the
beloved MacGregor series:

THE WINNING HAND

(SSE#1202)

October 1998 in

Silhouette ® SPECIAL EDITION ®

Innocent Darcy Wallace needs Mac Blade's protection in
the high-stakes world she's entered. But who will protect
Mac from the irresistible allure of this vulnerable beauty?

**Coming in March, the much-anticipated novel,
THE MacGREGOR GROOMS
Also, watch for the MacGregor stories
where it all began!**

**December 1998:
THE MacGREGORS: Serena—Caine**

**February 1999:
THE MacGREGORS: Alan—Grant**

**April 1999:
THE MacGREGORS: Daniel—Ian**

Available at your favorite retail outlet, only from

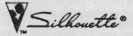

Silhouette Romance
celebrates the joys
of first love in

VIRGIN BRIDES

September 1998:
THE GUARDIAN'S BRIDE
by Laurie Paige (#1318)

A young heiress, desperately in love with her
older, wealthy guardian, dreams of wedding the
tender tycoon. But he has plans to marry
her off to another....

October 1998:
THE NINE-MONTH BRIDE
by Judy Christenberry (#1324)

A widowed rancher who wants an heir and a prim librarian
who wants a baby decide to marry for convenience—but will
motherhood make this man and wife rethink their
temporary vows?

November 1998:
A BRIDE TO HONOR by Arlene James (#1330)

A pretty party planner falls for a charming, honor-bound
millionaire who's being roped into a loveless marriage. When
the wedding day arrives, will *she* be his blushing bride?

December 1998:
A KISS, A KID AND A MISTLETOE BRIDE (#1336)

When a scandalous single dad returns home at
Christmas, he encounters the golden girl he'd fallen
for one magical night a lifetime before.

Available at your favorite retail outlet.

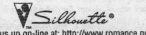

Silhouette®

SRVBSD

COMING NEXT MONTH

#1201 FATHER-TO-BE—Laurie Paige
That's My Baby!
When Celia Campbell informed honorable Hunter McLean she was carrying his child, he was stunned! He couldn't recall their impulsive night of passion, much less envision playing daddy the second time around. He knew that getting married was the right thing to do, but could he open his heart to love?

#1202 THE WINNING HAND—Nora Roberts
MacGregor Series
Sweet, unsophisticated Darcy Wallace was feeling very fortunate! After winning the jackpot, she caught dashing and dangerous millionaire Robert MacGregor Blade's eye. But she would need more than luck to convince this confirmed bachelor of her dreams to gamble on a future— with her....

#1203 FROM HOUSE CALLS TO HUSBAND—Christine Flynn
Prescription: Marriage
Heart surgeon Mike Brennan had a gentle touch, a soothing voice—and, boy, did he look sexy in his scrubs! But nurse Katie Sheppard had vowed *never* to marry a doctor—particularly one who was her best friend…and best-kept secret crush.

#1204 THE RANCHER AND THE AMNESIAC BRIDE—Joan Elliott Pickart
Follow That Baby!
Josie Wentworth of the oil-rich Oklahoma Wentworths didn't know the first thing about working ranches—or grumpy, gorgeous cowboys. But a case of amnesia had the socialite princess riding the range—and yearning for a lifetime of lovin' with the man least likely to say I do!

#1205 PARTNERS IN MARRIAGE—Allison Hayes
A housing shortage in Turtle Creek? Whatever was Shelley Matthews to do? First, the schoolteacher moved in with devastatingly handsome Blue Larson. Then, despite her misgivings, she offered to be the Lakota Indian's partner in marriage. Dare she trust in happily ever after again?

#1206 THE BODYGUARD'S BRIDE—Jean Brashear
Women To Watch
In the name of justice, Jillian Marshall vowed to avenge her sister's murder. Nothing stood in her way—except for dangerously attractive bodyguard Drake Cullinane, who had an agenda of his own. Only he could soothe the pain paralyzing her heart, but how much would she sacrifice for love?